ROUTE 666
CALIFORNIA DEMON
BOOK FIVE

DEBRA DUNBAR

debra dunbar
SENSUALLY FUN FICTION

ive days after the massacre, LA burned.

Since we didn't have a bat signal, Juke had been calling me every time they got a 911 call involving demon attacks, and Bishop would teleport us to the scene. But even with Juke running triage and only sending us to the worst of the attacks, there were too many for the two of us to handle. We couldn't go on like this.

My phone rang. I knew who it was even before I looked at the screen.

"We've got a situation downtown," Juke said, her voice somber.

I ignored Bishop's raised eyebrows, and immediately went to the giant bank of windows at the back of my living room so I could look down at the city.

The downtown area glowed red, fires clearly visible even from this distance.

"What's going on?" I asked, as if I didn't know.

This was the new normal in LA. Bands of demons attacked neighborhoods, looting, murdering, and stealing. The rich had abandoned their homes, knowing that even their hired security and purchased magic wouldn't protect them from the violence. The middle class had fled, driving to the border and bribing their way across. The poor were trying to escape, loading up any vehicle they could with their belongings and begging an unsympathetic U.S. for asylum.

I'd pleaded with Bea to leave with the girls, but she'd refused. She had her house, still had a job, and knew as well as I did what their chances would be at the border. Nevarra and Sadie could be taken away, placed with some foster family across the continent with Bea in detention awaiting her hearing. I understood her decision, but I still fretted about their safety.

"Groups of demons have attacked downtown," Juke told me. "They're bombing and burning buildings. Little Tokyo is rubble. The Fashion District is burning. Everything is either bombed, burning, or being looted."

I caught my breath. It wasn't just the loss of some amazing art and cultural centers that worried me. Skid Row was downtown, and that's where the poor and disadvantaged were along with the missions that served that community.

"We're evacuating," Juke continued. "Getting people moved to the arts district where we've got transport. The demons are slaughtering any human they find—slaughtering or taking them."

"Where do you need us?" I asked.

"Seaton and Palmetto at the Wisdome," Juke told me.

The Wisdome was an events center that I'd driven by but never actually been to. I assured Juke I was on my way, then turned to Bishop.

Guilt swept through me in a wave. And it wasn't the first time this week I'd felt that emotion. This wasn't Bishop's fight. If it weren't for me, he'd be up at his bar or his house. He'd had a deal with the demons—until he'd broken that deal for me.

"Teleport me downtown?" I asked as I disconnected the call. He'd come to stand beside me, looking out the windows at the fires. I knew he'd heard both sides of the phone call. "You can sit this one out. It's just evacuation security."

Bishop shook his head. "I'm going to fight by your side. I'm not teleporting you into a war zone full of demons and leaving you there."

He'd been by my side throughout this whole mess. As nervous as I was about being underpowered and unprepared for this task, having Bishop with me made me a little more confident that I'd at least come out of a fight involving a group of demons alive—even if I might not be the victor.

I nodded to Bishop and he reached out, putting his other hand on my shoulder.

In a flash we were out of my living room and in downtown LA. The smoke blinded me, choking me with a weird sulfur smell, and the sound of gunfire practically deafened me.

Bishop grabbed me, curling his body over my back and taking a hail of bullets. His wings extended their full width, and the gunfire halted.

"Angel!" someone shouted.

Juke ran forward, holding her badge up in the air and yelling, "Cease fire!"

"They're angels. Allies," she said as she reached us. "They're here to help."

I still wasn't sure I was an angel, but she could call me anything she wanted as long as it kept me from getting shot.

"Where do you need us?" I asked.

"We've got the humans gathered together inside Wisdome," Juke told us. "A group of demons attacked us, so we had to move the vans to Mateo and Conway. Once we get everyone loaded, we're taking them to Lincoln Heights where we've set up shelters at the rec center and the youth center with overflow at the high school. The demons are all over the downtown area, but if you two can clear a path for us to bring the vans back around and get these people out of downtown, that would help."

I turned to Bishop. "Would it be better for us to stay close to the vans, or to lure the demons away? Will the demons be more liable to flee when we attack, or come together to try and kill us?"

"Initially they'll flee, especially because there's two of us. But then they'll group together and attack." Bishop looked around. "Let's clear the area around the vans, then move west down Palmetto. If it seems we're drawing more demons toward us, I'll lure them off while you guard the vans."

I nodded. "Once the vans are back here and loaded, I'll escort them until they're clear."

"I'll distract the higher-level demons, leading them into the air," Bishop told me. "You handle the ones on the ground."

"Are you sure they'll follow you?" I asked. "According to Juke, these guys seem pretty fixated on killing or taking the humans."

"Yeah. I'm sure. The lesser demons and Lows will still go for the humans, but the higher-level demons will come after me. There's a bounty on my head. They'll want not just the money, but the prestige of taking me out."

Guilt rolled through me. Again. That bounty on his head? That was because of me.

"Let's do this," I told him. It wasn't the time for me to mourn the situation I'd put us in—not when there were people who needed our help.

Bishop and I jogged two streets down, while Juke stayed back with the other officers at the Wisdome. As Bishop and I approached Mateo, we saw the evacuation vehicles. The "vans" were armor plated tactical transport vehicles, and four demons were doing their best to pop tires and set them on fire, shooting electricity and stabbing at the vehicles with claws and spiked tails. I'd seen demons blow one of these vehicles sky high, incinerating both it and the occupants, so I was assuming these weren't particularly high-level demons.

"Hey!" I yelled. "Get out of here right now!"

They turned to face me and I sent a bolt of lightning toward the one farthest from the vehicle. He absorbed it without injury, but my attack gave Bishop time to dash in and grab the demon who was trying to stab the tires. The demon dissolved from the feet up into sand. The other three demons turned their attention from me to Bishop, rushing him.

I launched forward as they piled onto the angel, pulling my gun out as I ran. Jumping on one, I shoved the muzzle against his head and pulled the trigger. The demon's head exploded into a mess of flesh and blood. I leapt from him as he fell, turning toward the other two. Bishop was grappling with them, all three lit up with electricity and that weird energy I'd come to associate with demons. I grabbed one, yelping as the energy scorched through my body, singeing my spirit-being.

The demon sent more energy through me, and this time I was prepared. I absorbed it. Then I slammed my fist into his chest, bringing my knee up to his head as he bent over. Grabbing his horns, I beat his head repeatedly into the side of the tactical transport vehicle until he dropped to the ground.

Bishop had turned the demon he was fighting to sand. He stooped, grabbed my opponent off the ground, and did the same to him. Then he spread his wings, rising up above the street so he could be seen. His feathers glinted in the firelight: salmon, orange, and indigo.

From his vantage point, Bishop could clearly see any nearby demons as well as they could see him. As lightning and energy streaked through the air, he spun around, easily dodging blasts. Circling around, he pointed east down an alleyway.

I pulled my other pistol from my hip holster and took off, Bishop flying overhead as I ran. When I burst into the middle of Palmetto Street, I started shooting. Two demons fell by bullets before they started taking defensive maneuvers. Instead of head shots, my bullets were either missing or hitting the demons in their torso or limbs. Those might have taken a human down, but the demons were repairing their injuries as quickly as I could inflict them. With the element of surprise over, I switched to lightning attacks, which didn't do much more than the bullets. One of the demons threw that explosive energy at me. I grabbed it, ran forward, then slammed it back into him. Bits of flesh flew everywhere. The one remaining demon squawked in alarm and took off. I followed him, putting on a surge of inhuman speed and tackling him before he'd reached the end of the block.

The demon thrashed about, pummeling me with alternate bursts of electricity and demon energy. I held on to the demon energy, knowing I'd need to use it later, and instead blew a sizable hole through his head with a shot from my Glock.

I continued to straddle the demon, waiting for a few seconds to make sure he was truly dead. Head shots usually did the trick, but Blister had told me there were a few rare demons who were able to survive that, continuing temporarily as a freakish demon zombie, or recreating their head in a flash of light.

This guy stayed dead, so I climbed off him, my pistol and the demon energy I'd stored at the ready as I checked my surroundings. The vans had followed me, no doubt instructed to do so by Juke. I led them back to the Wisdome and the police sprang into action. I circled the area while people ran from the building, loading as quickly as possible into the vehicles. When the last human was on board, the cops hopped in, and the vehicles took off.

I looked up as they started down the street, realizing that Bishop was no longer directly above me, and that he was no longer the only one in the skies. Six other beings flitted around him with giant bat-like wings. A pair dove toward Bishop and he dropped low, darting to the side and grabbing one of the other demons. They tumbled in the air for a heart-stopping second before the demon exploded. Spinning around, Bishop deftly dodged another attack as the sand from the demon's corpse rained down onto the street.

I could have stood there forever, watching the beautiful dance of Bishop's aerial battle, but I needed to ensure the evacuation route was clear, so I reluctantly turned away. Never once did I doubt Bishop's ability to handle six flying demons—or more. I knew he hadn't wanted this endless stream of battles or the price on his head. He'd been happy living a semi-human life as a bar owner and a "finder" of lost things, but when he vowed to help me guard the city, when he'd broken his contract with the demons, the gloves were off.

He'd fought in the war between the angels millions of years ago. He'd guarded and protected the Nephilim and the shifters for ten thousand years. He might downplay his abilities, saying he was just a middling angel of no particular skill, but Bishop was far more than middling. That angel was one scary dude. I'd seen him face down an archangel, and I had no doubt that when he truly cared about something, he was darn near unstoppable.

I ran, circling a two block radius around the transport vans, shooting at demons and getting updates from Juke about the evacuation route on my phone. Most of the demons took off when they discovered I was more than a human with a couple of pistols.

After the vehicles had cleared the 4th Street bridge over the river, I kept up my protection, darting ahead to clear the path, then ducking behind to ensure they weren't attacked from the rear. The vehicles moved fast, and even with my paranormal speed, I was getting winded and tired trying to keep up. Even before this particular power had kicked in, I'd been quick and had incredible endurance, but racing around a bunch of trucks speeding down city streets was proving to be a strain.

There were fewer demons as we passed the 10. Juke had said they were evacuating the humans to Lincoln Heights, and for the first time I wondered if they expected me to escort them the entire way. I hoped not, because I wasn't sure I could keep up this speed for the three to four miles it would take us to get there.

My phone beeped and I slowed to glance at it. Juke had texted that they were in the clear, but asked if I could return downtown to do another sweep, just in case they'd missed any humans or if there were any of the police there in need of assistance.

Will do. Be safe, I texted back, grateful to be able to stop and catch my breath.

The armored vehicles speeded ahead, making a left on Brittania as they headed to safety. Turning around, I scanned the skies and saw nothing but heavy cloud cover with the flash of lightning in the distance. I'd always welcomed storms before the demons came, but now I eyed the lightning, wondering if it was a natural occurrence, or a battle above the clouds.

I'd lost track of Bishop. A slight trickle of worry ran through me. He was powerful, but as he'd said before, there was only one of him and tens of thousands of demons.

Pushing those thoughts away, I jogged back toward downtown. This time I was going slow enough to actually take note of my surroundings as I passed.

Past the Wisdome, the arts district was almost unrecognizable. Buildings that had stood tall this morning were piles of rubble, broken electrical wires sparking across concrete, rebar, and steel beams blocked sidewalks. Cars were melted blobs. Huge chunks were missing from the road, some of the holes going down six to ten feet. Street lights were smashed, signs twisted. Broken glass and shards of metal were scattered across the road and sidewalks, and everything was coated with a thick layer of white cement dust.

I slowed to a walk, trying to determine my location from the ruined landmarks. Finally I saw something I recognized. It all miraculously remained standing even though the building façades were pockmarked with damage and blackened with scorch marks.

It was an open-air shopping mall called the Bloc. As I approached I began to see groups of demons smashing in neighboring store fronts and looting the merchandise. I held back, watching and looking to see if there were any humans in need of my help. I really didn't care about the thefts, and while I wasn't happy about the damage, I wasn't going to risk my life to save a Nordstrom from being trashed. Corporations had insurance. And they knew the risks they took continuing to operate in a demon-controlled New Hell.

Looking around, I saw the darkness was only relieved by the glow of small nearby fires. The electricity here was completely out, and whatever backup system these high-end stores usually had in place to allow for alarms during a power outage must be out as well. The only sounds were smashing glass and the gleeful shrieks of the inhuman looters.

Greed demons, I thought as I watched the horned, scaled,

and furred beings carting off expensive clothing, jewelry, and accessories. It was kind of funny to see something that looked like a cross between a vulture and a goat walking out with a Louis Vuitton bag on its shoulder.

Blister had told me that all demons were greedy, but there was a certain type who'd taken avarice to an art. Some demons loved spreading rot and disease. Others fed off sexual energy of their human partners, like a parasite. Others thrived on destruction and violence. These guys were kicking down doors and smashing windows, but they were clearly focused on grabbing the goods.

The demons had stuffed their loot into a box truck that looked like it had been rolled over a few times, then they ran into the Bloc. I was about to move on, assuming any humans in this area had long since fled when the piercing sound of terrified screams filled the air.

Shit.

I took off for the mall entrance, thinking that some idiots had probably holed up inside, hoping to protect their inventory rather than evacuate when they should. Now I'd have to fight a dozen demons, all while trying to keep what sounded like another dozen humans alive. Running into the entrance hallway, I smacked into something with scales and fur and bounced into the wall. As I turned I saw that it was a fleeing demon who'd hit me.

That demon was followed by another, and another. I stared in astonishment as they tore out of the building in a panic. Some of them were on fire, others were missing limbs. I was astonished as I watched them run screaming down the street.

What. The. Hell.

Did the humans inside have flame throwers? Had they put down bear traps? Were they trained ninjas in addition to retail managers? I holstered my pistols, not wanting to further alarm humans tough enough to send a dozen greed demons running, then cautiously made my way inside, keeping to the wall. The hallway opened up into a large courtyard flanked by stores that went up for three stories. Some huge roofing section must have come loose from a neighboring building, because the center half of the courtyard now had a sheltering overhang.

Non-functional escalators were along the sides of the courtyard. The upper floor walkways around the open space were smashed and missing sections, leaving storefronts to dangle a few feet over the edge. Just like outside, there was broken glass along the courtyard. The store walls were scorched, with chunks of the once-glossy granite missing.

I didn't see any humans, but I did see an enormous pile of stuff in the middle part of the space that was sheltered by the overhang. Most of the stuff appeared to be jewelry, but there were a few purses, some large paintings and sculptures, and oddly enough, a Maserati. Was this what the humans had been protecting? It seemed weird for them to pile it all together like this, but with the condition of those stores on the upper floors, I supposed it was safer down here at ground level.

But where *were* they?

With tentative, tip-toed steps, I slowly made my way into the open space, expecting at any minute to be roasted by a flame thrower or have my leg snapped off by an invisible bear trap. Neither of those happened. Instead, I heard a throaty growl, then a high-pitched scream cut abruptly short. My eyes widened, and I froze, my feet rooted to the floor as an enormous dragon strolled into the courtyard from the hallway opposite me.

He was bright orange with glowing red eyes. A demon dangled from the dragon's mouth. The demon's empty, sightless eyes stared from a lizard-like face as the dragon crunched down on its body.

Then the dragon's gaze locked on me. I didn't breathe, hoping like a scared rabbit that the predator wouldn't notice me.

The dragon tossed his head up, flinging the dead demon in the air. As it came down, the dragon snapped the body into his mouth, swallowing the corpse with one gulp. Then he looked at me once more, opened his mouth and roared.

I ran, barely escaping a blast of flame that scorched the wall where I'd once stood.

CHAPTER 2

As I dashed down the hallway to the entrance, I heard the dragon coming after me, slowed down by needing to wedge his huge body into the smaller space. Concrete broke free from the walls, wood snapping and metal supports bending behind me. The ceiling shook, dust floating down into my hair. I ran faster, worried that the dragon was going to bring half the building down on my head. The greed demons and their vehicle were long gone by the time I cleared the building doorway. Making a quick left I darted down a side street, skirted a burned-out Porsche that was blocking the road, and turned left into an alleyway. There I stood, breathing heavy and hoping that dragons didn't track by sense of smell. If this had been Bob, Bishop's partner and were-dog, there would be no escaping him, but I wasn't sure dragon noses were as sensitive as the canine, or were-canine, ones. The dragon had reeked of sulfur, and spit fireballs. I was going to assume his olfactory function would be overcome with his own foul odor.

There was an enormous crash and a roar from the vicinity of the Bloc. I peeked around the corner, but didn't see anything after me. Another roar shook the air and the night sky lit up with a burst of fire sent heavenward. Sparks rained down, and flickers of light told me that a few more buildings had been set on fire. Nothing came down the street after me, and after a few minutes of quiet, I decided that the dragon had given up the chase. Just in case, I went in the opposite direction, heading east toward Skid Row.

There still was no sign of Bishop, although I saw some demons flying up just over the tops of the buildings, like giant bats searching for prey. Was Bishop okay? Was it him they were looking for, or were they just in search of opportunities to maim, kill, destroy, and steal? I tried to stay out of their view, lurking in shadows and watching them carefully.

Serpents with lion heads and talon-spiked feet roamed the streets accompanied by chicken-legged humanoids with shark heads and leathery tails. There were a few individual demons looting, blowing up abandoned vehicles, or throwing street signs like javelins through store windows, but most of them were in groups of five or six, organized and walking the streets like they were patrolling for something. Clearly they weren't policing against crime as they ignored the destruction being committed by the other demons. Once more I wondered if they were looking for Bishop. Had he been shot down out of the sky? Was he injured and sheltering somewhere while these demons tried to find him to finish him off? I followed one group and saw after they met up with another that they had split up to go in opposite directions.

The group I followed walked back down the street where the dragon's lair was, giving the Bloc a wide berth even though the front entrance had completely collapsed on itself. The dragon was nowhere in sight. I assumed he'd found another way in and was once more guarding his treasure.

Wary of getting anywhere close to the lair, I held back and lost the group.

Up and down the streets I went, doing my own version of a search while keeping clear of any demons I saw. I was just about to give up, assuming the police had managed to evacuate all of the humans, when I heard the sound of crying.

It was soft and muffled, as if whoever it was tried to stifle the sound. I crept forward, listening and trying to track the noise. As I got closer, I realized it was coming from behind a dumpster that had been tipped over, spilling refuse and black trash bags all across the alleyway.

"Is someone here?" I asked in a loud whisper. "Don't scream. I'm here to help."

A face peered around the side of the dumpster, smeared with dirt and tears. As the girl crawled into view, I saw she was only about fourteen years old with torn jeans and a filthy T-shirt. Her black hair had come loose from its braids and was sticking up around her head in tiny spikes. Her dark eyes met mine, a mixture of fear and hope in their depths.

"I'm Eden," I told her. "What's your name?"

"Jayla."

There was a slight hesitation that made me wonder if Jayla wasn't her real name.

"The police have evacuated downtown." I glanced behind me to make sure no demons were heading our way. "I'm doing a sweep to make sure no one is left behind. Are your parents still here? Brothers or sisters?"

She shook her head. "Just me. I…I have my stuff. I don't want to leave it behind."

The girl pulled a battered, dark green backpack from behind the dumpster, then a striped tote bag that looked like it had been dug up out of the landfill. I swallowed hard, realizing the girl had been living on the streets. I'd been there myself a few times. It was most likely why she'd been missed when the police were evacuating the humans. Wary of cops, she probably hid, thinking it would be safer to lay low and ride it out than risk going with them. I sympathized, but in this instance, the demons roaming downtown were a far bigger threat than the police.

"You can bring your stuff," I told her, knowing how important belongings were when you had so few of them. "Are you injured? Can I carry something for you, or can you manage on your own?"

"I'm okay." She slung the backpack on, and settled the tote on her shoulder. "Where are you taking me? Where's safe?"

"The police evacuated everyone to Lincoln Heights. There's a couple of community centers and the old high school where people are staying."

The girl hesitated. "I don't want to go where the police are. Or those other people. Can you just take me where there aren't any demons? I'll be fine on my own."

"The demons are everywhere," I warned her. "And there's safety in numbers."

The girl scowled. "There's danger in numbers. Sometimes one person can go unnoticed, where groups are a target."

She was right, but I didn't want to think about all the humans grouped together at the community centers and the high school, a convenient target for a mass casualty event.

"Where would you like to go? Hollywood? Central City?" I suddenly had an idea. "I've got some family in the Valley. You could go there."

Bea would never turn away a child in need. Even if Jayla only stayed a night to get some sleep and food in her belly before leaving, she'd be better off than under a bridge somewhere. I wanted her to have an option, a choice. Just like I'd been given a choice years ago.

She bit her lip. "I don't know the Valley too well. Maybe Silver Lake?"

That was Telaney's neighborhood. While I was confident that Bea would welcome this girl with open arms, I wasn't so positive about my best friend. She adored her house and her privacy. While I wanted to believe she wouldn't refuse to give the girl food and shelter, I just didn't know. And I hated to spring Jayla on her with no warning.

"How about Los Feliz?" My beloved home had sort of become a flop house for those I was now considering my "team." The neighborhood shifters weren't too happy about that, but one more overnight guest wouldn't make much of a difference.

She thought about that for a second, then nodded. "Okay. I've been up there before visiting the observatory and hiking in the park. I should be able to find my way around. Where's your car?"

That was a problem. I didn't own a car. And I'd arrived here by angel instead of using my motorcycle. Bishop was nowhere to be seen, and so far all of the vehicles I'd passed were melted, charred, or twisted into the shape of a pretzel.

I heard a hissing noise and spun around, realizing there was a more pressing problem at hand. A band of six demons had spotted us and was running this way. I could fight, but fighting and trying to protect a human girl from half a dozen attackers with supernatural skills wasn't a good scenario.

"Run." I took the tote from Jayla before she could protest, grabbed her arm to shove her in front of me, and pushed her toward the other end of the alley as I spun around to face the demons.

The demons advanced, clearly excited that they'd found some humans to play with. One threw a brick at me with disturbing accuracy. I dodged it, glancing behind me to check where Jayla was heading. The girl was making a left two blocks down.

Deflecting another brick, I ran after Jayla.

The demons followed, tossing various debris and taunting me. I kept myself to human speed, and they remained an even distance behind me, clearly believing I was human and wanting to prolong the fun of this chase.

Eventually I'd need to take care of these guys, but my goal was to get Jayla clear of downtown without her being snatched or killed, then face off with these jerks when I could do so without worrying about the girl's safety.

Jayla dodged in and out of side streets, obviously not realizing the plan. We headed north, then doubled back toward the arts district once more as I cursed under my breath and tried to keep from being brained from bricks and blackened car parts.

The girl turned down an alley. The moment I rounded the corner, I realized her mistake.

Two tall buildings flanked either side of the alley, and at the back was a twelve-foot brick wall. I spun around to see one of the demons jog into the alleyway. Giving up my human masquerade, I hit him with some of the energy I'd stored. He shrieked in surprise, dancing to the side, so my blast only nicked his leg, sending him spinning back into the street.

Jayla cried out, her eyes wide as she looked at me. Frantic, she looked at the buildings on either side of the alley, then tried in vain to scrambled up the brick wall.

I moved to shield the girl and prepared for battle. Six demons rounded the corner and blocked the entrance to the alleyway.

They were wary, uncertain what to expect from me. Their hesitation bought us a little time, but I wasn't sure that time would matter. I'd seen two metal doors into the buildings on either side of us but I didn't think I could blast through them before the demons killed us. And I wasn't sure what was on the other side. Those buildings were little more than hollowed out shells of rubble, and I was well aware that, even if I could get us through one of the doors, we might find ourselves blocked by several tons of stone and steel.

I heard scrabbling noises behind me and realized that Jayla was still trying to climb up the brick wall. Even if she could manage to climb that high, I wasn't sure she could handle the twenty-foot drop onto the pavement on the other side.

"You got some spunk," one of the demons said to me. "Is that little human girl your prey? Leave her and we might let you live."

It was the worst lie ever. Without waiting for a response, a chicken-legged demon launched an energy attack at me, while a rhino with a cobra head stomped on the ground. The pavement shook as if we were in the midst of an earthquake, but I managed to grab the energy from chicken legs and throw it back at them. Unfortunately I missed, my aim thrown off by the undulations of the pavement under my feet.

The rhino-cobra stomped again, and this time the other five blasted me. I grabbed what I could, trying to stay in front of Jayla. One blast blew a hole through the brick wall about eight feet up, and I heard Jayla once more trying to climb the wall, this time toward the hole which was big enough for a teenage girl to squeeze through.

The demons continued to attack, leaving me with no time to retaliate. It was too much. There were too many of them and unlike before, these weren't lesser demons that I could manage on my own. I missed grabbing one of their blasts and felt it sear straight through flesh into the part of me that wasn't human. Gasping, I shrugged off the pain, and tried to keep from doubling over.

All six demons shot at once, two of them going wide. I glanced over and realized that they were aiming at the girl.

Diving to the side, I threw myself in front of her and waited for the blasts to hit, hoping I came out of this alive. Something solid slammed into us. As we fell and rolled to the corner of the alley, I recognized the body pressed against mine, as well as the burn of a very familiar angel's energy.

The blasts meant for Jayla and me took out the back wall of the alleyway. Bricks and metal rained down on us and Bishop tucked my head under his shoulder, shielding Jayla and me from the debris. Before the dust had settled, the angel was up, wings spread nearly the width of the alley as he raced toward the demons. I jumped to my feet as soon as he was off me, once more positioning myself to protect the girl.

CHAPTER 3

"Holy shit," Jayla breathed, staring wide-eyed at the angel.

"Stay back," I warned her as I positioned myself off to the side behind Bishop.

The demons didn't flee at the sight of the angel bearing down on them, but they did retreat to the edge of the alley. Then they shifted their attack toward Bishop instead of me. The angel easily deflected each blast, sending them into the walls at our sides.

The air filled with dust, and I began to worry that if Bishop and I didn't take out these guys soon, the remains of these buildings would collapse down upon us. Keeping Jayla behind me, I used the energy I'd absorbed, and attacked. It wasn't easy trying to shoot around Bishop's giant wings, but I managed to hit two of the demons and was thrilled to see them explode into bits. Bishop darted forward and grabbed one of the remaining demons, turning him into sand.

I heard a scream behind me and spun around to see Jayla struggling with a lion-headed lizard. The demon shouted something to the others, then dragged the girl through the space in the debris into the ruins of a building behind us.

Leaving Bishop to fight the demons in the alley, I ran after Jayla at top speed, slamming into her and the lion-headed demon. He let go of her as I hit. Jayla spun to the side, falling into a pile of concrete and rolling. The demon grabbed me with both hands, then roared as he closed his jaws over my head.

This is it, I thought as he bit down.

Light. The cold of an endless void. The combustion of a sun going super nova.

I never felt the fangs on my head. I never felt anything. And a millisecond later I was standing in a mess of concrete chunks, unharmed, a blackened spot before me.

Jayla stared in horror, and I wasn't sure if her expression was because of the two demons running toward us or because of what she'd seen me do.

I had no time to think about what had just happened. Pushing Jayla back, I made sure the girl was in the corner of two large slabs of concrete. The demons attacked, and in between the blinding bursts of light, I saw Bishop leap through the space where the brick wall had once been.

"Go," I shouted to Bishop as I fought the demons. "Get her out of here."

The angel vanished only to appear a split second later beside Jayla. I heard her scream, but was too busy with the two demons to focus on her. Another demon dashed from the alleyway, diving toward Jayla, who was trying to flee from the angel. Bishop vanished once more in a flash of light, only to reappear two feet away, in front of the demon. The demon skidded, but couldn't stop or turn in time. Bishop gripped its neck and the thing exploded into sand. At the same time, he looped an arm around Jayla's waist and the pair disappeared before the demon-sand hit the ground.

I spun back around, but my second of inattention meant I was too slow to grab one of the two blasts coming my way. It clipped my side, burning through my clothing and my skin but thankfully not injuring my spirit-self. The second blast I grabbed, sending it back and hitting one of the demons right in the head.

He exploded, and the one left ran for it.

I should have let him go, but I was angry, so I gritted my teeth against the pain of my injuries and took off after him.

There was a time not so long ago when I'd believed myself to be a real badass. In human terms, maybe I was, but the last few months had taught me I was a little fish in a very large pond—a pond with sharks and killer whales. The pain of my injury radiated through me. I was exhausted after all the running and fighting I'd done tonight. I chased the demon for six blocks then I lost him, my legs unable to keep up my speed and my lungs on fire from trying to force oxygen into my body.

Bending over, I put my hands on my knees, trying to catch my breath. When I stood upright, I caught sight of Blister strolling down the street toward me. The Low demon had on a silk blouse and leather pants, both with the tags still hanging from them. Over her shoulder was a Louis Vuitton bag.

I recognized the bag.

Blister was now a member of my household, my team. We'd had a discussion on how household members did not loot human businesses or steal from either humans or shifters. There had been a bit of an argument where I tried to differentiate between what Telaney and I did as licensed Vultures and illegal looting. I had believed we'd come to an agreement. It had been one of those "do as I say, not as I do" things. But here she was, dressed like a rich Valley girl heading to meet her besties for some matcha lattes after a day of shopping downtown.

"Where'd you get that stuff?" I demanded. As soon as the words were out, I realized I *should* be asking what she was doing here.

"Stole it off some greed demons." Her eyes narrowed and she clutched the purse tighter. "You didn't say I couldn't steal from demons, just humans and shifters and their homes and businesses. Demon theft is totally fair game. They left it all unattended in a truck, so I helped myself. I would have grabbed more but they all came running and screaming out of some mall, and jumped in the truck. I barely got out of the back before they took off."

I already felt like a hypocrite laying down the law for Blister when I made a living from robbing the dead, and occasionally the not-dead. Plus I didn't really care if she stole from demons. Their moral code seemed to be "if you don't get caught, it's not stealing," and I wasn't really in any position to throw stones at that philosophy.

"You can keep the clothes." I eyed the tote with a twinge of envy. "And the bag. Now come on. Let's start walking home and hope we can catch a ride."

Or steal a ride. Either one suited me just fine.

e'd walked about two miles and were safely out of the Downtown area, but there was still no sign of any parked vehicle, or any traffic we could beg a ride from. It was as if LA were deserted, and for a city that continued to be bustling even after the demons came and half the population fled, the silence was unnerving.

Blister chattered on about her new purse, then switched to gossiping about the demons at the tax office. I half-heartedly listened until I realized she was talking about Desiree and Corundum.

"Is he in her household?" I asked the Low.

She waved a hand and I noticed that her two-inch-long nails were now lemon yellow, with the sharpened points a bright red. "No, he's not in her household. He owed her a favor. That's why he gave you up to her. He wasn't happy about it, but you gotta repay your favors or you get a bad reputation and no demons will work with you. Desiree bought out your debt from Corundum in exchange for the favor he owed her and some other stuff. He really wanted to keep your debt, so whatever she offered must have been a pretty sweet deal or he would have bargained her down to something else. Corundum is a good negotiator. That's why he's where he is in the tax office. So she probably traded him something really valuable."

I was trying hard to learn about demon society and politics, but the whole thing was ridiculously confusing. One thing in Blister's rambling explanation stood out, though.

"Desiree now owns my debt? *All* of it?"

Shit. That was just fucking wonderful. In addition to the favors I owed her, she now had the favors I owed the tax demons? How the hell did that work? I hadn't realized any of this was transferrable when I'd made these deals.

"Yeah, but if you kill her, then you won't owe anyone anything," Blister cheerfully informed me.

I'd be happy to kill Desiree, but it didn't seem likely given that I struggled to take down even the lower-level demons.

"I guess she's in charge of New Hell now, since she killed Doriel," I commented, depressed and more than a little anxious at the thought.

Blister snorted. "She wishes. As soon as Doriel died, a bunch of Ancients and higher-level demons raced here from Hel, trying to jump into the power vacuum. At first, they were all busy killing each other, but after a few days, the most powerful came out on top. The rest have gone on home."

"Who are the top contenders?" I asked, wondering if the destruction downtown had been some sort of demon celebratory inaugural party.

Blister shrugged. "I know Desiree is still around, but I'm not sure on the other demons. They might just agree to split New Hell up between them in a sort of cease-fire, or they could keep duking it out until one of them gets the whole thing."

Everything was happening so fast. People were fleeing

New Hell. The rich had hopped in their private jets and abandoned their swanky estates. There were caravans of people heading for the border. Every day the humans who'd vowed they were going to hunker down and ride it out rather than leave their homes were changing their minds, deciding their lives were worth more than their homes and belongings. Even some of the shifters were leaving.

I wished I could abandon all of this and go somewhere that Desiree would never find me. Except I had to protect Bea and the girls, and I doubted Bishop would leave.

And then there was that vow I'd hastily made in a moment of supreme hubris. I'd claimed this city as mine, envisioning myself as a powerful vigilante bringing peace to the residents. The joke was on me. I wasn't powerful enough to bring peace, or to protect this city.

"I do know that Desiree is pissed about the situation," Blister continued. "She's one tough bitch and she's got a very loyal household, but it won't be easy for her to take out Ancients and their households. I'm willing to bet that if New Hell gets divided up, Desiree will make peace, hold her section, then scheme to kill the others and grab their territories later. That's how demons roll. Well, except for warmongers who prefer direct confrontation. The rest of us are more on the sneaky side."

The best thing about having a Low in my household was the gossip. And the education. Bishop knew a bit about demons, but Blister *was* one. She'd navigated their convoluted society for centuries and was happy to tell me all about it.

Now if only I could find someone who could help me with my powers which so far had been rather disappointing. By human terms, they were pretty darned impressive, but as far as demons went...well, the daughter of the OG Satan, especially one that was supposedly thousands of years old, should be more of a threat than I currently seemed to be.

"Can you get me all the information you can on these other demons?" Maybe I should hold a team meeting. My fledgling household, plus Juke. If we knew what the demons were up to, maybe we could come up with a strategy beyond Bishop and me racing around every time the police got a call.

"You want me to ask around the tax office? They always know what's happening. Squeaky owes me a favor. He's the coffee and donuts guy, so he overhears everything."

That was a benefit of being a Low, Blister had told me. Other demons usually ignored them, acting as if they weren't even present. The Lows actually preferred it that way since whenever they got noticed it tended to be because some demon wanted to torture them for fun.

"I'd appreciate it," I told her.

Blister sighed. "If I do this, will you finally mark me?"

I winced. Once more my lack of knowledge about demons had caused me to make a major mistake. I'd accepted the Low into my household, and evidently that meant I was supposed to damage her physical person using my personal energy signature so that every demon who saw her would know that I'd done it. Horrible as it sounded, the "mark," according to Blister, would protect her from random violence, as whoever hurt a member of my household would need to deal with me.

Not that dealing with me was all that much of a deterrent. I'd told Blister that along with my insisting that I wasn't going to break her finger or remove one of her toes. She'd informed me that as Low it was an honor to be invited to join a household—even one headed by a truly shitty demon such as me.

"It's important for you to be stealthy. Like a double agent." I told her, hoping she'd forget about this whole marking thing. "If other demons see that you belong to my household, they might not talk to you."

She shot me a look filled with disgust. "Most demons don't even know who you are. And while I've been told your energy signature seems like Samael's, most demons think that's a fluke. I mean, if the Fallen archangel were to have a child, she surely wouldn't be slumming around LA in a human body, shooting demons with bullets, barely able to do more than toss electricity around."

She wasn't wrong. I thought for a second, looking around as we walked down the street. Few buildings were intact, and those appeared to be shuttered and closed—except for one that still had a blinking red neon sign in the window.

"You can't change your form, right?" I asked Blister.

"I'm a little different back in Hel, but this is all I can manage here. Outside of my hair and nail color, this is it."

She sounded defensive about that. It wasn't like *I* could change how I looked—not even my nails or hair unless I went to a salon or bought a box of hair dye and some nail polish at the store. But I didn't ask her this because I wanted to rub her lack of power into her face.

"I'm not going to mark you by injuring you." I held up a hand to stop her protest. "I'm going to mark you my way. It'll be just as permanent." I pointed to the tattoo parlor.

She rolled her eyes. "That's how human gangs do things, not demons. I don't want a gang tattoo, I want a demon household mark."

"That's not my thing, Blister," I said for what felt like the millionth time. "I don't hurt my family or friends."

Well, not on purpose, anyway.

"The first household I've ever been invited to join, and it's headed by some shitty human wannabe," Blister grumbled.

"I'm pretty sure any other demon would take your head off for that disrespectful comment," I told her.

"I *know*. At least then I'd die being marked. You're not even demon enough to discipline me."

"I'm demon enough to steal that purse," I teased.

She shrieked and took a few steps away, wrapping her arms around the bag. "No stealing from household members. You said those are the rules, as stupid as those rules are."

"I said no stealing from humans or werewolves." I bit back a smile. "Other demons are fair game, remember?"

She whimpered a little then held out the purse. "Any belonging of mine is technically a belonging of yours as head of my household."

Huh. Another thing I hadn't realized.

"I'm not taking your purse," I told her. "I was just kidding. I'm going to totally covet it, but you're the one that stole it. It's yours."

"More proof that you're a shitty demon," she muttered.

The words were harsh, but I could sense the relief in them. Once more I bit back a smile as she stroked the bag.

"If I want one that bad, I'll steal it from that dragon," I told her. "Dragons are fair game, by the way."

She abruptly halted, her mouth open. "Dragon?" she squeaked.

"He seems to have taken up residence at the Bloc. There's a pile of stuff in the center of the courtyard. Designer stuff, artwork, even a Maserati," I told her.

"That's…that's horrible." She started to laugh and continued walking. "The other demons are going to shit a brick. A dragon downtown."

I glanced over at her. "What's the big deal? There have been dragons in New Hell since the demons arrived. Why would they suddenly be bothered about this one?"

"Because *this* one's got a hoard." Blister chuckled, shaking her head. "The other dragons were just raiding for loot and hauling it to wherever they called home. Any dragon that looked like they might want to claim a territory got bribed to go nest elsewhere."

"So with the chaos of the power vacuum, one showed up and settled in before he could be bribed away?" I laughed myself at the idea, then I realized that meant *we* were stuck with a dragon. "How big are their territories, geographically speaking? Is it only the Bloc that's off limits now? Or do we need to warn everyone not to venture closer than a three block radius?"

Blister shrugged. "Fuck if I know. It's not just territory that's the issue, though. The thing's gotta eat."

I shivered. There were no livestock beyond chickens and a few goats in the LA metro area anymore to serve as dragon dinner. That meant humans, shifters, or demons would be on the menu. I'd already seen the dragon chow down a greed demon, so hopefully he restricted his diet to them. Although that didn't exactly bode well for me or Blister.

We walked another six blocks, me worrying about the dragon downtown while Blister petted her purse. I was waiting for her to begin calling it her "precious" any moment now. Turning a corner to head north, I saw a car parked along the roadside. It was half on the sidewalk and the left fender had been torn off, but I was willing to bet it was still drivable.

"I'm going to jump that car," I told Blister. "Can you drive?"

She gasped. "You're letting me drive you home?"

"No, I'm letting you drive *you* home," I corrected. I'd been in car with Blister at the wheel once, and had no desire to repeat that experience.

"But what about you?" she asked.

"I'll either find another car to jump or I'll walk." I knew that if Blister drove me home she'd find some excuse to come inside, drink and eat, and eventually spend the night. I was hoping Bishop would come back at some point because I really needed to talk to him. And screw him. We'd been a bit busy the last few days, and this girl had needs.

Needs that wouldn't be fully met with a Low snoring on my couch. Although I'd offered to put Jayla up for the night, so I'd need to keep Bishop's and my sexcapades to the bedroom, and ensure the volume remained low.

The driver's door wasn't locked. I leaned in and looked under the dash, thankful that this was a twenty-year-old Ford Escort and not something new with a keyless start. I popped the hood, took a look, then yanked a few wires and got to work. Five minutes later the thing was running, although there was an alarming knocking sound coming from the engine.

"Should get you home," I said, as I closed the hood.

Blister wrinkled her nose. "This thing is a piece of shit. It smells like someone barfed on the upholstery."

"Drive with the windows open," I suggested. "A barf-mobile is better than walking."

"True." She climbed in and shut the door. "Sure I can't give you a lift?"

"I'm good," I assured her. Then I watched her drive off, making sure she was out of sight before I headed home.

CHAPTER 5

$\mathcal{I}$'d been unable to steal any of the other cars I'd come across, and everyone driving by me had declined to pull over and give me a ride. After all the running I'd done tonight, the walk home just about did me in. I limped my way up the road to my house, noting that my shifter neighbors were peering at me out their windows.

Unlocking the door, I flipped on the lights, and saw that my house was empty. No Bishop. No Mittens.

No Jayla.

Looking around I couldn't see any sign that the girl had been here. Maybe she'd decided to bed down somewhere else once Bishop dropped her off. I didn't blame her. I would have felt a little uncomfortable staying in a strange house that belonged to a woman I'd just met, let alone one who had some freaky supernatural powers. That plus the nosy neighbors probably had her heading for the hills.

Assuming the girl could take care of herself now that she was out of the center of a war zone, I kicked off my sneakers and got a glass of water out of the jug I kept filled on the counter. Then I tried the sink, nearly cheering when the water poured out of the spigot. Electricity. Water. What more could a girl want?

Shedding clothes as I went down the stairs, I made my way into the bathroom, turned the shower on hot, and waited for the steam to rise before getting in. I'm not sure how long I just let the water cascade over my body before I started with the shampoo and soap, but it was glorious. This house had a truly supersized water heater, and when the power was on, I took advantage of every drop.

By the time I finally climbed out of the shower, I was warm, relaxed, and felt oh-so clean. The steam hung in the air even with the fan turned on. I wiped a spot on the mirror clear with the edge of my towel and took my time drying off. Wrapping myself in a soft velour robe that had been left at my doorstep by some shifter as a tribute, I headed back upstairs.

The third step from the top squeaked as I put my weight on it, and I felt a sudden warmth that had nothing to do with my shower or the temperature in the house. It was an electric warmth that burned and tingled, and it was accompanied by the brush of an affectionate touch against my spirit-being.

I took the last few steps at a run and launched myself into his arms.

It sounds strange, but that hug was everything. Being wrapped in Bishop's arms, his spirit-self exploring mine for any injuries just as his hands were doing the same under my robe. Right then I wanted nothing more than to leave LA behind and go somewhere we could be alone—somewhere without violence and warring demon groups. Some isolated cabin in the woods. Or even his Aaru that he talked of sometimes.

After a long hug, Bishop led me to the sofa, pulling me down beside him.

He touched the scrape on my side that was almost healed

as well as the portion of my spirit-self that had been clipped during the fight in the alley, then he let out a long breath, obviously relieved that I had suffered nothing more serious than these small wounds.

Bishop had fared worse. Any physical injury he'd healed, but I could feel the lacerations to his spirit-self, and some were deep.

"Does this hurt?" I asked as I gently touched the wounds. I'd had plans for tonight, but maybe we'd need to restrict our lovemaking to our corporeal selves.

"It would be painful to join with you right now," he admitted.

I'd come to love the merging of our spirit-beings, but that could wait until these injuries had scarred over.

"But my body is willing to do what the spirit cannot," he added with a grin.

He reached forward, brushing his thumb across my lip before kissing me. He might be an angel, but he tasted like sin itself. I climbed onto his lap, fisted my hands in his hair, and tangled his tongue with mine.

His lips left mine to trail kisses along my jaw. He dropped his head and I felt his teeth nip their way down my neck. Shivering, my stomach clenched with need.

"Bedroom," I said, my breathy voice catching on the word.

With a throaty chuckle, he stood, carrying me across the room and downstairs. It was a short trip, but I kept myself busy, kissing his neck and gently touching my spirit-self to his. He picked up the pace, bursting into my bedroom and practically tossing me onto the bed. In a flash we were both naked, him staring hungrily down at me sprawled across the sheets.

I stared too.

"For once I'd like us to remove our clothes the old-fashioned way," I complained.

He raised an eyebrow. "Do you want me to put them back on?"

"Hell no. Now get over here."

He did as commanded, dropping his head halfway up my body to skim his lips across my abdomen. His warm breath tickled my skin, his hand reached up to gently pinch one of my nipples. I gasped, digging my hands into his hair and tugging.

"Get up here. And inside me. Now."

"So demanding," he teased as he climbed further up me.

I wrapped my legs around his waist as he entered me and began to move, slowly at first, then with increasing speed. Digging my nails into his shoulders, I urged him on. Pleasure built, starting low and deep. My muscles tightened and I clenched around him. With a groan he buried his head in the hollow of my neck and we came together, my climax roaring through me.

Holding him tight, I floated through the aftershocks and once more gently touched his spirit-self with mine. We lay there, entwined in each other's arms, and I wished this would never end. I wished I didn't have a city to save, that we could just fly away somewhere remote and spend our hours making love and enjoying each other's company, even if only for a few days.

Bishop's hands stroked my hair. "Hungry?" The word was followed up with a soft kiss on my neck.

Suddenly I was definitely hungry for round two, in spite of the sated feeling that still warmed my body. Then my stomach growled—loudly.

Bishop chuckled as he kissed me once more. With a gentle tug on my hair he eased himself off me and stood. We went upstairs and raided the fridge. While Bishop put together sandwiches, I pulled out a bag of chips and the a couple of bottles of wine. It was three in the morning and we were both starved, so we ate while standing in the kitchen. For a few minutes we did nothing but eat. As I dug into the second half of my sandwich, my desperate hunger was replaced by a need for a recap of the evening's events.

"What happened to you after the fight in the alley?" I asked Bishop in between bites. "Did you get ambushed after dropping Jayla off? Was there an emergency at Suerte?"

"The first emergency was that girl you stuck me with," Bishop informed me. "I delivered her here as you wanted, and she immediately freaked out. Said she couldn't be here and that I needed to get her out right away. There was no calming her down. I wasn't about to leave a teenager suffering a full-blown panic attack in your house alone, so I teleported her to Suerte."

I frowned wondering what was so terrifying about my house. Maybe it was me she was afraid of? She'd seen me fighting the demons and must have realized that I wasn't human. Either way, she'd clearly changed her mind about staying with me.

I wasn't sure it was a good idea to have a teen staying in a bar, though—especially a bar that catered exclusively to shifters.

"She was just as unhappy about Suerte," Bishop continued, "but I was done transporting the girl around. I told her she could sleep on the cot in the back room, or walk somewhere else."

I made a sympathetic noise, understanding Bishop's frustration. "Did she take off? Or decide to stay in the back room?"

"Neither. We weren't open, but HB was still there closing up, and she's a softy when it comes to kids. Said she'd handle the situation and told me to get lost."

I laughed. HB was amazing. I wasn't sure even *I* could get away with telling Bishop to get lost. Even if Jayla decided not to stay, I felt sure that HB would ensure she had a full belly, and drive her to her choice of locations. She'd probably even give the girl a blanket and a pillow, and show up in the morning with coffee and donuts, just to check on her.

"Afterward I had to deal with some demons who decided to bring it to the bar," he continued. "HB and I took care of them, but I'm going to up security on the area—especially if that girl decides to stay."

That guilt swept through me again. Before me, the only fighting Suerte had seen was between their shifter patrons.

"So what happened with you?" Bishop asked. "I fight off a dozen demons in the air then show up to find you cornered in an alleyway, protecting some human teen."

"Once the caravan of evacuees was clear, Juke sent me back to see if there were any humans they'd missed." I proceeded to tell him about the dragon, the roving bands of demons, and finding Jayla.

Then I told him about my conversation with Blister.

"Unless a very high-powered demon takes control, be ready to expect decades, if not centuries, of violence," he warned me. "There might be brief periods of peace, but demons will never be content with splitting the territory up. They'll fight until someone comes out on top. And even then, the demon on top will be determined to expand the borders of New Hell with the goal of eventually ruling the whole planet."

So the choice was endless fighting, or fighting until some megalomaniac achieved world domination. Great.

"Is that what would have happened with Doriel?" I asked him. "Was she planning on expanding New Hell's boundaries?"

"I don't think so. Doriel was an Ancient, one of the Fallen, and even before the Angelic War, she was more driven by the sin of sloth than anything else. During the war she was absolutely dedicated to Samael, the original Satan. When the angels and demons fought over New Hell, and the territory eventually went to the current Satan, Doriel pledged to her."

"So the current Satan isn't interested in expansion?" I asked. "Isn't she pissed that Desiree killed the demon she put in charge of the territory? Why hasn't she flown in here to kick ass and take names?"

"I don't know." Bishop scowled. "I've made inquiries through some contacts, but haven't gotten any concrete information. Some believe she's against even a minimal bit of order and that the current situation of chaos is what she wants. There's gossip that Doriel was put in place to placate the Ruling Council, and the Iblis, Satan, is who orchestrated her assassination. Gabriel is ignoring my requests for a meeting—which isn't all that surprising given what happened the last time we met."

I winced. Add that one to the problematic situations I'd caused. Gabriel had not only claimed I was an angel, but insisted I was the offspring of his prodigal brother—the OG Satan. He'd been pushy and a total jerk, and Bishop had ended up threatening the archangel in defense of me.

But that wasn't what really worried me about what Bishop had said. I'd never met this new Satan, or the old one that I could remember. The current Satan was a woman with black feathered wings and a ceremonial sword that evidently came with the title. From what I'd read and seen on TV, she was batshit crazy and a total loose cannon. The theory that she was behind all of this and in support of the situation in New Hell shouldn't surprise me. Actually it didn't surprise me. But it *did* bother me.

Batshit crazy or not, I wanted to like her. I wanted her to be of a like mind, to be on my side. I wanted her to swoop in here and save the day when I clearly couldn't. And if she didn't fly in on black wings of salvation, I wanted a damned good reason for her negligence. I didn't want to believe that she'd abandoned us, that she didn't care, or that she actually approved of the destruction and slaughter. If I were an Angel of Chaos, if Samael was truly my father or whatever, then this Satan was kind of my boss. I didn't want to hate my boss.

Bishop sighed. "There's someone I know who I haven't seen in a long time, but who might have some insight as to what's going on with the Ruling Council and the Iblis. It's been a few hundred years, so I'm not sure if she'll tell me even if she knows, but I'm willing to go see her if you want."

I looked down at my plate, focusing on pushing the few remaining potato chips around while I thought. *She.* Who was this that Bishop had known and hadn't seen for a few hundred years? I assumed she was an angel, or possibly one of the Fallen?

It was hypocritical for me to be jealous of Bishop's past when I'd also had a slew of relationships before I knew him. He was with me now, and he'd given me not the slightest hint that he wasn't one hundred percent in love with and committed to me. But still…

What had he had with this woman? And what had he had with Desiree? The demon had claimed that she and Bishop had been an item, and I'd never had the courage to confront him about it.

I didn't want to know. Sometimes it was best not to know.

"I'd like that," I finally said, looking up from my plate. "It would be good to find out if this is the way things are going to be, or if there might be a chance of some outside help."

He nodded. "I'll leave first thing in the morning. I should be back in a day or maybe two."

My heart sank at the thought of him being gone for even a few hours. It wasn't just that I'd miss him, I'd come to rely on Bishop and I was unnerved at the prospect of having to handle things in New Hell without his assistance.

"I'm having a team meeting tomorrow," I told him as I scooted the chips around my plate again. "Blister is nosing around the tax office to find out who the major players are in this war. I'm hoping she can also get some intel on where the fighting might be so we can plan some sort of defense."

"Have everyone meet at Suerte," Bishop offered. "HB and I are arranging for twenty-four-hour security around the building, so there won't be any chance of a surprise attack."

Living in a neighborhood with big cat shifters, I was pretty sure there wouldn't be any chance of a surprise attack here either. But I knew my neighbors were getting irritated with me and wouldn't be thrilled with five or six outsiders converging on my house for a meeting. In the interest of an improved relationship with the neighbors, having the meeting at Suerte would be a better plan.

"Would ten o'clock be okay?" I asked him.

Bishop nodded and pulled out his phone. "Sure. I'll text HB and also let the security team know."

I pulled out my phone as well, texting those I'd considered to be my "team" with the details. It was sad, Bishop and I typing away at our phones while standing in the kitchen eating sandwiches and chips, but this was the world we now lived in.

CHAPTER 6

Bishop left at eight after a quick breakfast. After cleaning up, I left some food and water out in case Mittens returned, and left soon after Bishop, driving north to the Valley on my motorcycle.

I pulled in the parking lot at Suerte at quarter to ten, noting that there were only two other vehicles in the parking lot besides mine. As I entered, I looked around the bar, surprised to see it empty of patrons.

Suerte was in the Valley, but not close to any major freeways and a good distance for some of my household. It wasn't as crazy as asking everyone to hike to Hawthorne or Torrance, south of LA, but Suerte wasn't exactly centrally located. Still, having my meeting here wouldn't piss off my neighbors, and it was nice knowing that we wouldn't be ambushed. And it was also nice knowing that if there were a fight, some fierce shifters would have our backs.

HB was behind the bar, so I wandered over in that direction.

"Where is everyone? I'd figured this place would end up being a safe spot for shifters with you and Bishop to defend it," I commented to her. "Why isn't the dining area filled with wolves, bears, and big cats?"

She shrugged and continued wiping the water spots off wine glasses. "After Bishop's house got torched, everyone thought Suerte would be next. It's no secret that he's broken his deal with the demons, and that they're going to come after him. Everyone figured they were safer in their own communities than here."

"But right now Desiree and the demons have more pressing things to deal with," I told her, thinking that I wasn't the only one who'd been given a much needed reprieve by the demons fighting over control of New Hell.

"Everyone is waiting to see how it all shakes out," HB told me. "Hopefully whoever ends up on top of the heap will be willing to work out some deal with Bishop again."

I flinched, knowing that I was the reason he'd broken his deal. Because of me, he'd endangered not just himself and his home and business, but his partners, his friends, and the shifter communities that had allied themselves with him. They should all hate me, and I was sure some of them did.

"I'm sorry," I told HB, hoping I hadn't lost her friendship over this.

She shrugged again. "Even angels do stupid shit for love. It's not your fault. You were born in chaos, and anyone who is going to stand by Bishop is going to need to learn to live with your chaos as well or cut ties and leave." She looked up at me, a sideways grin on her face. "Good thing I like chaos. And a good fight—especially when the odds aren't in my favor."

She'd faced Desiree once and been horribly injured. She'd almost died. I was surprised that hadn't changed her mind about chaos and fights, but I really didn't know much about HB. Maybe her past had been full of fights that had almost ended her, and she was one of those where defeat and adversity only strengthened their resolve.

Bishop was lucky to have her by his side. And so was I.

"Your little friend has stuck around," HB said.

It took me a second to realize who she meant. "Jayla."

HB nodded. "She pitched a huge fit when Bishop brought her here. For some reason, she decided to live in that shed out back. Good thing, too. That girl stinks to high heaven. I kept telling her to use the outdoor shower behind the kitchen, but she refused. There's no way I'd want her in the bar smelling like she does. It's even worse now than when she arrived. I swear that girl has been rolling in garbage and poop or something."

I wrinkled my nose, remembering that the girl had definitely smelled like someone who'd been living on the streets for a while, but I couldn't understand her not wanting to clean up when she was offered access to the facilities here.

I didn't know what the girl had been through, but I'd had my own odd habits and rituals after being bounced around foster homes as well as my short stint as a homeless runaway. I wasn't going to push Jayla into anything she didn't want to do—which included showering.

"I feel like I've got a feral cat living out back of the bar," HB continued. "She won't answer the door of the shed, so I have to leave food on the step for her. I put out three squares a day, and I still caught her raiding the dumpster. And she's been hunting." HB said the last with pride.

"With a pistol?" I hadn't seen a rifle among her belongings, but everyone in New Hell had some sort of gun, even the homeless.

"I haven't heard any gunshots," HB replied.

HB was a mountain lion shifter, and would absolutely have heard gunshots, unless Jayla was trekking over the other side of the mountain range.

"She's setting traps then?" I'd seen some of those survival reality shows before the demons came and remembered people using snares and box traps to catch rabbits and squirrels.

"I've never known any of the downtown homeless to be skilled in trapping. Plus it was a deer and a coyote she caught." HB shrugged. "I'm guessing it was some sort of knife from the marks on the bones. Unless she caught them with her bare hands and was using a knife to take the flesh off."

I shrugged as well, doubting that a city-streets homeless girl could catch a deer and a coyote with her bare hands. But we'd all learned to adapt since the demons came. Even people who were used to living in the shadow of high rises needed to gain new skills to survive.

HB angled her head to the side, and looked toward the door. "Car coming. Sounds like the engine's about ready to blow. Just saying whoever this is might need a ride home."

Five minutes later Blister came through the door, demanding food and tequila shots. HB handed her a bottle and shooed her back into the kitchen, telling her that she could "make her own damned burgers."

The Low had just vanished behind the swinging door when Telaney came in with Addy right behind her. Juke came the same time as Isha.

"Thanks for coming," I told the detective.

"It's the least I could do after your help last night." Juke smiled at me. "Everyone is safely in the temporary shelters. Over the last week you've proved to the police that you and Bishop can be counted on to help keep the peace—and assist when humans are in danger."

It was a heavy burden, and one that I'd assumed willingly. But now I felt the weight of that, and worried that I wouldn't live up to Juke's and her department's expectations—especially if Bishop wasn't available to help, or if I ended up facing demons that were more powerful than the ones we'd come across downtown.

Juke patted me on my shoulder. "You done good, Alvaro. And I'm happy to be the police liaison to your group of vigilante helpers."

I couldn't help but laugh at that, thinking that two years ago the police would have rather slit their throats than work with a group of vigilantes, especially ones that weren't human.

Juke headed toward the others at the bar, but Isha stayed behind and reached out to pluck the sleeve of my T-shirt.

"Eden. I'm sorry, but Fi…well, she's kinda with Kevin on this. And I don't blame her. I mean, pack is pack. My pack is neutral on the whole thing, but I owe you a personal debt, and honestly that makes me part of *your* pack, if that makes any sense to you."

It did. I impulsively hugged her, thrilled to have the wolf by my side. I'd seen her fight in the arena and again at that disastrous press conference where our governor and Doriel, the demon who was supposed to be in charge of New Hell, were killed.

That gave me a team of four, not including my actual family, or Bishop and HB. Telaney, Addy, Blister, and Isha. These four were what I'd consider to be first-round draft picks, and I was thrilled to have them on my team.

Although it wasn't like poor Addy really had any choice in the matter. Still, looking at her over at the bar, chatting with Telaney and Juke, she seemed happy. And that was a huge improvement over the angry, lost, depressed woman she'd been less than a week ago.

"Go over to the bar and get a drink," I told Isha. "We'll begin soon."

I went into the kitchen to herd Blister back into the bar only to find her eating two raw hamburgers on buns with an excess of condiments. She'd tucked a dish towel into the collar of her shirt, and it was splattered with blobs of ketchup, mustard, and mayonnaise.

Rolling my eyes, I left the kitchen.

Giving everyone a moment to get settled with their drinks, and for Blister to finish the rest of her burgers, I hopped up on the stage the bar used for bands, and got the meeting started.

"Everyone's here," I announced. "We're getting ready to start."

"Cool." Blister took off her makeshift bib and tossed it on a table before pulling a large square of paper out of her backpack and waving it at me. "Map's right here. I marked it."

We both stared at each other for a few awkward seconds. Didn't she understand that I needed her to present at this meeting? We couldn't exactly strategize and plan if we didn't know what the fuck was going on in New Hell, and it wasn't like she'd had the opportunity to brief me ahead of time.

"Go ahead and tell us what you've found out, Blister."

"Me?" she squeaked, pointing at her chest with a long, pointed nail.

I hopped off the stage and walked over to her. "Yes you," I whispered. "You're the one who's been gathering intel. You're the one with the vital information. I need you to share that with the team."

She gaped. "But I'm a Low. You're supposed to get the information from me, then announce it as if you found it out yourself through some special, super-secret means. That's what the heads of demon households do."

"I don't have time for that bullshit," I said. "And my ego isn't so fragile that I need to claim your work for my own. You're my spy, my information gatherer. The team, or household or whatever, needs to respect your skills and know that they'll also be recognized and valued for what they bring to the table."

Oh my fucking god. That sounded like some middle-management motivational speech. But the weird thing was, I meant it.

"You want *me* to present the information?" Blister hissed. "Fine. But that's one more reason you're a shitty demon and a terrible head of household."

It was a common refrain from the Low, but this time, the words didn't carry the heat they normally did. She was flattered. And she liked getting the recognition and respect. I might not be a typical demon, but I got the impression that Blister was starting to enjoy my unconventional ways.

We pushed a few tables together and Blister spread a giant map of the greater Los Angeles area on top of them. It drooped over the sides, making it a little hard to see the places around Torrance to the south and the upper part of the Valley to the north. Oh well. We'd just have to scoot the map around when we discussed those locations.

"Where...where did you get this thing?" HB wrinkled her nose.

"Bus station," the Low told her.

It *was* the perfect place to get a giant map of the city. Besides, it wasn't like they were using it any more. Public transportation had left as soon as the demons had arrived.

"What's that stain?" the mountain lion shifter pointed, her face scrunched with an expression of disgust.

"Probably pee," Blister told her. "Just ignore it."

I knew HB couldn't ignore it. It was just a faded, yellowish patch to the rest of us, but the shifter could probably smell the ancient urine from halfway across the room. Isha probably could as well. That was most likely the reason she'd held back, standing a good ten feet from the map.

"Wait." Telaney went behind the bar and came back with a

bottle of clear liquid. She sprayed the corner of the map, then blotted it with a rag. HB's eyes stopped watering and she sighed.

"Good idea," HB said. "I picked up that enzyme spray a few months ago when the wolves and the big cats literally got into a pissing contest at trivia night. Didn't realize it would work on human urine as well."

I eyed the bottle, wondering if it would work on hellkitty pee too. Mittens liked to poop at random locations of my house in spite of the multiple litter boxes with a variety of litter in different rooms. Thankfully he hadn't peed on the floor yet, as I assumed it would burn right through the hardwood.

"It looks like you've already marked the map sections in highlighter." I gestured to the the Low demon. *Take it away, Blister.*

She glanced around, slugging down a gulp of tequila from the bottle gripped in one hand and eyeing the crowd for a few seconds before speaking.

"Within days of Doriel's murder, the demons trying to gain control of New Hell went from twenty to five. In the last twenty-four hours, two of those demons have been killed, and we now have three major players. My current intel says that the three have reached a tentative agreement to split New Hell among them. These are their territories as they stand right now. The northern sections from the Valley up to the Alaska border are still being disputed, as are the areas south of Tijuana. But all three demons are drawing clear territory lines here in LA."

Everyone leaned close.

"This area outlined in yellow." Blister stabbed a pointed nail at the map, poking a hole in it. "Is being claimed by a demon known as Itinder."

I snorted at the name, thinking immediately of the dating app.

"He's a high-level plague demon," Blister continued. "Normally plague demons work solo or with small households of four or five, but this guy's household is basically a standing army of two thousand."

Juke sucked in a breath. "He's claiming the Valley. What does that mean for us that a plague demon is claiming where we live?"

"Death and disease, that's what it means," HB said. "Spanish flu? Small pox? Polio?"

"They were all due to plague demons?" Juke eyed the map nervously.

"Assisted by plague demons," Blister told her. "They mutate normally occurring diseases to make them more deadly, or faster spreading, or whatever. In the past, plague demons couldn't stick around for long or they'd get dusted by the angels, so either human medicine had a chance to deal with it, or the disease itself burned out without the plague demon around to spur it on."

"But that's not the case here." Telaney's voice was low and halting. "We've got no angels to chase this guy out, and our medical care here in New Hell is shit at best."

We did have an angel—two of them if I was counting me. But I understood what she meant. We weren't back in the times when a handful of demons who'd made it through the gates from Hel would be harassed and possibly killed by a squad of hunter angels, here specifically to hunt them down. New Hell was overrun with demons, and Bishop and I would have no other angelic help.

"Are all of them plague demons in this army?" I was really worried at the thought of two thousand plague demons tearing through northern section of New Hell.

"Some are." Blister shrugged. "Most of the are mid-level

generalized demons. He's got a few greed demons and imps, and a handful of low-level war demons. About ten are pestilence demons, since pestilence and plague tend to get along —well, get along as much as any two demons can, that is."

I frowned, thinking of the demonology book I'd been studying. "But warmongers and greed demons don't seem like they'd be all that friendly with plague demons. Imps either. They all want healthy humans to fight, embezzle, and play tricks on. Bedridden, dying humans aren't their thing."

Blister jabbed one of her pointed nails at me. "True. And that's something we might be able to exploit. These demons with large households have constant power struggles and arguments. Sometimes they can quell them with their own clout. Sometimes they've got a strong steward to keep the rabble under control. But even in the best household, there are weak points. There is always that one demon who felt slighted that one time, or one who resents another who got recognition he believes he deserved. And there are often demons who don't like the direction their leader is taking and are actively planning a way out."

I nodded, but wasn't sure how I could exploit that weakness. These demons would laugh if I offered them a spot in my household to betray Itinder. I could keep an eye on them, watch for signs of factions, and do what I could to help them implode, but how could I watch two thousand demons? Especially when there were two other major players to deal with as well. Plus, I only had one actual demon in my household. The rest of us were in no position to get close to disease-spreading demons. And my only demon, Blister, was a Low, and would be at just as much risk of being killed on sight as the rest of us would be.

So…this Itinder," Addy said. "Any idea what his plans are? And does he intend on keeping his army of two thousand in his new territory or sending them back to Hel once things are solidified as far as the power structure here?"

Blister shrugged. "He'll probably keep at least some of them here in case he gets challenged by the other two players. I can't see him keeping all two thousand here for long because if he can't keep them busy, they'll start fighting amongst themselves."

"How about the other two territories and the demons who hold them?" I asked.

"Here we've got Barstonel." She stabbed at the blue outlined section of the map. "He's a warmonger, but an Ancient. That means he was an angel during the war and part of the Fallen. He's not top-of-the-heap as far as the Fallen go, but he's no weakling. His household isn't as big as Itinder's but he's got better control over them. He wants to fight. Doesn't matter if it's humans, shifters, or the other demons. He's probably the biggest threat over the other two face because he just doesn't give a fuck about boundary lines or peace treaties. The other two will probably try to keep him occupied fighting someone or something else, just so he leaves them alone."

I eyed the blue section, realizing that it encompassed the south LA area where the Disciples had their home base. The gang was formidable, and might keep the warmonger busy for a few months at least. There were a few good-sized shifter groups in that area as well. I looked over to Isha and saw from the worried frown on her face that she was thinking the same as I was. Her pack was in that warmonger's territory. And shifters defended their pack and lands with their lives.

"And this..." Blister shot me a sympathetic look then stabbed one of her fingernails into the orange outlined section. "This is Desiree's territory."

Everyone was quiet, eyeing me while trying not to make

it obvious. Desiree had most of LA proper, including the Los Feliz neighborhood where I lived, and the Silver Lake area where Telaney's home was located. Hollywood. Bel Air. Beverly Hills. Brentwood. Everything from the mountains to the shore, bordered by the Valley to the north, and stopping at Santa Monica and South LA to the south.

"She's a greed demon," Blister continued. "Desiree has a huge household and they're very loyal. She's a master at negotiating and getting demons what they want so they'll ally with her. Plus, she's been here even before the demons claimed the territory two years ago. She knows this area. She knows the humans and shifters and the power structure here. That's her primary advantage over the other two. Power-wise, she's less of a threat than the other two. But given her knowledge and her allies, in my opinion she's the biggest threat. She's wily and a total weasel—no offense to any weasel shifters here—but she's not likely to cause mass casualties like the other two. Well, not unless it would ultimately be to her benefit."

Everyone eyed me again. If this wasn't Desiree, I might think about approaching her and working out a deal to take the other two demons out. But this was the woman who'd bought the favors I'd owed the tax office. That plus the favor I'd promised her myself meant she didn't have to do anything for me. I wasn't in a good position to negotiate. And I didn't trust Desiree to hold up her end of any bargain I made with her.

"What about this section?" I pointed toward the area Downtown where none of Blister's highlighters surrounded.

"No one's claimed that right now because of the dragon," Blister announced.

CHAPTER 7

 veryone inhaled.

"Hell no, a dragon?" Telaney muttered.

"Maybe he'll do us all a favor and eat the demons," HB drawled.

"Or eat the humans and shifters," I pointed out. "I'm not sure that just avoiding his territory will keep anyone safe. The guy's gotta eat, and anyone in the neighboring area is probably on his menu."

"Before now the dragons just looted and left," Blister told the group. "They'd come, fly around, steal shit, then go back to wherever their home was. Sometimes demons would cut a deal with them where they'd basically pay the dragons to hurry them along. No demon wants a dragon mucking up their game. From what I've heard, dragons are smart. They have egos the size of a small planet. They're really hard to kill and really easy to piss off. And once they make a nest somewhere and start stashing their hoard, they're not gonna budge unless you kill them. Which is pretty fucking impossible."

"Can we make a deal with him?" Addy asked. "Offer him a

museum if he takes out the plague demon and his army. We can even stuff the dead demons in industrial freezers so he'll have food for at least a few months."

"It's not a bad idea," I mused, thinking of all the shops on Rodeo drive as well as those abandoned mansions. There were a couple of problems with that plan, though. One, most of the posh places were in Desiree's territory. Two, I wasn't sure that the dragon wouldn't fry me before I managed to get one word out about our offer.

It was still worth further consideration, though.

"Any other suggestions?" I asked, because I had nothing.

After a few seconds of silence, Telaney stepped forward. "I say we leave the dragon alone and focus on trying to take out this plague guy somehow. I don't know how. A whole warehouse of Lysol, maybe? Tons of Clorox wipes? If we attack him with a pressure washer full of bleach, can we kill him?"

"Not before his two thousand demon army takes us out," Addy scoffed. "I'm voting that we approach the warmonger and partner up with him to kill the plague demon and his crew. And then maybe Desiree."

"Which leaves us with a warmonger in charge of everything," Isha pointed out. "I agree that he's probably the lesser of three truly terrible evils, but if we go that route, we need to have a plan to get rid of him as well."

"Desiree would be eager to cut a deal to take out the other two," Blister said. "And while her household is loyal, she's probably the least able to manage a territory as large as New Hell on her own. I don't want to deal with any of them one-on-one, but if I had to pick, I'd choose working with her over a plague demon or a warmonger."

I glanced over at HB and Isha.

"Shifters will be less affected by the plague demon than the warmonger," Isha told me. "We could help fight against this Itinder, but we'd at more of a disadvantage fighting a warmonger. And I really don't want to think about what Desiree could do to us."

I was sure Desiree could do plenty to hurt the shifters. She'd nearly killed HB, and she was the one luring shifters into traps and making them fight in the gladiator games south of the city.

"I think we should focus on taking out Desiree first," Addy chimed in. "She might not be the strongest of the three, but I think she's the most dangerous."

"I say we partner with either Desiree, the dragon, or the warmonger and take out the plague demon first," Telaney countered. "He sounds like the biggest threat to me."

I turned to Juke, wanting her opinion on this.

"Every option sucks," she informed me. "But no matter which we pick, we need a combination of offense and defense. We need to work at dismantling these mini fiefdoms, and protecting the residents from harm."

"We're not going to be able to protect everyone," Addy said. "We can't. New Hell is too big—especially with people spread out all over the place."

"I think we can help with that," Juke spoke up. "I mean, we the police, although we, this group, could certainly assist. Lots of people are fleeing the area, and those who remain are moving closer together and forming neighborhood groups. I'll work with my department to see if we can designate certain high-density spots as sanctuaries or safe-zones, and focus patrols on those areas. If people clump together, we'll have an easier time defending them."

"Shifters won't go for that," Isha warned. "They won't leave their packs or their homes, and they have thousands of years of distrust for human organizations baked into them."

"Bishop and I know what packs are where, along with their leaders, and their sizes," HB spoke up. "We've already put out the call that unaffiliated, or solo shifters are welcome at Suerte. Right now everyone is kind of taking a 'let's wait and see' approach, but if the violence heats up, we should have a good number here to help defend the area. And humans are welcome as well—as long as they are shifter friendly."

"We'll do what we can to assist in defending human neighborhoods as well as these sanctuary zones," I told Juke.

But defense wouldn't be enough. We needed a plan to take back LA.

I just had no idea what the plan was.

* * *

JUKE, HB, and I remained behind when everyone else had left. We still didn't have a plan beyond gathering further information and helping anyone who was being attacked.

"Once we get the sanctuary areas nailed down, maybe we can assign some of your team to help in protecting each one. Assuming they're within a reasonable geographic distance, that is," Juke said.

"Sounds good," I told her, even though the proposal didn't sound good at all.

One of my team. Addy had magic, but when she was kicked out of her magical cult, she'd been forced to leave behind all of her spell books and supplies. There were some things she could do on the fly, and she had been busy trying to gather what she needed to do more than those three or four spells, but she was still a long way from being the powerful mage and illusionist she'd once been. Telaney could shoot the head off of a pin, but would be at a severe disadvantage if she had to face off against any but the lowest level demon

Isha and HB were an asset in a battle, but again, shifters had their limits when dealing with demons. HB had nearly been killed by Desiree. I had no doubt a pack could put up a formidable defense, but they'd lose facing an army of two thousand demons. Or even a few hundred demons. And Blister was a Low. She was great at spying, but probably not so great at fighting.

That left me. Until Bishop got back, that was.

And Mittens. Maybe. The hellkitty came and went as he liked. Sometimes he showed up to assist me, but other times he was missing in action. Mittens was definitely a valuable weapon when it came to the demons, though. He was pretty much feared on the same level as the dragons, despite his diminutive, fluffy, adorable appearance.

The dragon. I wished there was some way to leverage him, but I knew nothing about dragons beyond what Blister had just told us.

But there was someone who *did* seem to know everything about everyone. Alfie.

HB suddenly stiffened, pulling a shotgun from behind the bar. My internal musings over dragons and Mittens vanished. Seconds later a man burst through the door. He had a strangely elongated mouth and jaw, almost like a muzzle. His eyes glowed, and his furry hands ended in long claws.

"Incoming," the werewolf announced in garbled tones.

HB tossed me the shotgun and vaulted the bar, by the time she hit the floor she was in the form of a giant cougar. To give Juke credit, the detective didn't even blink. She pulled a white-muzzled pistol from a leg holster with one hand and the whip from her hip with the other.

The whip shimmered, the black leather turning as bright red as Juke's tight curls.

HB snarled and the werewolf interpreted, telling us to fight out front of the bar so we didn't wreck the place. I held back a laugh, a whole lot more confident since HB's concern seemed to be for the bar furnishing rather than our surviving this battle. I got the impression the shifter patrons did more damage than she expected these demons to do, but that she didn't feel like cleaning up the mess.

We went out into the parking lot where my motorcycle and two cars stood. I had a moment of anxiety and moved over toward the empty side of the lot, hoping to draw the demons away from my bike.

We stood there and waited. Juke finally turned to me, her eyebrows raised. I shrugged, wondering how fast the werewolf had run to outpace the demons by this margin.

HB lifted her head, sniffed the air, then made a low growling noise deep in her throat. The werewolf squatted down, like a sprinter at the Olympics. Juke and I took their lead, the cop racking the pistol before extending it out, one-handed, the whip sparking as it pooled on the asphalt.

Four of those lizard things that I'd seen destroying cars and trucks on the freeway burst out of the trees. One of them spit, and Juke danced out of the way, the spit burning a ten-inch pothole in the asphalt. I fired the shotgun, hitting one of the demons. He slowed, staggering slightly, then kept running even though his torso was torn and bloody flesh.

Okay. New plan. As I placed the shotgun on the ground, and prepared to use my own paranormal weaponry, Juke shot her pistol. Blue paint splattered across one demon's chest. The werewolf leapt forward, and in a blur of speed, was on the demon, tearing it to shreds.

The other three lizard demons continued their charges, spitting as they ran. We dodged the acid phlegm, me throwing electricity at them with the same shitty result as the shotgun. Juke was taking her time, aiming carefully and making sure each expensive magical bullet wasn't wasted.

I heard the pistol fire and another lizard sported a blue splat, this one on his shoulder. The werewolf darted over to finish him off and Juke got off a third shot before the lizard demons were on us.

Snatching the shotgun up from the ground, I took out the blue-splatted demon, leaving us to deal with the remaining one. HB snarled, crouching low then dove forward, knocking the demon sideways before he could reach Juke. The lizard spat at the cougar, singing her fur and burning right through flesh. I saw the white gleam of bone, but HB never flinched, her jaws closing tight around the demon's throat. Picking it up, she shook the thing like a dog toy then tossed him aside. Juke snapped her whip, and the glowing red tip cracked through the air, striking the demon in the hip and removing one of his legs. The demon howled, but before he could regenerate, HB and the werewolf were on him, ripping him apart.

I stood there, feeling completely useless. I was an utter fool for doubting the shifters and the humans. They'd kicked ass, taking out these three demons, when all I'd done was give them the equivalent of a static shock. Yes, I'd killed one with the shotgun, but the weapon would have been completely ineffective if Juke hadn't first shot the demon with her anti-magic gun.

Four demons dead. And the only injury we'd suffered was HB's shoulder, which didn't seem to affect her one bit.

But we barely had time to take a breath before the air changed, growing heavier and thick, like just before a storm. Every insect and bird went abruptly silent. HB and the werewolf stood, backing away from the lizard demon corpses. The cougar shifter's fur rose upright on her back, the wound on her shoulder healed before my eyes.

I turned to look where she faced, and saw the air shimmer. Smoke rose from the ground, forming a somewhat insubstantial humanoid form. This demon wore armor, blurred with the smoke of his form. Horns rose from his head and curled backward. His eyes glowed red, and his arms were wreathed in fire.

"Give her to me." His voice was like an autumn wind over dry leaves.

Did he mean…me? Had Desiree sent him? Or had some other powerful demon taken notice at the press conference where Doriel had been killed and decided I needed to go?

Either way, it was clear that those lizard demons were the pre-show, the spear fodder. This was the real threat.

I eyed the shotgun in my hand, then set it down again on the ground. Not that my lightning weapon would be any more effective against this guy than it had been on the lizard demons, but it was probably better than the shotgun. Juke readied her whip, checking the pistol and cursing under her breath.

Was she out of bullets? Or maybe she doubted her aim with only one or two left in the magazine. That would leave us with her whip, the physical weapons of the shifters, and my puny ass lightning.

Unless…

"I'm right here, you *puta*," I shouted, walking forward and ignoring Juke's hissed warning. "I'm gonna fuck you up, you fireworks freak show. Your last thoughts before your spirit-self shreds into oblivion will be filled with fear."

The demon gave me what was clearly an annoyed look. Then he shot a blast of energy my way.

I grabbed it and held on, dramatically staggering back. "*Dios mio!* That demon shot me. I might have a bruise."

"You annoying insect," he hissed. Then he unloaded a huge burst of energy at me.

I sucked it in, falling to the ground with the impact, but managing to hold it all.

His form coalesced into something more substantial and

he stared at me. I stayed on the ground, praying my friends wouldn't do anything stupid.

HB and the werewolf held back, but Juke clearly hadn't gotten the memo. She cracked her whip at the demon. It just passed through him with a shower of sparks, but did nothing except draw the demon's attention to the cop.

The demon directed his next blast at Juke. She dove to the side to evade it, firing her pistol at the same time. The bullet went wide, painting a blue splat on a nearby tree. The demon's energy blew another chunk out of the parking lot. Not pausing, he threw a second blast at Juke. HB and the werewolf leapt forward. Juke fired her pistol once more.

Everything felt like it shifted into slow motion. I heard the empty click of the weapon, saw the demon fling out his hand toward the attacking shifters, saw the blast heading straight toward Juke and knew that the second blast of energy was going to reach HB and the werewolf before they managed to hit the demon.

With a shriek of frustration, I *pulled*. The energy heading toward Juke made a hard left, zooming into me instead. But I wasn't fast enough to yank all the second blast my way before it connected with HB and the werewolf. Fur singed off HB's side, burning through flesh and leaving ribs, her shoulder, and the side of her hip nothing but torn muscle and bone. It hit the werewolf head-on and he dropped to twitch on the ground, his ears burned off and his skull visible.

In spite of her horrific injuries, HB kept going. Her open muzzle sank through the black smoke of the demon, closing with an audible snap on something solid. The demon grabbed her with his hands, and I knew another blast at that range directly into her torso would kill her.

Scrambling to my knees, I consolidated the energy I'd collected into a tight ball and sent it toward the demon, hoping that what I was doing wouldn't kill my friend. The ball of energy flew with a burst of bright white. It hit the demon and there was a second of stillness, when nothing happened.

Then the demon exploded. The area lit up as if someone had just flicked on high voltage lights. When the light dimmed, I saw no demon-shrapnel, no remains beside the curling of smoke drifting to the sky.

CHAPTER 8

I ran to HB, praying the whole way that she was still alive. The cougar shifter had been blown nearly fifteen feet from the demon and was laying on her side, her wounds speckled with bits of dirt and debris. She opened her eyes to look at me and lifted her head.

"Stay down," I told her. "How bad are you? What can I do?"

She chuffed and swung her head toward the werewolf. Her eyes were pleading, so I left her and jogged over to the other shifter, pretty sure that he was already dead.

The werewolf looked horrible. His injuries were primarily to his head, and I wasn't sure if the burns had been enough to affect his eyes and ears, or the base of his skull that I knew was essential for life functioning. I didn't know how extensive shifter healing was. In a human, this would have been non-survivable, but HB's injuries would have been non-survivable in a human as well.

The werewolf's legs twitched. He opened his eyes and I saw that they were completely white. He coughed, and flecks of blood sprayed the ground.

"It's okay." I put my hands on his back and his bicep, knowing full well that it was not okay. "Just relax. I'm here, and I'll try to make you…comfortable."

Should I put him out of his misery? I wasn't sure whether shooting him or electrocuting him would kill him or just increase his agony.

He opened his jaw and whispered mangled, blood-flecked words. "Dying. Save me."

I gasped, nearly recoiling from the shifter. He didn't know what he was asking. I'd saved a dying person once and inadvertently bound them to me. Addy was now basically my minion, unable to refuse any request from me, even something implied. She couldn't kill herself. She couldn't kill me or harm anyone I considered friend, family, or household. This binding had caused her to be kicked out from her cult-like mage group, to lose everything she'd valued and cared about in life. She'd hated me then for that, and I wasn't sure she *still* didn't hate me.

I swore I'd never do that again.

"Heal me. Save me," the werewolf begged, his blind eyes rolling in their sockets.

"I can't. If it works, you'll be bound to me. Even if I try not to give you direct orders or requests, or even suggestions, sometimes I can't help it. It turns you into a puppet, and I swore I'd never do that again."

"Serve," he gasped. "Honor to serve another warrior. Duty. Willingly yours. Serve you for life."

I wanted to deny him, to think that he was making a choice in fear and desperation that he'd regret later, but then I thought of the shifters I knew, especially the werewolves. They were intensely loyal. Those in packs had this type of relationship with their alphas or heads of their families. They were either loners, leaders, or served a leader. And those who served were proud of their role, especially if their alpha was someone they respected and admired.

Isha had left her pack to join my household. Was that much different from what this werewolf was agreeing to?

"Serve." The werewolf coughed again and began to seize.

I had to make a decision right now. Let him die. Mourn him. Celebrate his fighting spirit. Or interfere in his destiny, heal his body, hold his soul in place, and bind him to me for what might end up being far more than his normal lifespan.

I should have held fast to what I knew was right, but he'd made his wishes clear. I'd brought all of this to Suerte's door, and I owed this werewolf, I owed all these people. I needed to do whatever I could to help them. And if that went against what I'd vowed, then so be it.

Laying my hands on the werewolf's head, I sent myself into him. My spirit-self touched his soul, anchoring it to his form as I swept through his body. Muscle, nerves, flesh—all of it formed, knitting together as some weird creation energy poured from me. I thought I'd emptied all of my resources taking out that demon, but as soon as I decided to heal this werewolf, some untapped resource opened up to me.

The moment he was healed, that resource vanished. It was like a door slammed shut on an endless ocean of power and energy, leaving me tired, depleted, and unable to do more than throw electricity around and shoot my human weapons.

I pulled away from the werewolf, looking down at him once more. He'd reverted to a human appearance, but my healing hadn't been completely successful as far as his appearance went. His reddish-blond hair was patchy, bald in spots and an inch long in others. His ears were scarred and deformed. And his eyes as he turned to look at me were still solid white.

Fuck.

"Are you...can you see?" I asked, terrified that I'd screwed up somehow and left this werewolf blind for the rest of his life—which might end up being thousands of years.

"Yes. But I see more."

The werewolf reached out a hand and touched my jaw. I wasn't big on physical demonstrativeness from people I didn't know, but since this dude was basically my minion now, I figured I should probably allow it.

"You're...like the sun. So much power." His voice sounded awestruck.

It made me terribly uncomfortable. "And you need to lay down and rest." I took his hand from my jaw, squeezing it to keep him from thinking this was some sort of rejection on my part. "Can you get up? I can help you."

He shook his head and sat up. Now that the most severely injured of us was okay, I turned to look at Juke. Outside of dirt and a tear at the knee of her pants, she appeared unhurt. She'd gotten to her feet and was standing near us, staring with shock at the werewolf.

Yeah, I'd need to explain that one. I hadn't told many people about Addy, but it was clear that Juke would need to understand the extent, and the limitations, of this weird power I had.

HB had changed back to her human form, but was clearly still hurting. She hobbled over toward us, grimacing and holding her side.

"Never shift until you've cleaned the dirt and grit out of your wounds." She winced. "Damn. I'll be picking open my skin and digging out gravel for months until this all works its way out of my body."

That sounded horrible. It made me thankful for my own weird supernatural healing ability that didn't seem affected by whatever debris was in my wounds.

"What was that?" Juke asked, inclining her head toward the werewolf.

"I can heal," I told her. "It comes with a horrible price. He begged me, knowingly accepted the price. I only hope he doesn't regret it."

"I don't regret it." The werewolf stood. "Thank you for honoring my request. I'm pleased to serve you, Protector, for the rest of my life."

Juke's eyes widened as she looked at me.

"Werewolf thing," I said, embarrassed to admit the truth. "And I should probably know your name," I added to the werewolf.

"Kellan Marlboro."

I nodded. "And I'm Eden. Please call me Eden."

I'd meant to cut off his use of the awkward title, but when I saw him flinch, I realized what I'd done. Crap. I needed to be more careful about how I worded things in the future— both to Kellan and Addy.

We went inside, HB refusing any help as she hobbled along still clutching her ribs. She collapsed in a chair and I went behind the bar, deciding we all needed something stronger than iced tea.

"This calls for the good stuff," HB informed me. "Whiskey."

"Me too," Juke said.

"How about you, Kellan? What's your poison?" I asked.

"Just water. I'm still feeling a little shaky." The werewolf gave me an apologetic smile, as if he were worried that I'd be offended he wasn't drinking. Clearly we both had a lot to learn about each other about how this thing between us would work going forward. Would his bond be the same as the one between Addy and me? Were there differences based on my questionable skill, his being a werewolf and not human, or the nature of his injuries?

I walked back to the table with three whiskies and a bottle of water. Hopefully this was the "good stuff" HB had wanted. It all tasted the same to me, so I'd just grabbed a random bottle off the top shelf.

Everyone sipped their drinks except me. I tossed mine down and pushed the glass away from me. "So…what the hell was that demon, and why was he looking for me?"

Juke shrugged. "You know more about demons than I do. Do you think maybe Desiree sent him? She's the only one I can think of who is gunning for you."

"She's taking a big risk sending someone into another demon's territory to grab Eden," HB pointed out. "Desiree isn't stupid. I'd think she'd be more likely to try to grab Eden when she was in Los Feliz or elsewhere in her own territory."

"I'd assumed she wouldn't want to face an entire neighborhood of big cat shifters to get me. Or potentially run across the hellkitty that comes and goes from my house," I said. "Plus, I assumed Desiree would want to stabilize her territory and her authority before coming after me. She strikes me as someone who is comfortable playing a long game, and she wouldn't want to spread herself too thin, leaving herself and her territory open to attack from the other two contenders."

"Maybe you pissed off this plague demon or one of his minions and didn't even realize it," Juke said, clearly only half teasing.

"Or Desiree has made some sort of deal with the plague demon, and this is the favor she owes him," HB suggested.

Shit, I hoped not. The idea that Desiree would partner up with a plague demon was horrific.

"Or someone else is after you." HB sent me a look filled with significance and I suddenly realized what she meant.

Rumors were flying that I was the offspring of the OG Satan, Samael. That might be a good reason for someone to want to take me down. Either they had a beef with Samael, and figured I'd pay the price, or they thought it would do their reputation good to take down the Morningstar's daughter.

None of those theories was the slightest bit calming. At all.

"I'm going to step outside for a bit," I said, getting up from my chair.

While everyone else continued to sip their beverages, I went out through the kitchen door into the area behind Suerte. There was a strip of gravel that ran the length of the bar and extended out fifty feet. A rusted trailer frame was parked over to one side, with a dumpster at the other, easily accessible from the parking area. Further back, where the gravel met the woods, stood an old shed. The metal roof was rusted, and the wood trim around the double door was chipped and rotted in a few places, but the building was sturdy and hopefully didn't leak.

I'd come out back for some fresh air and to work through the mess that had become of my life, but while I was out here, I might as well check on the teenager I'd rescued from downtown last night.

Approaching the shed, I noticed the window on the side of the building was propped open. The faint sound of someone humming reached my ears. It was a happy sound— one that reassured me that Jayla was okay even though she was living in a dilapidated shed behind a bar. I guessed it was better than sleeping in an alley downtown.

Walking around to the door, I realized the humming had stopped even before I knocked.

"Jayla?" I called out. "It's Eden. Just wanted to check on you and see if there was anything you needed."

I heard some scurrying around, and waited, not sure if she would answer. If she refused, I wasn't going to push it.

Everyone deserved privacy. Hell, I wouldn't want to answer the door for an unexpected visitor either.

After a few seconds one of the double doors opened and Jayla peered out. HB was right, the girl did stink. But in spite of the odor of dead possum and rotted bananas, her face was reasonably clean and so was the hand that held the door open. She'd smoothed and re-braided her hair, tucking in the wayward pieces that had been sticking out when I'd seen her last. Opening the door wider, the girl slipped outside. Before she closed it behind her, I caught a glimpse of inside. She had an inflated pad and a blanket against the wall with the open window. There was an old apple crate that she'd repurposed as storage and a table. A couple of books were inside, and on top were an assortment of trinkets—plastic Pokémon figures, polished stones, one of those scented candles in a glass jar, and small battered teddy bear.

"Are you okay? Bishop said you were kinda freaked out at my place, but didn't seem happy about Suerte either," I said. "You're welcome to stay as long as you want. But you're also free to leave."

She looked down at the ground, nudging some loose gravel with one of her feet. "I'm okay. Your house was pretty, but it felt…exposed. The overlook to the city on one side, and the mountains on the other? Only one road in or out? I felt trapped. And I got a bad feeling about the neighbors there too." She glanced up at me and grimaced. "Sorry."

I wondered if she could sense shifters. Addy had told me so many humans had magical abilities that went unnoticed or unbelieved. But if the shifters in my Los Feliz neighborhood gave her a bad feeling, then Suerte must feel equally menacing.

"I had a bad feeling here too," she confessed. "But that blonde woman was very nice. She didn't make me do anything I didn't want to do, and let me have this place for my home. Plus there are only people here sometimes. Mornings there's usually only that blonde woman, and a cook. I like it. As long as no one bothers me, that is."

What did this girl's past hold where she'd rather be isolated in a shed behind a bar than in a warm house, clean, with hot food and companionship. It wasn't my place to pry, especially since I barely knew her, so I kept those questions to myself.

"Is there anything I can get you?" I asked instead. "Food? Personal supplies? Clothing?"

She shook her head, but there was a moment of hesitation, a wistful expression, that made me realize Jayla was too proud to ask for anything.

"Okay. If you think of anything, let HB know and I'll bring it by," I told her.

Jayla snuck back inside and I returned to the bar, vowing to get Nevarra and Sadie to put together a care package for her. No one knew what a fourteen-year-old girl would need and want more than two other young girls. And certain hygiene supplies might be less embarrassing if they came from kids more her age. Maybe after a few care packages and some letters, she might feel comfortable meeting them. She might be more willing to open up to kids her own age as well, and I knew that Sadie in particular had a way with others who felt lost and afraid.

It was a perfect idea. In the horrible mess that was New Hell, with death, destruction, and demons tearing us apart, if I could make one girl's life a little better then I'd feel like I was a success.

CHAPTER 9

Kellan asked for a lift back to his house in Burbank. The dude had run the equivalent of a marathon already today, and he was understandably a little weak from his near-death experience. Plus I felt like I at least owed my newest minion a ride.

The werewolf refused my helmet, insisting he'd be fine with just some sunglasses. He was probably right since one of the other side effects of my healing seemed to be near indestructibility. I doubted I had the same, so I put the helmet on, waited for Kellan to get settled behind me, then fired up my bike.

It was about eighteen miles to Kellan's house. He navigated there, pointing out where he lived. I parked on the street and pulled off my helmet.

"You walked to Suerte from here?" I asked the werewolf.

He climbed off the bike and smoothed a hand over his patchy red hair. "My roommate gave me a lift. I was supposed to call him later if I needed a ride home, but I thought I'd ask you. Come on inside. We probably need to talk."

He was right. This guy and I were tied together, and I knew nothing about him other than his name and that he was a werewolf. Turning off my bike and putting down my kickstand, I followed him up the walkway to a three-story townhome. We were a couple of blocks from a small airport, and this street had once been home to stately trees and nearly identical Victorian-styled townhomes. Now the airport looked like someone had bombed it, the runways overgrown with weeds. The once white townhomes were gray and dingy with boards over broken windows and plastic sheeting nailed to the roof. A few were nothing more than burned out shells. The green trees lining the road were rotted and dead.

"I live here with two other guys," Kellan told me. "We used to work together before the demons came and managed to grab this place as squatters. It's not in bad shape. We rotate shifts so one of us is usually home to defend it in case somebody gets ideas about moving in."

That was always the danger with life in New Hell. Squatters' rights meant if you lived somewhere, you owned it. Abandoned or empty houses were fair game, and some felt that empty for a few hours in the middle of the day meant fair game as well. That's where having good neighbors helped. Or roommates who could greet any intruder with the business end of a shotgun.

"Are your roommates werewolves?" I asked Kellan.

"One's a bear shifter. The other is human." He did a complicated knock pattern on the door, then turned the knob. "It's me. And I've got someone with me."

Kellan opened the door and I saw a man with a shaved head and dark skin lowering a shotgun. He was wearing blue striped boxer shorts and nothing else. I'll admit I stared, impressed with the guy's muscular physique and his unconcern with his near-nude state.

"Jesus, Mosi. Put some clothes on," Kellan complained.

Mosi ignored him, frowning as he set the shotgun aside. "What happened to your hair? And your ears? Oh, my God, your eyes! Kellan, what is wrong with your eyes?"

"I'm okay. I swear I'm okay even if I look really weird right now. A demon nearly burned my head off, but I'm fine. Mosi, this is Eden. Eden, my roommate Mosi. We're going into the kitchen to talk. Join us if you want." Kellan turned to me. "There are no secrets between the three of us. Just letting you know in case that's a problem."

"I trust who you trust."

Kellan was now bound to me. He could never hurt me or anyone I claimed as mine. I knew from personal experience that if his roommates turned against me or mine, Kellan would stand by my side, no matter how much it hurt him to do so. It was less about me trusting his friends, and more about me trusting him to do the right thing if his friends turned out to be enemies.

Mosi led the way through a narrow hall into a small kitchen. He motioned Kellan and me toward the tall barstools on the other side of an island with a chipped, brown laminate surface. As we sat, he lit a small camp stove, and put a kettle on top.

"We haven't had electricity for two weeks," Kellan explained.

"Or water for two months," Mosi added. "We've been carting all of this from the reservoir and either boiling it or running it through a filtration system. Good thing Lucus was an avid camper and backpacker and had all this stuff or we would have probably died from giardia by now."

I turned to Kellan in surprise since I'd assumed shifters were immune to those sorts of bacterial issues.

"He means Lucus would have died from giardia." Kellan grinned. "Mosi and I would have just wished we would have died. Being a shifter means you're hearty, but it doesn't mean you don't get the occasional bout of diarrhea."

"Kellan got kennel cough last winter." Mosi laughed. "He was a big baby about it, too. So, are you a chamomile or green tea kind of woman?"

"Either one is fine." I really wasn't a tea person, but worried I'd offend him if I refused.

"So, how does this work?" Kellan asked me. "I've never been a demon's minion before, so I don't know what to expect."

There was a crash as Mosi dropped a mug. "A what? Kellan, what have you gotten yourself into. Is this why you're missing chunks of hair and your ears are all chewed up? Is this why you look like you've got the cataracts of a ninety-year-old woman?"

"My head was incinerated," Kellan explained. "A demon attacked Suerte during my watch. He burned most of my head off. I couldn't regenerate it and was dying. Eden healed me, and now I'm her minion."

Mosi glared at me and I tried to explain before he went out into the hall to get the shotgun.

"I've only done this once and didn't realize that saving someone's life involved binding them to me. I swore I'd never do it again, but he was okay with the whole minion thing. It's kind of hard to watch someone die when they're begging you to help them and they're willing to pay the price," I said.

Mosi turned back and getting another mug out of the cabinet. "Well, I don't like it," he growled.

That made two of us.

"It was *my* choice. I didn't want to die. She's Bishop's mate, and HB trusts her, so it was a risk I was willing to take," Kellan explained.

His roommate grunted, but didn't reply.

Kellan sighed and turned to me again. "What are the rules on this thing? Am I only able to be a certain distance from you? Can you communicate telepathically with me? Summon me to your side via teleportation?"

"Uh no. None of that. At least, I don't think so." I held up my hands. "I have to be really careful how I word things because even casual requests become orders you can't refuse. You can't harm me or anyone I care about—I'm not sure how far that extends and whether it includes casual acquaintances or not. You also can't kill yourself. I think you might be inde-structible. Or possibly immortal. I don't know if you'll age or not. Nobody gave me an instruction manual on these things. Hell, I didn't even know I had these powers until this month. It's all new to me too."

"Is it like having an Alpha?" Mosi asked.

"I've got no idea what having an Alpha entails," I confessed.

"Normally packmates live near their Alpha, sometimes in the same neighborhood or development, sometimes just in the same city or town," Kellan explained. "It's important to be reasonably geographically close though—at least for werewolves. Some shifters are more social than others, and some have tighter community bonds. The Alpha lets their packmates know when they need them to do something, or when there are meetings, or social obligations like group hunts."

"So the Alpha texts you? Posts on a group chat? Sends an e-mail?" I asked.

"Pretty much. If a pack member attacks him or his family, it's a challenge and there are formal rules that are different for each pack surrounding that, including what happens to the loser. Some packs also require monetary contributions to help support the Alpha and pay for community lodges, group hunts, and feasts." Kellan shrugged. "That's about it.

Everyone defends the pack. They all fight together for their common good."

"Okay. That sounds reasonable," I told him. "I don't need any money though. I live over in Los Feliz, and I don't see any reason to have you live any closer to me. Stay here. Basically live wherever you want. I don't think there's any distance requirement to this thing. The other person who is bound to me is in Silver Lake, but none of us have really tested to see if there's an issue if you decide to vacation in Denmark or something."

Mosi snorted. "Like he's gonna go to Denmark. Guy's never been out of SoCal in his entire life." The bear shifter handed us our tea mugs and we all took a sip. Mine was a green tea with a nutty, slightly sweet flavor.

"We'll just exchange phone numbers and text or call if one of us needs to get in touch." I pulled my phone out and we shared contact info, including my address just in case.

"Am I okay to continue patrol and guard shifts at Suerte?" Kellan asked.

"Absolutely. Can you let me know your schedule, though? I want to make sure there's no conflict with your other commitments." Suddenly I remembered something. "Is there going to be an issue with your current pack and Alpha? Will you need to leave them, or will they be okay with this arrangement? Will your Alpha be pissed about this? Am I going to need to fight him or her?"

"No. I'm a lone wolf," he said. "Left my pack six years ago. Most of the werewolves I'd grown up with had moved away and joined other packs, and we'd gotten a new Alpha I didn't really connect with. Spent a year checking out other packs in the area, but ended up really enjoying the solo thing. Bishop has always served as a kind of Alpha for the packless. Actually, he's sort of the Alpha-Alpha." Kellan eyed me. "I heard you were a co-Protector with him, but I'd never met you before, so I've always considered myself as ultimately belonging to Bishop."

I almost told him that he belonged to himself, then I remembered what I'd learned in the past year about shifters and their different cultures. Community was important to werewolves, as was a sense of belonging, and having a leader. It wasn't my place to impose my own culture and beliefs onto this guy.

"I'm solo as well," Mosi chimed in. "Black Bear and Polar Bear shifters tend to stay in family units. Grizzlies are solo."

"Unless they have mates," Kellan added.

Mosi gave me a sheepish smile. "Actually most are solo even if they have mates. Usually they only hook up a couple of times a year, but a few of them do form bonds and have a more conventional relationship."

I glanced from one to the other, feeling as if I were missing something here. It wasn't my business, though, and I needed to be careful not to ask Kellan any question he might feel pressured to answer because of our bond. So instead I gulped my tea, and pushed my curiosity away.

"I just texted you my schedule," Kellan said. "Is there anything this week you need me to do?"

"I'm still trying to figure out what my priorities are going to be going forward," I replied. "For now, any assistance will probably be last minute with little notice. I want you to let me know of any conflicts or difficulties you might have in assisting me. That way I can modify or rescind my request. Okay?"

He nodded.

"One more thing," I added. "When you came in to Suerte, you were in human form except for your face and your hands. I've never seen a shifter do that before."

"Half-form," Kellan told me. "Shifters generally take ten to twenty minutes to change form, and during an attack, that's not usually optimal. About half of us can instantly assume this half-form, which gives us claws and fangs and a sturdier body. It helps in a fight. Personally, I like to assume half-form when I'm on patrol since it means I've got natural weapons, increased speed and endurance, and still have opposable thumbs. I can do things like climb and grasp tools, and even shoot a gun, although that's kind of awkward."

"The downside to half-form is that you look like a monster from a B horror movie," Mosi said. "You'd think it wouldn't be so much of a problem now that the humans know about shifters, but plenty of them get freaked out. It sucks to heal half a dozen bullet holes because some Karen is afraid you're going to eat her."

I could absolutely sympathize. Even though I didn't have a "demon form" that I was aware of, I'd encountered my share of fear and distrust once people realized I wasn't human.

"Ten to twenty minutes to shift," I mused. "But HB instantly turned into a cougar today. Why doesn't she need a longer time to change form?"

I saw Kellan shudder. His mouth opened, and I quickly spoke before he could.

"Do not answer that if it's a private matter that you don't feel comfortable sharing."

Kellan sighed, slumping in his seat. "Thanks. I do know why, but that's something you'll need to ask HB. Other people's secrets aren't mine to share.

CHAPTER 10

*L*eaving Kellan's, I headed to Bea's, wanting to make sure that she and the girls were all right, and to let them know about the situation in the Valley.

I'd nearly lost my family to bounty hunters this year. I wasn't about to lose them to a disease-spreading demon. But how could I protect them? Even if I stayed at Bea's house full time, I still had no idea how to defend against disease. Would the plague demon's magic ooze in late at night, sliding under the door and through the walls to take my family while they slept? Would we have no warning at all of the attack? No way to even *try* to defend ourselves from illness and a horrible death?

I felt the sting of Genevieve Planteaux's wards as I drove down the block. It was a nice, cool fall day, and several of the neighbors were outside working on house repairs or in the small gardens everyone was struggling to grow in their front yards. I saw Nevarra and Javier sitting on the tailgate of Javier's truck. Their shoulders touched, and their clasped hands were in Nevarra's lap. The girl waved at me, kissed Javier's cheek, then hopped down from the truck. She was jogging up as I'd parked my bike in Bea's driveway next to her faded, tomato-red car.

We hugged, both of us letting the embrace go on longer than we would have a year ago.

"How are things?" I asked when we finally stepped apart.

The girl glanced a few houses down. "Tense. Marissa's cousin moved in after her neighborhood was destroyed. She said most of the others on her street fled for the border. She didn't want to leave because they're so short-staffed at the hospital, but the last few days she and Marissa are both talking about going. They've got some family in Florida that might help get them across the border."

"But you all have been safe? Right?" I asked, feeling a little guilty that I hadn't called or been by for the last three days.

Nevarra blew out a breath. "We're good."

I narrowed my eyes, because she didn't sound as if they were good.

"Eden!"

I turned at Sadie's voice just in time to brace for impact. The girl slammed into me and we hugged.

"Bea's down at Dave Rickard's," she announced. "She's helping him with the fence."

I assumed she meant the electric fence that extended across the backyards with solar powered motion alarms on the posts. It was very useful in deterring human intruders, but I knew it wouldn't do much to prevent any demons from getting into anyone's yard.

"Later tonight, we're all getting together to make bombs," Sadie continued. "You should come, Eden. There will be popcorn and sodas."

"Bombs?" I choked out.

Nevarra jabbed an elbow into her sister's side. "They're not *really* bombs. Just stuff that falls and breaks and…kinda explodes if someone trips a wire."

That sounded like a bomb to me.

"Why are you all making bombs?" I glared at the two girls. "What happened?"

Nevarra sighed. "We've been getting attacked. Used to be just those demons breaking into cars, peeing acid on the lawn, and busting out windows, but two nights ago a group of three demons set fire to the Hannicks' house and grabbed Mrs. Hannick when they all ran out. They blew right past Genevieve Planteaux's wards."

"The watch shot them, but it didn't slow them down," Sadie said. "Then Javier's whole family came running out of their house, all of them these giant wolves with glowing eyes."

"They fought the demons and rescued Mrs. Hannick," Nevarra said proudly.

"Genevieve came out and did some spell that made all the demons scream and clutch their heads," Sadie added. "They ran off, but since then we've been adding physical barriers and defenses as well as making bombs."

"Genevieve remade the wards," Nevarra said. "And Javier's brothers and sisters moved back home. Because when family gets attacked, defending them is a priority."

I flinched, even though I knew Nevarra wasn't directing that comment at me. Nevarra had initially been concerned about her boyfriend being a shifter, as well as the fact that a werewolf family had lived in our neighborhood for over a decade, posing as humans. But as she and Javier had grown close, Nevarra had clearly changed her viewpoint. Now she seemed proud of her boyfriend's heritage, and his shifter family's priorities and values.

It didn't change the fact that I felt guilty, though. My foster mother and sisters' neighborhood had been attacked and I hadn't known. I knew Bea hadn't called me because she didn't want me to worry, that she wanted me to live my own life as a grown woman. But just like Javier's siblings, I felt a tie, a responsibility toward my family. They'd needed me and I hadn't been there.

They should've been my priority. Not a bunch of humans and shifters I didn't even know. Not the residents of a sprawling city. Not even my team should take precedence over Bea and the girls.

"Eden!" I looked over and saw Bea hurrying toward us. "How are you, honey?"

She folded me in her arms, and I suddenly felt safe, loved, and very much at home.

"I'm fine," I told her, not planning on letting her know the details of last night or the fight at Suerte. Bea worried about me just as much as I worried about her and the girls.

"Let's all go inside and sit," Bea announced after giving me one more squeeze. "I'll put on some coffee and we'll catch up. I do need to tell you about what's going on here in the neighborhood."

"Sadie and Nevarra already spilled the tea," I told her as we walked into the house. "How is Mrs. Hannick? It must have been terrifying for her to be snatched like that."

Bea sighed. "They're packing their van today. Rick's been saving and thinks they have enough to bribe their way through the border. I can't say I blame them. Helen is really shaken."

I didn't blame them either. Poor Mrs. Hannick. If those demons had managed to get away with her, the woman's fate would have truly been horrific.

Waving for us to sit, Bea went to make coffee, talking about the new wards and the improvements on the electric fence. A few minutes later she'd placed mugs in front of each of us, pouring a healthy splash of shelf-stable milk into Sadie's and Nevarra's, and a scoop of sugar into hers before sitting down.

"Mrs. Vandergriff is staying with Carlotta and Luis," Sadie said as she sipped. "Do you remember her from school?"

I thought for a second, then nodded. "She was my biology teacher, I think."

"Yes, she was," Bea said. "She'd moved in with her son and his family about ten blocks north of here when the demons came. Yesterday morning she went out to get groceries. She walked, because she didn't want to take the car in case her son or daughter-in-law needed it so she was gone a few hours. When she came back, the whole street was silent. She went into the house and found them all dead—son, daughter-in-law, two little kids."

I sucked in a breath. Violent death of children was not unusual in New Hell, but it still affected me every time it happened.

"She dropped the groceries and ran screaming to the neighbors, but she found the same thing in every house. They were all dead. For two square blocks, everyone was dead."

"Do you know what happened?" I asked Bea, knowing it was probably the plague demon. The gangs still killed people, but they wouldn't have taken out two blocks of families, and the victims wouldn't all have died in their homes. There would have been signs of fighting, as well as a few fallen gang members and at least one or two injured survivors. Not this weird mass death.

Bea's brow creased with worry. "Mrs. Vandergriff said they were covered in sores—red, infected sores. Some had blackened vein-like marks on their bodies. Her family was fine when she'd left to do the shopping. Her son was making breakfast, his wife was changing the baby. The older child was playing in the kitchen. There was no sign of a struggle. It was like they were suddenly stricken with a disease and died within minutes—or at most an hour."

The plague demon. But as horrifying as Mrs. Vander-griff's experience was, I had another worry.

"She's staying with Carlotta and Luis? What if she's contagious?" I had my own family to worry about, and Carlotta and Luis's son, Javier, was Nevarra's boyfriend.

Bea got up for more coffee, talking as she poured. "She's in quarantine in their garage and Carlotta is the only one who has even minimal contact with her for now. Carlotta assured me that werewolves aren't susceptible to most human diseases. They do have their own illnesses, but whatever killed Mrs. Vandergriff's family won't transmit to them."

"But this isn't a regular human disease," I protested. "These people went from healthy to dead in less than two hours. They were covered in sores, infection, and necrosis. Who's to say that a demon-fueled plague won't cross over to shifters?"

Bea sat down. "I know. I'm worried too. But we couldn't just abandon Mrs. Vandergriff as upset as she was. She's just lost her whole family and needs help. If we start turning our backs on people out of fear, then the demons have already won."

I understood that, but fear for my own family overshadowed concern for Mrs. Vandergriff.

This plague demon was a serious threat—more so than the warmonger or even Desiree. He'd killed two blocks of people in one morning. No survivors. No one had time to get medical attention or even attempt to fight back. Had they known what had happened? Was there a demon walking down the street, spreading germs and viruses as he went, like sowing seeds? Could they have killed him, and if they had, would it have made any difference at all? Or had the damage already been done, the whole neighborhood doomed the moment he'd appeared?

"Enough about our problems," Bea said with a wave of her hand. "Tell us what's going on in the rest of the city?"

I told her about New Hell being divided into threes, but I couldn't offer them even a glimmer of hope that anything might change soon. Or ever. Maybe the Hannicks had the right idea. Maybe the humans and shifters should give up and flee, leaving the whole mess to the demons.

It was a depressing idea—one I wasn't quite ready to embrace.

"Where's Bishop?" Sadie asked.

"He's off trying to get us some help." I was purposely vague, not wanting them to think that Satan was going to save us, even if she decided to show up.

"I heard from Javier that the demons set fire to downtown," Nevarra commented.

I winced. "They did. The police were able to evacuate the humans to safety. And at least one of those demons was eaten by a dragon, so there's that."

"A *dragon*!" Sadie squealed. "I *love* dragons! What color is it? Can we see it? Does he look like the ones in the picture books?"

Oh, good Lord. "He's orange. He looks like a dragon. And no, you can't see him because he shoots fire out of his mouth that can burn you to a crisp. And if he doesn't incinerate you, he'll eat you."

"Maybe he'll eat all the demons," Nevarra said.

"The demons know now to avoid that area of downtown, and humans should do the same," I told her, thinking that the dragon was just as much of a threat to us as the demons— maybe even more.

But talking about last night and downtown reminded me of something.

"There's a favor I need to ask you both," I said, looking at Nevarra and Sadie.

"What?" They said at the same time.

"There's a girl living in the shed behind Suerte. Her name is Jayla and I think she's about fourteen years old. She's homeless and was living downtown before last night, so she doesn't have a lot. I think she would really appreciate a care package, if you both could put together one for her."

"I'll bet she needs things like toothpaste and stuff. Oh, and clothes! What size is she?" Nevarra asked. "I've got some clothes that are too small for me and too big for Sadie that she might like."

"She's shorter than you and thinner, although I'm hoping now that HB is getting her regular meals she fills out a bit," I told Nevarra.

"We can ask around the neighborhood," Nevarra told Sadie. "I'll bet a lot of people have stuff in their attic from when their kids were younger. I know Javier's parents probably have a ton of things."

"Does she like stuffed animals? Is there anything she collects?" Sadie asked. "How about jigsaw puzzles or books? Maybe a pretty notebook for her to write in?"

I held up my hands. "They all sound like good ideas. I'm not exactly sure what she likes, but she has a bunch of polished rocks on a box beside her sleeping bag, so maybe pretty trinkets like bracelets and stuff. Oh—I think she's into Pokémon. She had a couple of the figures on a crate next to her bed."

Sadie clapped her hands, hopping up and down. "I have some extra Pokémon decks. Maybe we can play? Do you think she'd like it if we stayed and played some games, or just talked? She must be lonely in that shed by herself."

"Some people like being alone," I cautioned her. "Why don't I take the care package to her and ask how she feels about company. If she's open to it, I'll borrow Bea's car and take you for a visit one day. How about that?"

"Okay." Sadie turned to Nevarra. "Let's put together two or three care packages. Eden can give them to her every couple of days. It'll be like Christmas for her."

My heart ached at how wonderful my sisters were. They were so excited to help a girl they didn't even know, ready to befriend her and give her a fun set of gifts. I loved them, and I was doubly committed to making sure they had a future here.

"There are some extra blankets and throw rugs in the attic," Bea said. "You girls can look through those and see if there's anything suitable to give Jayla. We'll text Eden when you've got a box ready and she can come by to pick it up."

They stood, racing upstairs while I sat and drank coffee with Bea.

"Think you'll be able to carry all that on your bike?" Bea asked. "You can borrow my car if you like."

"We'll see what they put together." I was used to stuffing Vulture salvage into the saddle bags on my bike and my backpack, and had rigged up a way to tie stuff across the back fender. Hopefully I could make it all fit. If not, then I'd take Bea up on her offer.

"Why don't you stay here today and have dinner with us?" Bea offered.

I was tempted, but I had at least one other errand I wanted to run before nightfall.

"Rain check?" I said as I stood. "Let me know when the girls have their gift box ready. I'll try to make time for dinner later this week."

Shouting a "good-bye" up to the girls, I gave Bea a hug and left, driving to a strip-mall bookstore that was far from ordinary.

CHAPTER 11

BISHOP

It took me most of the morning to find Ahia. Alaska was a huge state, and the last time I'd seen her, she'd been transitioning from living with a community of natives to a pack of werewolves.

Nephilim and their descendants, the shifters, had been under my questionable protection for the last ten thousand years. Initially I'd made my home in what was now Syria, teleporting around the globe to check on the children of angels. Gabriel usually alerted me to a Nephilim birth, but the archangel wasn't all-knowing, so I had to rely on gossip and folktales as well as sensing energy signatures to find those who might be targeted for extermination.

I'd found Ahia by accident, checking out stories of a "child of the moon and sun" in the north of this continent. What I'd found hadn't been a Nephilim, but an angel—an Angel of Chaos.

I'd kept my mouth shut, not even letting Gabriel know about her existence. I'd also kept my true nature a secret from her until my last visit, when Ahia finally connected the visits from a shaman of neighboring native tribes, a shifter, a gold rush prospector, and a fisherman and called me out. I'd told her who I was, but never revealed who *she* was. Ahia believed herself to be a Nephilim, an Alaskan native, and a member of a werewolf pack. It wasn't my place to disrupt her life.

It was one of the reasons I was so pissed at Gabriel for outing Eden. The woman was just beginning to explore who and what she was. She didn't need some asshole shattering her world and yelling at her about a parentage she'd had no control over.

Eden.

I'd loved her the moment I'd seen her in my bar, fighting a group of shifters and begging me to help her family. It wasn't just the siren's call of her unique spirit-being, of her ridiculously overpowered and locked-away powers. Everything about her shone with a light of protective fury. She'd do anything for those she loved—kill for them, die for them, barter her very soul for them.

It had been a long time since I'd seen such conviction, and it had been intoxicating. I wanted her. And more than that, I wanted her to look at me with the same love she felt for her family.

But millions of years had taught me that love could be a fleeting thing, and that I should not pin my hopes on this fantasy. So I'd scowled at her, quote her my price, and tried to make it just another job.

It hadn't been just another job. And Eden had been far from just another client.

Which was why I was scouring Alaska, looking for a werewolf pack with a Nephilim named Ahia.

I finally found her at a dive bar in Juneau called Fjords Landing. The place was dimly lit, grimy, and filled with shifters. Ahia was at the back of the bar, doing shots with a grizzly and a female wolf with flaming red hair.

Her eyes widened when she saw me. "Bishop? Holy shit, I haven't seen you since the Russians were here. When was that? 1820? 1840?"

"1820," I admitted, turning to smile at her friends. "Hi. I'm Bishop."

"This is Karl and Sabrina," Ahia introduced me before turning to shout at the bartender. "Arnold! Get Bishop a shot! And another round for us!"

Arnold was another werewolf. He brought a tray with four shots, then sat the bottle at the end of the bar, telling Ahia he'd just put it on her tab. We clinked glasses, downed the alcohol, then took a few seconds to savor the burn.

Sabrina's gaze went back and forth between me and Ahia, then she elbowed Karl. "Thanks for the booze, Ahia, but we need to get going."

Karl grunted and left without a word, Sabrina following behind him and mouthing that she'd call Ahia later.

"So, what's up with this unexpected visit, Bishop?" Ahia grabbed the bottle and filled our glasses.

"I've just heard you were recently made aware of your true nature, and that you're now on the Ruling Council." I wasn't sure about either of those rumors. It had only been a matter of time until Ahia found out she was an angel, but the Ruling Council? Those spots went to powerful angels who'd politicked their way up through the various choirs in Aaru, not a random post-war offspring that had been living with humans and shifters her whole life.

"It's true." Ahia eyed me. "You're not surprised I'm an angel?"

I shrugged. "I've been here ten thousand years. I've seen some things."

She laughed. "I'll bet you have."

"How'd you manage the Ruling Council position?" I asked as I brought the glass of whiskey to my mouth.

"I'm fucking the archangel Raphael."

I nearly spit the whiskey out. Ahia laughed as I coughed and thumped my chest.

"Seriously," she said. "He showed up for some angel-business, outed me, and we fell in love. He weaseled me a spot on the Ruling Council. He's good at that. Weaseling, that is. I swear he's more of an Angel of Chaos than I am sometimes."

I'd heard that about the archangel Raphael. "I'm actually here hoping to get some information."

I told her about the situation in New Hell as we drank whiskey, about the murder of Doriel, about the increased fighting and violence, about the factions dividing New Hell, about the desperation of the humans and shifters. Ahia had always been protective of humans, having lived as one for most of her life. I was hoping she'd feel sympathy for what we were going through south of her, and be willing to spill some confidential information at least.

"Do you need help fighting?" she asked when I was done. "Raphael and I have a lot on our plate, but I feel bad that you all were hung out to dry like this. We can come down for a week or two and help clean house."

It was a generous offer, but with the number of demons in the LA area, extra help for a few weeks wouldn't do more than put a small dent in our problem. We needed a way to solve our own problems, long term.

"I might eventually take you up on that," I said, just in case the situation got dire. "But what we really need is the Iblis. No one has been able to tell us where our current Satan is, or what her intentions are regarding New Hell. Does she plan to replace Doriel? Is she comfortable with what's going on right now? I need to know if this is going to be our future, or if we can expect her to come in and help support some stability in the territory."

Ahia shifted her weight from foot to foot, pouring herself another shot and downing it before responding.

"I can't…we're not supposed to talk about it."

I tamped down a surge of frustration. "I understand confidentiality issues, but this is personal for those living in New Hell. The Fallen who was supposed to be running things was murdered, and honestly she was pretty damned useless before she was killed. We deserve to know where the Iblis is and what her intentions are."

Ahia glanced around the bar then leaned in closer. "She's gone. Poof. Vanished. She's not in Hel. And she sure as fuck isn't in Aaru."

I frowned. "Dead?"

She shook her head. "I don't know if you're aware that she and the archangel Michael are mated. He'd be a wreck if she was dead."

"And he'd be downright psychotic if she'd vanished," I pointed out. "So I'm guessing he at least knows where she is and isn't sharing that with the rest of the Ruling Council."

Ahia nodded. "We all have our guesses. Raphael and I think it has something to do with the fae, but beyond that we're as much in the dark as anyone else."

"So there won't be any immediate help from that quarter," I said, thinking that even when the Iblis returned, we still might not be able to count on any help from her.

"Is there anything the humans can do to fight back against the demons?" Ahia asked. "There are a lot of shifter packs in the area. Together they might be able to force the demons away from a decent enough sized area to give the humans and shifters an oasis in the shitstorm."

I thought about that for a bit. "There are too many demons, and the area has already been claimed by those with power and sizable households to help them hold on to that power. We might be able to force them out of a small town, but we'd spend the rest of our lives having to defend it. And we'd be vulnerable to a siege. No, we need a longer-term solution."

"Then you need magic," Ahia said. "Outside of a very powerful demon willing to exert their influence over the others, the only thing they'll respect is magic. If you had one sorcerer, even a Fallen would think twice before attacking their city."

"We've got mages in the city, but they're loosely affiliated at best," I told her. "I wish we had a sorcerer on our side."

"If you can get the mages working together, you might be able to secure and hold something the size of Burbank," Ahia said. "But there needs to be a combined effort, otherwise they'll just pick the mages off one at a time. Everyone is stronger working together—even demons."

It was such a shifter mentality, but then again Ahia had been raised in tight-knit native communities, and spent the last few centuries with a shifter pack. Still, her comment gave me an idea. We were stronger together. If we could manage to splinter the demon households and alliances, and gather our most powerful into a joint effort, we might have a chance of winning this war.

CHAPTER 12

EDEN

I parked in the lot beside a Honda minivan that looked as if it hadn't been washed since the turn of the century. Every time I came here, there were a few more potholes in the asphalt of the lot, and a few more boarded-up windows in the other strip mall stores.

The familiar burn of the security spell swept through me as I walked in the door. Alfie was helping an elderly man who I assumed must be the owner of the van. I smiled in reply to the bookstore owner's nod, and headed to the rows that I knew contained grimoires and texts concerning mages and sorcery.

Basic summoning. Elemental magic. Herbal gardens. Necromancy. Maybe I should have asked Addy a bit more about her particular branch of illusion magic before I'd come here. Would Alfie allow me to return a spell book if I bought the wrong one? I would hate to come home with an expensive tome only to find out Addy had no experience with those sorts of spells.

"Hello Eden. What a pleasant surprise." Alfie came around the corner only to jerk to a halt, eyeing the book on necromancy in my hands. "Uh…you don't want that. I can't in good conscience sell you that."

"Oh it's not for me." I stuck it back on the shelf, pretty certain it wasn't for Addy either. "I know a mage who lost all of her spell books. I'm thinking of bringing her by in a day or two so she can maybe replenish her library."

Alfie rubbed his hands together with an eager smile. "Wonderful. Send her on in."

I didn't have the heart to tell him that Addy probably didn't have enough money to buy more than the cheapest of his stock, so I instead switched to conversation to a more pressing topic.

"I was hoping you could give me some information about the three demons who seem to have split New Hell between them. Itinder, Barstonel, and Desiree."

He pursed his thin lips. "Barstonel is one of the Fallen. Groneski's *Infernal Peerage* should have a decent section on him."

Alfie turned and I followed him down another aisle of bookshelves. Stopping midway, he pulled a giant tome off the shelf and handed it to me.

"Is there anything on the other two in here?" I didn't feel like spending the money for this doorstopper just to read about one demon.

"If they've ever been a member of a Fallen Angel's household, then they should be in the index." He took the book from me, went to the front counter, and opened it up.

I peered at the miniscule typeface as he ran his finger down the index. "Itinder originally belonged to Asag's household, but left after five thousand years of service. He was briefly in Haagenti's household, but after two hundred years he left and formed his own small group. After a century-long blood feud with Misorol, he killed his rival and assumed his household, rising in the ranks to level five." Alfie looked up at me. "The book won't have anything on him after that since he's not considered one of the Fallen and is only at the fifth level in the hierarchy."

"Interesting stuff, but none of that really helps," I complained. "I need to know about his strengths and weaknesses, and how to defeat him. Blister said he has a two-thousand demon army at hand. How do I kill two thousand demons and the plague demon who leads them without dying?"

"I have some books on military strategy during the angelic war, and another on major demonic feuds. Those could give you some ideas," he said.

Great. More books. "I'll pass on that, thanks."

Alfie shrugged. "Suit yourself. Do you want me to look Barstonel up?"

I nodded. Might as well since Alfie seemed to be letting me have this information without making me buy this book.

He flipped through the pages. "Barstonel served in the angelic war under Samael. Originally he commanded twenty-thousand demons, but after the Fall he went dormant, so the surviving members of his household went elsewhere."

"Dormant?" I frowned, wondering if this was some Rip Van Winkle thing, or if Barstonel had just flounced off to pout somewhere.

"Samael vanished soon after the Fall, although he was rumored to be seen here among the evolving humans roughly fifty thousand years ago." Alfie's shoulders slumped and his eyes focused on some distant point over my shoulder. "Those were dark times. For so long most of the powerful Fallen slept. Those who remained awake interbred, creating the demons. Hel...Hel was a pit of chaos and violence. The elves had their territories. The demons had theirs. The dwarves had theirs. Then something shifted about a hundred thousand years ago. The demons remained ruled by chaos, but some order now stabilized their society. They began to interact with other races in Hel—and to sneak through the gates into this world."

I was fascinated. And I was sure that none of this was in that fat book on the counter. "What do you think happened? What changed?"

He shook his head, as if clearing away the memories. "No one knows. But slowly the sleeping Fallen began to awaken. There was commerce. Vows were once again considered binding. The demons evolved, although the angels would say they devolved. In the last few years, change has occurred at the speed of light, but then again, that's what happens when an imp holds the Sword of the Iblis."

"The new Satan," I commented.

"The gates to Hel are open. Demons rule a portion of the human world. And for the first time in nearly three million years, Angels of Order are bonding with Angels of Chaos—and demons as well."

None of that had turned out so well for the humans, but I wasn't about to rain on Alfie's happy-parade, so I kept my mouth shut about that.

"Is there anything else about Barstonel?" I asked.

"He lives for conflict and battle." Alfie skimmed the text. "He'll never refuse a challenge for single-hand combat. He keeps his vows and promises, and is honorable when beaten in battle or in a duel. After a hundred years here in the eleventh century, he returned to Hel, so I'd assume his preferred fighting methods would be very dated."

"Then he wouldn't be expecting things like guns or grenades, or trucks and attack drones," I mused.

Alfie smiled. "Don't count on that. Even if he remained in Hel, he might have received information from those who'd crossed the gates. Plus, he'd be knowledgeable about magic and the sorts of weapons a sorcerer might employ."

"Anything on Desiree?" I asked.

Alfie shook his head. "Lots of demons who have resided here for extended periods of time change their names. If you know her other names, I might be able to find something."

I didn't know her as anything but Desiree. I vaguely remembered Bishop mentioning something about her name change, but I really didn't want to talk to him about Desiree —not when I believed that they had history together. There were times when I preferred to shove my head in the sand and ignore a potential conflict, and this was one of them. I loved Bishop. And deep down I was afraid that me finding out the details of his and Desiree's former relationship might take a lot of the shine off that love.

But there was one more thing I did want to know about.

"How about dragons?" I asked. "Some orange dragon has taken up residence downtown in a mall known as The Bloc. He's got a pile of goodies in the courtyard and is incinerating or eating anything that comes close to him or his hoard."

"Well, that *is* unfortunate," Alfie said cheerfully. "I'd advise you and anyone you care about stay away from downtown."

I waved my hand. "I figured that out myself. What I want to know is if I can leverage this dragon in any way. Can I cut a deal with him to help me take out these other demons?"

"I'm sure I have something on dragons." Alfie headed down another aisle of books while I trailed behind him. "Ah. Here."

He handed me another giant doorstopper of a book, this one a foot long, ten inches wide, and about seven inches deep. I nearly dropped it.

"This will tell you everything you need to know," Alfie

announced.

I glanced at the book, despair pooling in my stomach. "Any chance of a Cliff Notes version? Dragons for Dummies? An executive summary?"

"Nope. It's three hundred dollars, but I'll give you a discount and let you have it for two-ninety."

I glared at him. "Ten bucks? That's your discount?"

"Since you're referring your mage friend here, I'll let you have it for two-fifty," Alfie offered.

"Twenty bucks," I countered.

He gasped, clutching his chest. "That's insulting. Two-twenty."

"Thirty." If he didn't come down considerably in price, then this purchase wasn't going to happen.

"One fifty, and I'll let you make payments," he said.

I hesitated. Then I pulled the contents of my pocket out and counted it. I had seventy-five bucks on me, and I knew there was another hundred back at the house. Vulture jobs had become a low priority the last week, and I was a little nervous about my dwindling finances. Did I really need this book? Did I even have time to read the fucking thing? And was the dragon even going to be of help, or would I spend time and money only to find out a bunch of random, useless facts about the creatures?

As always, I went with my intuition.

"Deal." I handed over a twenty. "Here's my down payment."

Alfie went back to the register to enter the deal in a ledger book that he brought up from under the counter. The book was too big for a bag, so he wrapped it in paper, tied it in twine, then handed it over.

Outside, I strapped the thing to the back of my bike, hoping it wouldn't fall off on the freeway. Then I kicked my bike to life, and headed home.

$\mathcal{P}$arking my bike in the drive, I glanced around the street, taking the mood of the neighborhood. My brief elevation to "Protector" seemed to have ended. I got the impression I'd been demoted and no one had the guts to tell me. No more presents appeared at my door and I found myself once more struggling to come up with the money for food and basic necessities. The shifters had always lingered around outside, watching me while pretending to do yard-work or buff their vehicles, but now they stayed inside, eyeing me through gaps in their curtained windows. There were no more visitors. Fi, who'd been the neighborhood representative assisting during the press conference that had ended in mass slaughter was no longer a part of my house-hold. And that sucked, because she had some serious leader-ship and strategic skills where I seemed to have none.

I was a little down as I walked up to my front door, feeling as if I'd lost both friends and my welcome here. I had no concrete plan for dealing with what was happening in New Hell. I was worried about Desiree and the inevitable confrontation with her. I still wasn't happy about my creating another minion, no matter what Kellan said regarding his willing acceptance of the costs of not-dying. I was worried about HB's injuries, worried about the attack on Bea's neighborhood, worried about everything.

Then I opened the front door to my house and everything changed.

The smell of steak, butter, and onions hit my nose. I saw the table set with two place settings, candles alight and an open bottle of wine next to two crystal glasses. Mittens greeted me by jumping up into my arms, her breath smelling of tuna.

And there was Bishop, in the kitchen.

He said he'd be back, but I hadn't known when, and his presence opened the floodgates of my heart. All the fears, doubts, and emotions poured out as I set Mittens and the giant book of dragons on the counter and rushed into his arms.

"Hey." He gathered me close, wrapping his arms around me and squeezing tight. I felt the brush of his spirit-being along mine, the touch of his lips to my hair. "What's up? Is everything okay?"

I stayed right where I was, telling him my worries with my face against his chest. His worn cotton T-shirt was soft, the muscles under it firm, and all I wanted to do was get naked and stay in bed with this angel forever.

He rubbed my back, burying his face in my hair and inhaling. "You're doing what you can here, Eden. You're making a difference. And every person in this city should realize that."

"But I'll spend my whole life in constant battle if I can't somehow manage to make this city a safe place," I told him. "It's all more than I can manage, and I don't know where to go from here. Plus I'm scared about my family, and I worry that my presence is endangering those I care about. That demon at Suerte was there for *me*. Am I really doing good, or am I just making things worse?"

"It sounds like you did a good job helping protect Suerte today." He kissed the side of my head. "And that attack is not your fault. Demons have been targeting my home and business since I broke my contract."

Which was my fault, too.

"HB was *seriously* hurt." I was whining, but I knew that Bishop wouldn't hold that temporary lapse in character against me.

"HB will be fine. She is far stronger than you realize. It'll take more than one smoke demon to kill her. And don't worry about the neighbors here. Shifters can be fickle in their loyalties. It comes from millennia of fear and distrust. When the crap hits the fan, they'll be here for you. Because if they aren't, they'll lose both your support and mine, and they don't want that."

"But Kellan..."

"You need to stop with this anxiety over the minion thing. There's nothing wrong about what you did. Everything in life comes with a price, and that includes what amounts to resurrection. I get that Addy didn't have a choice, but that wasn't your fault. Kellan willingly accepted the price. I know him. You don't need to feel the slightest bit of guilt about tying him to you. Not the slightest."

Bishop always made me feel so much better. When an angel that was millions of years old told you everything was going to be okay, you believed him.

But...

"My neighborhood was attacked." I choked back a sob at that. "I mean Bea's neighborhood. I wasn't there. I left them, moved out, and I wasn't there to protect them. They're family. I swore I'd never let anything bad happen to them, but I can't protect them while I'm living here. I should have never left."

"It sounds like they did a pretty good job of fighting the demons off on their own," Bishop said. "You are a grown woman and as Bea has told you herself, you have the right to start a life on your own. But if you would feel better moving back into your old neighborhood, then do it. I'll make sure this house remains yours when you feel your family is safe enough to move back."

I hugged him tighter, pushing my spirit-being slightly into his. Bishop was my rock. He might claim I was more powerful than he was, but I'd yet been able to do anything to confirm that theory. And beyond the alleged circumstances of my parentage, he had the knowledge, the wisdom, the strength that I didn't. He anchored me. He gave me confidence. Without him, I would be floundering in doubt and anxiety.

"If I move home, Nevarra will feel obligated to give me back my old room, and I don't want that," I told him. "She'll feel bad if I'm sleeping on the couch, even though I'm honestly okay staying there. Plus I don't want Bea to feel like I don't trust her to protect the girls without me. She's my mother in every way, even if she was never legally able to adopt me. I think she'd be insulted if I acted like my own mother couldn't protect my sisters without my help."

"Is there another house you can live in temporarily?" Bishop rocked me slightly, still rubbing my back.

"I…I don't know." Mentally I ran through the houses on the street. Maybe the Hannick's, although living in that peach-and-lavender hued nightmare would be worse than sleeping on Bea's couch. There were a couple of abandoned ones further down the block, but I wasn't sure if they were in any condition for occupancy.

"You're never going to be able to effectively plan and fight for New Hell while you're worried about your family. Do what you need to do to make them safe, so you can actually focus on the other matters."

I opened my mouth to counter that I couldn't fight anything else if I was there twenty-four-seven to defend my family, then an idea hit. Why did it have to be me? If I could get my family and neighbors the tools and resources they needed, they could defend themselves. The last few days had proven that I wasn't the end-all, be-all of New Hell. Gutsy humans, shifters, and mages were holding their own. Genevieve's wards. Javier's werewolf family. Juke with her gun and whip. They just needed to band together with the right tools, and then *all* of us could make New Hell safe.

Bishop kissed the side of my head again, then pulled back to look down at me. "Your priority always needs to be those you love. Human life is short. These demons will be here to fight for centuries."

"I know. And you're right. But I made a vow. I claimed the city and I feel a responsibility to the people who live here." I told him.

Bishop hugged me close. "I've lived for millions of years. Taking decades or centuries to assert your claim is perfectly acceptable in the lifespan of an angel. The humans you care about can't wait that long."

"I know, but neither can the other humans in the city," I said.

He sighed. "Humans have died—some horrifically—long before you were here to save them. There are eight billion humans on this planet. You cannot assume responsibility for all of them—even if you limit yourself to the ones in New Hell. Your priority right now is to protect those closest to you, then work to make the long-term future of New Hell a better place."

He was right. And I had some ideas on how to make that

all happen. I'd left Suerte frustrated and without a plan, but fifteen minutes with Bishop had brought clarity to it all.

"Let's eat," he said, pulling away from me and turning toward the stove. "I've been keeping these steaks medium-rare the whole time we've been talking. Go sit at the table. Pour the wine. I'll bring out dinner in just a minute."

I did as he said, thinking how impressive it was that he'd known exactly how close I was to home and how to time dinner exactly right. And keeping the steaks from over-cooking while I'd unloaded on him? That was a trick I really wanted to learn.

I poured the wine, sipping it as I sat at the table. Bishop brought out steak smothered in butter-sautéed onions and mushrooms, baked potatoes with crispy, salt-crusted skin, and salads full of crunchy vegetables. We ate, and I snuck Mittens little bites of steak under the table. When we were finished, I insisted on doing the dishes. Once everything was clean and put away, I joined Bishop in the living room to snuggle up on the sofa with more wine. We looked out the bank of windows down on the city, Mittens snoozing on the coffee table in front of us.

"How did your trip go?" I asked the angel, realizing that so far the evening's conversation had been all about me.

He sighed. "Worrisome. Unsuccessful. I spent most of the day gathering information and none of it is good. Just between you and me, the world outside of New Hell is facing some pretty dark shit. The angelic host is causing issues among the humans. Interdimensional rifts have opened up across the globe. There are threats that mean those that I'd hoped would help us are only able to provide short-term assistance. And the Iblis, the new Satan…she's gone."

"What!" I turned to him in surprise. Doriel, the demon supposedly in charge of New Hell, the one who had been assassinated, had serve under the new Satan. She, the Satan, was ultimately in charge of New Hell, and both Bishop and I had hoped she'd intervene on behalf of the humans and other residents here.

I'd been bitter that she'd seemingly abandoned us, but hadn't expected much from a demon, especially one who'd taken the title of Satan. Still, a small part of me had been hopeful, despite all signs to the contrary, that she or one of the archangels would help us.

"No one will tell me exactly what has happened, but they're all worried," Bishop said. "I'm assuming she's still alive since her mate, the archangel Michael, isn't burning the world down in a display of grief. Besides, no one else has assumed the title of Ha-Satan. Although, the title has gone unclaimed and dormant for millions of years in the past, so that's no real clue as to what's going on. There's no saying it wouldn't go unclaimed for millions of years again."

I sucked in a breath. "Then I guess we're on our own."

He put an arm around my shoulders. "We've got each other. We've got friends and family. We're never on our own."

Still, it meant I needed to formulate some sort of plan—whether it be short or long-term—for helping the residents of New Hell. There would be no Satan to ride in on a black horse to save us all. It would be up to Bishop and me, and our merry band of followers.

"I spoke to my friend, and she said that we might be able to leverage magic against the demons," Bishop told me. "I haven't heard of a sorcerer in the area, but if the mages were to work together, they might be able to create enough of a magical defense to secure a section of the Valley for humans to live in peace. Plus they could provide weapons that might be able to level the playing field between humans and demons."

He had a point. Again. Magic…it might be the very

thing that turned our small army into a force to be reckoned with. Thinking over the meeting and the fight at Suerte, I began to set priorities. There were still plenty of humans left in the LA area, along with the police force that had stuck it out through budget cuts, dwindling resources, all while fighting an enemy that far overpowered them. I'd been guilty of thinking they were nothing more than cannon fodder, doomed to fall at the hands of the demons they fought. Then I'd seen Juke today.

The woman had been a total badass. With an anti-magic gun and a whip that clearly had been magically enhanced, she'd more than held her own against those demons. We needed more Jukes in this world.

We needed to arm more humans like Juke was armed.

"I'll talk to Mathias," I said, hoping the mage would be willing to put me in touch with other magic users in the area, and help organize a joint effort to protect the city. But we needed more. Even if there were a hundred mages, I didn't know if they all had the skills to produce weaponry on the scale that we needed.

"Do you think we can manage to get more anti-magic bullets and weapons?" I asked Bishop. "They're in very limited supply. I'm not sure whether it's a cost issue or if the demons are blocking their import, but either way I'm sure it's going to be more difficult to get them going forward. If we can manage to bring as much as we can into New Hell and arm the police force as well as some trusted individuals, it be a game changer."

Bishop frowned. "I might be able to leverage a few contacts to get us some supplies. It will take me a while, though. Can you hold down the fort for a few days?"

I swallowed my fear and nodded. A few days without Bishop would be hard. But I needed to be able to stand on my own two feet and not constantly be relying on Bishop for support.

"Can I suggest something?" Bishop asked.

"Please do. I'm floundering here and have no action plan whatsoever beyond gathering information and getting the humans anti-magic weapons and ammo."

He rubbed my shoulder. "Make alliances where you can. Then pick one target and focus on that one."

I snorted. "Alliances. Let's see… Desiree has bought out my jobs from the tax demons. She wants to punish you, wants me working for her, and I have no leverage whatsoever to use in a negotiation."

"Offer to help her get rid of one or both of the other demons and clear your debt with her," Bishop said. "There's always a negotiation point. You just have to get creative and think what each of these demons really wants."

He was right. I snuggled against him and thought out loud. "I think Desiree would go for that, but she's tricky and would figure out a way to twist the deal so I did the work and still ended up owing her. She'd know full well that I couldn't take out those other two demons on my own. She'd agree just to enjoy watching them kick the shit out of me."

"You do know that eventually you're going to have to deal with her," Bishop commented.

"Yeah. But I'm trying to put that off for as long as possible." I thought for a second. "From what I've heard, the warmonger dude is motivated less by territory and more by actively fighting battles and one-on-one duels. He's got a bit of an honor code, I've been told. So that's a plus."

"Sounds like you two would have a lot in common," Bishop teased.

"Hey!" I swatted him.

"Do you know who this warmonger is?" Bishop asked.

"His name is Barstonel. He's one of the Fallen, what

Blister calls an Ancient. He's taken the south section of New Hell—basically from the airport south and west of downtown. I'm going to assume he'll be picking fights with the shifter packs and other groups in the area. The Disciples will most likely be high on his to-do list."

"He might be open to attacking one of the other two demons with your household's assistance, and he might not demand much in exchange," Bishop said. "Like you said, for this warmonger, the reward is in the fight."

"Okay. Moving that possibility up on my list. The other dude is Itinder, a plague demon. He's got the Valley north, and I'm particularly concerned since that's where my family lives. All I know about him is that he was a member of a bunch of notable households, then struck out on his own. He killed some other demon, got a bunch of followers, and leveled up."

Bishop was silent for a few seconds. "If it were me, I'd try to make a deal with the warmonger to get rid of the plague demon. Then you can decide whether you're going to switch sides and fight him with Desiree, or stay allied with him and go after her."

I winced, not liking all this duplicity and changing sides thing. I didn't include many people in my friend—or even in my household—circle, but once in, I was loyal. The idea of a double cross made me ill. If I allied myself with this warmonger, I couldn't betray him—unless he did something horrible or broke my trust first.

But how would I find the warmonger, get an audience with him, and convince him I was worthy of an alliance. Yeah, there was the whole "her energy signature is like Samael's, the OG Satan," but that might not count for much when I couldn't do much more than a Low.

"What about that dragon?" I mused. "I mean, it isn't like I can negotiate with him. He pretty much would attack me on sight. Maybe we can use him as a weapon, though. Although, according to Blister, the demons are staying clear of that downtown area. She said they bribed the other dragons to leave, but this guy seems to have made a nest and established a hoard, so I guess he's here to stay."

"I don't know much about dragons," Bishop admitted. "If we could manage to drive opposing forces into his territory, then I assume he'd take care of them for us."

Getting the plague demon's army from the Valley into Downtown didn't seem all that probable, but I decided to keep that option in my back pocket.

I sighed. "I think the most concerning thing for me right now is my lack of power. I mean, if I really am OG Satan's daughter, then I can't imagine he would have produced a dud. Why am I not kicking ass and taking names? Why am I such an underpowered loser compared to the other demons?"

Bishop chuckled. "You're hardly an underpowered loser. Every now and then something happens that reveals hidden levels of immense power. I don't know why you can't always access that. Maybe there's some sort of damper on your abilities that will only let you use them when you are actually able to control them. You're still young. Not twenty-three years old young, but anything under a few hundred thousand years is young by angelic standards. It might be a good thing you can't destroy the whole world in the blink of an eye."

"I still feel like an underpowered loser," I grumbled.

He sighed, pulling away slightly. "You absorb deadly amounts of energy, store it, then launch it back. You heal others—and even with the minion thing, that's not something demons can do. It's not something most Angels of Order can do either. You've created on a huge scale using absorbed energy—"

"With your help," I pointed out. "That shit would have killed me dead if you hadn't helped me."

"I'm not so sure," Bishop told me. "I never really knew Samael on a personal level, but he always struck me as brilliant and immensely powerful. I'm pretty sure whatever is blocking your power is there for a reason, and if you truly need it, it will be there."

I hoped so. Because I couldn't save New Hell as I was. I needed to be more if I was going to truly make a difference in this city.

CHAPTER 14

Bishop and I made love, snuggled together and dozed in bed. I woke up around two in the morning to him kissing me goodbye.

"I'll be back with weapons and bullets," he promised.

I reached out to grab his hand, still half asleep. "Thank you for this. Love you."

He bent down and kissed me, his spirit-being brushing against mine. "Love you too. Stay safe."

He teleported away and I immediately felt cold and lonely. When would all this be over? When could we just be together and explore this thing between us without the constant battle for New Hell? It was all my fault. If I was just some human, or even a part-demon, then Bishop would never have broken his vow. We could be snuggling in his house right now, letting the rest of the world pass us by. Why had I claimed this territory, vowed to defend the innocent and fight for peace? Why couldn't I put myself first, like I'd done for so much of my life?

Because then I wouldn't be me. And Bishop probably wouldn't have loved that other version of myself.

I felt the mattress sag and opened my eyes to see Mittens, walking up from the bottom of the bed. He purred, curling himself against my side and I reached out a hand to stroke his soft fur. Such a tiny kitten. So adorable, and yet so lethal. Mittens was an inspiration. He gave me hope that as human as I looked and felt, somewhere deep inside me was the strength to truly make a difference.

SWIRLS OF LIGHT AND ENERGY. Vast swaths of deepest darkness. A pulse of conversion, of destruction leading to creation. Nothing was sacred beyond the transition of something into something else. Occasionally I would pause to admire a form, a structure, or even the beauty of the nothingness. Then I reached out and reshaped. Even my creations were in a constant state of change. Atoms splitting and forming anew, excess energy swirling out to fuel another formation.

"You are ready."

The voice boomed, and I didn't know who this was or what they meant. Ready for what?

Suddenly I was ripped from my home of light and darkness, plunged into a place where everything felt compressed, divided, hindered. My vast being was compacted into something small. A strange feeling raced through me. Cold. Hungry. An unbelievable limitation of my self.

I opened my eyes to see my former home above me, far away and blurred through the lens of a strange atmosphere. Confusion. And fear. I was defenseless, and terrified.

I bolted upright, breathing heavy, my heart pounding in my chest. The confusion and fear from my dream remained. Glancing around, I realized I wasn't in my bed, in my home, or even in Los Feliz. I was on the couch in Bea's living room.

Immediately I relaxed, comforted by the familiar, loving

surroundings. It had just been a bad dream. Had the house in Los Feliz been a bad dream as well? Bishop? I looked down at my hands and patted my body, unsure that I wasn't actually still a teenager living with my foster mother and sisters.

I heard a creak on the stairs and looked up to see the barrel of a pistol pointed my way.

"It's me! Bea, it's me!" I squeaked, not wanting to shout and wake the girls.

The pistol lowered and Bea put a hand against her chest. "Lordy, Eden. You scared me half to death. Why didn't you call or text that you were coming over? And why so late? Has something happened? Why are you naked?"

Crap. I snatched the crocheted afghan off the back of the couch and wrapped it around myself. I tended to sleep in the nude now that I had my own house—especially when Bishop was over.

"No, nothing's happened—at least that I'm aware of. I was fast asleep in my bed at home, had some weird dream, and woke up here on your couch."

I got up and pushed the curtain aside to look out the window. My bike wasn't in the drive or on the street.

"I think I might have teleported here," I said, not sure what was more strange—that I might have driven my bike all the way here while naked, and not remembered it, or teleported. I definitely hadn't walked. My feet weren't dirty, and I was pretty sure if I'd gone that far in some naked sleepwalking state, I'd be dirty, sore, and exhausted.

Bea came down the stairs and put the pistol on a bookshelf. She was wearing a cotton pajama set with lavender stripes and a blue plush bathrobe. I felt a wash of love and homesickness and went over to hug her.

She folded me against her soft body, hugging me tight and putting her cheek against the side of my head. We stood there for a few minutes, then she stepped back, looking at me, her hands on my shoulders. "Teleported. Eden, that's something to be happy about. You can quickly remove yourself and others from danger. You can be where you're needed in an instant."

"Let's not get too excited here," I told her. "I *think* I teleported. In my sleep. I doubt I could do it again on purpose."

"Try," she urged.

I stepped away from her, not wanting to inadvertently take Bea with me, or scramble her molecules in a shitty first attempt. Closing my eyes, I imagined myself back at my house. Opening them, I found myself still at Bea's, with her watching me expectantly.

"Maybe if you're not watching me it would help," I said.

She turned around and I tried once more. It didn't work. I kept up with the attempts, varying whether I was sitting, laying down, eyes opened or closed, verbalizing where I wanted to be, praying—nothing worked.

After a few minutes, Bea had gone into the kitchen to make coffee. I finally gave up and went in after her, sitting at the kitchen table, still wrapped in the afghan. I watched as she turned on the stove, waved a hand over the burner, then turned it off and got out the little butane cooker we'd picked up a few years back when we realized electricity was no longer a reliable utility.

Filling a kettle with water from one of the jugs on the counter, she put it on to boil. The nice thing about the little camp stove was that it was insanely fast. The water boiled in a minute. Bea poured it into a drip setup we'd engineered to replace the old coffee maker that needed electricity to work. As the brown liquid slowly poured into the carafe, she walked over and sat down across from me.

"Work called last night and told me not to come in the rest of this week," she said.

Dread settled in my chest. "I'm sorry. Do you think they'll have you back soon?"

She shrugged. "I think they're waiting to see how things settle here in New Hell. Might be that we don't have any sort of trash disposal going forward."

This was so Bea. She was more concerned about sanitation than her wages. We were in a better position than most. The transfer station was right across the street and it would take our neighborhood years to fill the thing up with untransferred trash. We'd begun composting earlier this week, and there was probably some trash we could burn, but it would eventually pile up. And with the trash would come rats and disease, and a smell that we'd never be able to escape.

The more immediate problem would be the loss of Bea's wages. Her sewing and soap making only brought in a small amount of food and supplies in trade. With Bea unemployed and my Vulture work drying up, we'd really be in trouble. Keeping my family safe from the plague demon wasn't my only worry now.

"We'll be okay, hon. Don't you worry about us when you've got so much more to think about right now." Bea patted my hand and got up to pour us both a mug of coffee.

"I've got some extra cash back at the house to help you get through the week," I said, thinking that Alfie would just need to wait for his next payment. "And the pantry is stocked with canned and dried foods too. I'll bring some by for you all."

I might not be getting tributes from the local shifters anymore, but their former generosity had resulted in more dried beans, canned vegetables, rice, and noodles than I could possibly eat myself.

"Thanks, Eden. The girls and I appreciate it." Bea set a mug in front of me and took her seat.

I went to take a sip of my coffee and froze. Something

dark and foul curled like smoke into my awareness. With a gasp I dropped the mug, jumped up, and ran for the door. It took a few frustrating seconds for me to unlock the half-dozen deadbolts Bea had put on the steel door, but I finally got the thing open and ran outside.

The street and all the houses were dark from the power outage. The dump that served as a transfer station across the street was a black expanse with the garbage forming vague hill-like shapes in the distance. To my eyes, nothing seemed amiss, but I felt that oozing darkness at the end of the street. Then I felt the flare of Genevieve Planteaux's wards spring to life.

Bea appeared in the doorway, her pistol in hand. I waved her back, putting a finger to my lips to tell her to remain silent. Staying on the grass and using the vehicles on the curbs and various shrubberies to conceal myself, I made my way to the end of the street. The wards flared again and again, the third time feeling slightly weaker than they had before.

The fucker was trying to force his way through. Stepping into the street, I caught my first look at what I was about to battle.

Three demons stood on the other side of Genevieve's wards. The one with a boar's head and a human body was battering the wards with his fists. A lizard-like demon stood a respectful distance back, and by his side, arms folded across his body, was a demon wearing a grim reaper cloak. A black whiplike tail and massive clawed feet stuck out from under the hem. He glanced my way, and from the hood of the cloak, I saw glowing green eyes.

Genevieve appeared beside me and I started at how quiet and stealthy she'd been. Her ebony skin glowed in the faint light from the wards. Her silk robe billowed from a magical breeze. Her full lips pursed in disapproval.

"The wards will not hold much longer." She spat out a curse. "It took me three days to make those and strengthen them. Demons. They have no respect for the magical craft. Just going to bash their way through like a wrecking ball. I will have the headache all day from this."

"If you drop the wards, would they be undamaged? Can you bring them up again without needing days to work on them?" I asked her.

"Yes, but then the demons will come in." She shrugged. "Either way, demons will kill us. And if I am dead, it does not matter whether the wards are broken or just damaged. They will quickly fall without me alive to power them."

"If I walk through, will the wards remain intact? *Can* I walk through right now?" In the past I'd been able to, but I wasn't sure what sort of enhancements Genevieve had done and if they'd block me since I was also a demon. Or angel. Or something.

She shrugged. "They should be okay. Originally I made them so residents, friends, and family could get through. I want to try to add on a layer that blocks anyone with evil intent, but I am not sure how well that will work."

It was worth a shot.

"I'm going through and hopefully the wards will hold and keep out any attack. If I fail, everyone needs to get out of here as fast as possible."

I had no guns. I had no clothes. I was literally naked and wrapped in an afghan—an afghan I had lots of fond childhood memories of.

The boar's head demon smashed the wards again.

Fuck it. I took off the afghan and draped it on the hood of a car. Then I went for the demons, ripping a metal pole that once held a street sign from the ground as I ran. A circular hunk of concrete came up with the pole, some grass and dirt clinging to the edge.

The wards flared as I ran through, sparking red and burning my skin. I kept going, not stopping to assess any damage. The boar head dude was closest, so I plowed into him, using the pole as a spear. Surprisingly, it impaled him. He staggered back a few steps, blood pouring from the entry and the exit points. I kept going until everything but the chunk of cement was in or through him, then stepped back and yanked.

The pole slid out with a wet sound and the demon laughed, moving forward and again impaling himself. Then he punched me.

It felt like I'd been hit by a truck. Everything went hazy as I flew back into the wards. It was the burn of the magic that brought me back to my senses.

Jumping away from the wards, I dodged another punch, grabbed the pole still sticking through the center of the demon, and danced to the side. He staggered, turning with the pole, so I kept going, speeding up with the idea of using centrifugal force to throw the demon back and free my only physical weapon.

I heard the lizard demon say something in a language I didn't recognize right before he began throwing high voltage electrical bursts at me. They hit me with surprising accuracy, doing absolutely nothing.

Realizing I was more than just a gutsy, superstrong human, the lizard demon shouted something else and began waving his hands around. By this point I had increased speed to the point where everything except for the boar-head demon was a blur. With a grunt, he lost his footing and came free of the metal pole, flying backward straight into the wards.

They'd burned me, but they did far more to the boar-head demon. With a fireworks display of colored sparks, they held the demon three feet in the air. He screamed, jolting around.

Five seconds later the wards spat him out, and the demon corpse lay smoking on the ground.

Wow. I would never doubt Genevieve Planteaux's magical abilities ever again.

The lizard demon was still jumping up and down, waving his hands and shouting. The dude with the cloak just looked at me, green eyes glowing in the blackness behind the hood. I hefted my pole and watched them, hoping they'd just give up, go away, and mark off this neighborhood as "don't mess with these fuckers."

I wasn't so lucky. The hooded guy spread his arms, clawed hands opening. Small black blobs that vaguely looked like ants rained down from his fingers onto the pavement, rushing toward the wards. I knew instantly that this was a plague demon, although I doubted he was *the* plague demon. That guy was probably too busy poisoning the water supply or unleashing chlorine gas into the air to bother with destruction on this small scale.

Another thing I knew—Genevieve's wards were too depleted to keep all of these diseased ants out. And it would take only one of them to start a chain reaction of disease that would kill off most, if not all, of my neighborhood.

I ran forward, stamping ants with the cement end of the pole, then also with my bare feet. They spread out and sped up, and I realized there was no way I could squash thousands of ants before they reached the wards. So I dropped the pole, put out my hands, and *pulled*.

This weird method had worked before with demon energy, with electricity attacks, with fire, and even with bullets. I hoped this skill, one of the few I could reliably count on, worked just as well on plague ants.

Their forward progress halted, even though their little legs kept moving, then suddenly thousands of tiny bugs flew toward me, covering my skin.

I couldn't help it. I screamed and flailed. Thankfully the ants remained on my skin in spite of my panicked movements. The plague demon released more, and once again, I pulled them toward me.

This was truly beginning to freak me out. Every inch of me was coated with ants. At least they weren't crawling around or trying to get into my eyes, nose, or mouth, but it was still incredibly gross. More ants poured from the plague demon's hands, and I continued to gather them to me. The thick layer of ants began to melt together until I felt like I had a black rubber wetsuit on. Then I felt them seep through my skin. Nausea twisted my stomach. My burned skin heated with fever. My breathing grew wet and labored.

Oh no. This was not going to fucking happen. I wasn't going to die naked, covered in ants, because of some plague demon virus. Not. Going. To. Happen.

More and more ants coated my skin. I dropped to my knees, my hands hitting the pavement. The fever tore through me, making my teeth chatter and my mind wander. I tried to focus, tried not to let any of the ants through the wards.

The asphalt felt cool in the morning air, chipped and rough from two years of no maintenance. My fingers felt a long crack, felt the grass that had sprouted through, determined to grow and live no matter the challenges it faced. My vision faded and I saw dandelions. Stars. Constellations. The garden Bishop had helped me create when I'd absorbed all of Doriel's energy and thought I was about to die.

Energy. Destruction. Creation. Nothing ever ended, nothing ever began. All of existence was transformation. Constant transformation.

Something opened up inside of me and I screamed as light and sound ripped through my physical being.

Nothing was exempt from transformation. Nothing.

It was as if I'd exploded into an Eden-sized sun. The black coating shattered and flew from my skin. I saw the plague demon throw his hands up to shield his face, but it was a futile action. Nothing was exempt from transformation—not him. Not even me.

The shards of black turned to brown dirt as they hit the ground. The plague demon froze, solidifying into a column of white, as if he were Lot's wife turned to salt. Then the column collapsed, a patch of sand in the middle of the roadway. From the sand sprouted flowers—a thick patch of daisies in full bloom.

I remained on my knees, trying to steady my breathing. My fever was gone, my vision restored, but I had the mother of all headaches and my stomach still churned with nausea.

"Eden?"

I heard Bea's voice and gave her a thumb's-up, not able to do much more at the moment. Several minutes later, I felt I might be able to actually get to my feet. Using the pole for leverage, I struggled upright, then clung to it for a few minutes more. Finally feeling stable, I let go of the pole and carefully made my way through the wards.

They burned just as bad going in as coming out, and I muttered a few choice words for Genevieve Planteaux as I came out the other side.

Surprisingly, only six people stood outside of their houses at the end of their lawns, silently staring at me as I passed. Maybe the wards had dampened the sound of the fight, or people had heard the commotion and figured they would be safer inside behind locked doors. Either way, I was glad they were all okay. No one in my neighborhood had died this morning, thanks to me and Genevieve. And if no one besides Bea patted me on the back, so be it.

I slowly staggered my way to Bea's house, feeling like I'd

been burned, hit by a truck, and in the process of recovering from a bad case of the flu.

Patty Wilson stepped into the street, shaking a finger at me. "Put some clothes on, Eden Alvaro. This is a family neighborhood. Public nudity will not be tolerated."

Nice to know Patty's priorities. She'd rather die from a plague than be subjected to my unclothed boobs, ass, and hoo-hah.

Well, fuck her. I gave the woman the finger, and kept going.

CHAPTER 15

"That Patty Wilson is a piece of work," Bea raged as I drank my cooled coffee at the kitchen table. "You save us all from a horrible death, and she scolds you for being naked? Humph. She's probably jealous."

"Because she couldn't kill those demons?" I asked.

"No, because you look a whole lot better naked than she does," Bea huffed.

She'd scooted me into the bathroom once I'd gotten home to wash up with what precious little water they had in the sink. Then she'd handed me antibiotic cream, burn cream, and some clothes. I'd foregone the creams, knowing that I'd heal quickly and figuring at some point they'd need the medical supplies more than me. The clothes I accepted, although Bea was significantly larger than I was. It felt like home being enveloped in one of her T-shirts and a pair of drawstring shorts. I'd stolen one of Bishop's shirts to sleep in, and I might decide to keep Bea's outfit as well, just to lounge around in when I was feeling homesick.

"Do you think that lizard guy will be back?" Bea asked.

I frowned into my coffee, worried about the one that had

gotten away. Outside of his electrical attack, he hadn't seemed to be able to deploy any other offensive weapon. Did that mean he was a lower-level demon? Was he there as cannon fodder? Or to loot our houses once we were all dead? Or maybe just to watch and enjoy the carnage? Either way, he'd escaped sometime between the ant launch and me turning the plague demon into a patch of daisies.

"I doubt he'll come back. I'm more worried what he's going to tell his boss about this, and what his boss is going to do." Would the plague demon retaliate? If so, I needed to be here to protect my family. Actually I'd need backup to protect my family. Just because I'd taken out the boar-head demon and what I assumed was a mid-level plague demon, didn't mean I could deal with the higher-level version. And if I were honest, Genevieve Planteaux's wards had played a major part in killing the boar-head demon, so I'd really only managed to take one of them down solo.

Bea sighed. "We'll deal with that when we need to. In the meantime, I'm going to get some breakfast going."

"Eden!"

I turned to see Sadie and Nevarra in the doorway. They both ran toward me, and I turned to pull them in for a group hug.

"What are you doing here?" Nevarra stepped back and eyed me. "And why are you wearing Bea's T-shirt?"

"I think I teleported." I waited for their squeals of excitement to stop. "And since I now live alone, I tend to sleep without any clothing on. Bea was kind enough to loan me some, so I didn't need to be streaking around the house."

Sadie giggled.

Nevarra's eyebrows went up. "So Bishop spent the night last night? Isn't he going to be worried when he wakes up and you're not there."

"Now, Nevarra," Bea scolded. "None of us need to be prying into Eden's private life."

"Oh I definitely need to be prying into Eden's private life," she said with a grin. "Is your hottie angel joining us for breakfast too?"

"Sadly no." I wrapped an arm around her shoulders and pulled her close once more, loving having both my sisters in my arms like this. "He had to leave late last night. He's going to try to get us more anti-magic guns and bullets, so the humans in New Hell will be able to better defend themselves when attacked."

"Will the anti-magic bullets work on plague demons?" Sadie asked. "Like against the ones that killed Mrs. Vandergriff's family and her neighbors?"

"I'm sure those bullets would work on plague demons just as well as they work on the other demons," I told her, already having planned to set aside a few of the weapons and at least a case of the bullets for them. It would make me feel a lot better about leaving them alone if they had some way of neutralizing any demonic disease before it happened.

Although Genevieve Planteaux seemed to be doing a pretty damned good job of defending the neighborhood herself.

Sadie put a hand on my cheek. "Are you sunburned? Were you at the beach? You never get sunburn, Eden."

No, I didn't. Not unless I went through activated magical wards twice. If she'd seen me thirty minutes ago, I would have had blisters on my face, but thankfully my speed-healing seemed to be speeding up even more.

"I wish I was at the beach!" I kissed her forehead. "When all this crazy shit settles down, we need to go to the beach. Bea and I'll pack a picnic. We'll body surf and build sand castles. If that ice cream place is still open, I'll buy you both cones."

Bea placed a bowl of oatmeal in front of me. "You girls sit and let Eden eat. I've got your breakfasts coming right up."

Nevarra went to pour herself and Sadie a drink from one of the containers of shelf-stable milk I'd found last month on a salvage job. I dug into my oatmeal, surprised that Bea had added milk and dried cherries to the mix. By the time we'd all finished our breakfasts, I was feeling less battered and was formulating a plan.

"Bea, can you go over to Genevieve Planteaux's house and ask her if she'd mind a houseguest for the foreseeable future? I'm thinking of asking Addy to come here and help add some magical defenses and protections."

"Genevieve might like the company of another mage," Bea said. "And the neighborhood can chip in for food and magical supplies, since Addy would be helping us all out."

"How about Mittens?" Nevarra asked. "Can he come help us as well?"

"I'll ask him," I replied, worried the hellkitty might cause more destruction than the demons. Plus Mittens tended to come and go on his own terms. There was no saying he wouldn't hang out in the junkyard and ignore demons attacking our neighborhood, or wander off when he was needed most. He thought of *me* as his possession, but I wasn't sure he considered either of my homes as his territory. So defending them might not be anywhere on his priority list.

"Are you going to stay too?" Sadie asked.

My house in Los Feliz was more centrally located, but Bishop was right. I couldn't fight all three major demons and their followers, and I couldn't protect all of New Hell. I needed to pick one fight, strategize, then pivot once I'd defeated that foe.

My priority was going to be this plague demon. Desiree and the warmonger were less of a threat when it came the possibility of human death on a large scale—at least right now. And they were definitely less of a threat when it came to my family

"I might," I told her. "But there are a lot of things I need to do away from here, so I can't be here every minute of every day. I'm hoping that Addy and Genevieve will keep you all safe, and that Bishop will be back soon with some anti-magic weapons."

"You can have your old room back," Nevarra said.

"No, I will have the couch." I shook my finger at her. "That is your room now, and I'm just here temporarily."

"We have a box of things ready for your friend Jayla," Sadie told me. "When you leave, maybe you can take it over to her? We're working on a second box for her now."

"Sure. I'll take it to her." It was then I realized I had a problem. Not only did I have no clothing besides the borrowed ones from Bea, I was without a vehicle.

"Can I borrow your phone?" I asked Bea. "I'm going to need to call someone for a ride."

* * *

AN HOUR later I was in Juke's sweet muscle car, a box on my lap.

"You owe me for this one, Alvaro," she scolded. "I'm supposed to be doing neighborhood checks, not hauling your ass to a bar and then to your house."

"I do owe you one," I promised, glad that owing a favor to Juke was a much less dangerous experience than owing a favor to a demon. "And I appreciate both the ride and the detour." I'd promised the girls I'd deliver their first care package today, and Suerte was sort of on our way to my house.

She grumbled, then shot me a quick glance. "So…do you think you can figure out this teleportation thing? Because you being able to zip around like Bishop? That would be extra helpful, you know."

"I don't even know *how* I did it last night to attempt to duplicate it," I told her. "I was asleep, and just woke up at Bea's house."

"Do you think it was the dream?" she asked. "Or did you have a subconscious premonition that your mom and sisters were going to need you? That a threat was on its way?"

I shrugged. "I've never had premonitions before, and my abilities seem to come and go. I'd love if I could teleport reliably, but don't count on it happening in this lifetime."

She glanced at me again. "So you killed a plague demon and some asshole with a pig head?"

"Boar," I corrected.

She sniffed. "Whatever. I'm impressed either way. Think we'll ever be able to get rid of this plague demon and his army? This is the second hit in two days. I get a feeling we'll see daily attacks if we can't do something to stop this guy. People are already panicked. Ones that can afford it are fleeing New Hell, but many just don't have the means to even get to the border, let alone start a new life. These people have nothing, Eden. Their homes, their jobs, their belongings, their friends and family—everything is here."

"I'm working on it," I told her. "I was thinking of maybe trying to get a meeting with the warmonger who has the southern part of New Hell to ask him if he'd help us get rid of the plague demon."

Juke made a garbled noise. "So we'll be swapping a disease for murderous violence?"

"Hopefully not." I sighed. "I have to at least give it a try. We need powerful allies, and I don't think we can afford to be choosy right now."

"Don't make a deal with the devil," Juke cautioned. "If Bishop can get us more ammo and anti-magic guns, we might be able to take out this plague demon without needing to sell our souls to some warmonger."

"I won't make any hasty promises," I reassured her.

"Good. But speaking of deals with the devil, I need to tell you that this Aries drug is making a comeback."

I sucked in a breath. "No! I thought the supply chain had been disrupted. And that we warned people about the addictive nature and side effects."

"Evidently the supply chain disruption was only temporary," Juke said. "And desperate people do desperate things. I don't know if it's true or not, but there's a rumor that people high on Aries are immune to plague demon attacks, just like shifters supposedly are."

I winced. "I wouldn't bet on either of those being true. I know shifters don't normally get the majority of human diseases, but I'm pretty sure a powerful demon can concoct something that would kill them too. Can you and the rest of the police force try to convince people not to take the drug?"

"Sure. That'll work. Don't take the scary drug. Demons are going to rip you and everyone you love apart or kill with a fast-acting plague. This drug might help, but is addicting so don't bother to take it. Just lay down and accept death instead of fighting it with every weapon you have."

"Okay. Point made." I scowled. I didn't like this drug. It was dangerous, and it made humans susceptible to manipulation. Once they were hooked, they'd do anything to get more. Starting out with good intentions didn't mean we wouldn't end up with a ton of addicts stealing, killing, and being just as much of a danger as the demons they'd originally wanted to protect their friends and family from.

"How do you plan to contact this warmonger?" Juke asked.

Hell if I knew. It wasn't like I could look him up in the directory. I didn't have a whole lot of contacts south of the city. The Disciples and I were on shaky ground. I'd helped them end the gladiatorial games at SoFi Stadium, but I'd also stolen Piers's motorcycle helmet, and threatened a gang member—one who had some important family connections in the Disciples. I didn't know if they'd help me if I asked, or if they even knew how to get in touch with this warmonger. Bags had a friend who owned a pawnshop down in Torrance, and pawnbrokers tended to be in the know about the powerful in their areas, but Shavonne also had reasons she might not want to give me any assistance, even as a favor to Bags. I'd still try both, just in case. And if those didn't work, hopefully Blister would come through with something.

"I've got a couple of leads," I told Juke.

Luckily she was turning into the parking lot at Suerte which didn't leave her with an opportunity to grill me about those leads. As soon as the car came to a stop I hopped out, box in hand.

"I'll only be a few minutes," I told her before pushing the door closed with my hip and heading around behind the building.

No one came out of the bar, but given that everyone inside was most likely a shifter, they would have heard us coming and HB would have identified us by smell long before Juke put her car in park. I went around the dumpster and headed toward the shed, seeing a flash of movement from inside.

"It's Eden," I called as I knocked. When no one answered, I added, "My sisters put together a box for you as a gift."

I waited but didn't get a response. I couldn't even hear anyone moving inside, which made me wonder if what I'd seen earlier had just been a reflection of tree leaves off the glass. Feeling foolish, I knocked again. It wasn't like the shed was so large that she couldn't have heard me knock or call out before, and it certainly wouldn't have taken her more than a couple of seconds to get to the door.

Deciding that she was either not inside or not wanting visitors at the moment, I set the box down, then went around the side of the building. Out of curiosity, I peeked back around and saw the shed door ajar with two hands sliding the box inside.

My errand done, I jogged to Juke's car and climbed in.

CHAPTER 16

"**D**amn," Juke muttered as we turned down the road to my house.

I glanced up and saw some vehicles on their sides or upside down. Juke had to slow down and weave around the wreckage. On the other side of the car blockade I saw roof shingles, an uprooted tree, and someone's concrete fountain smashed and strewn across the road.

Holding my breath, I eyed the houses as we passed. Their yards were torn up, and some had scorch marks along the exterior stucco walls, but it didn't look like there was much in the way of major damage.

As Juke pulled in my driveway, I saw that my house hadn't been spared. If anything, it seemed to have more scorch marks than the others. We both climbed out and stood, looking around to assess the situation. A few of my shifter neighbors came out of their houses, arms folded across their chests as they stared at me with grim expressions.

Was this my fault? How the fuck could this be my fault? Los Feliz was in Desiree's territory, wedged between the plague demon's and the warmonger's sections. I'd assumed she still had her hands full consolidating her own holdings right now and wasn't in any position to make attacks into my neighborhood, but maybe I was wrong. The demon knew my real name, knew where I lived, and had made it clear she wanted me working for her. Was this her way of getting to me? Attack my home, and hope that I either gave in and went to her, or that my neighbors grabbed me and handed me over?

Juke followed me inside, in spite of supposedly having official police work to do. I quickly glanced around the open floor plan and didn't see any interior damage. Mittens meowed, strolling toward me from the kitchen, his eyes glowing bright green and his tail lifted and bushy.

"Did those mean demons attack your home?" I picked him up and cuddled him against me. "Was your daytime nap interrupted?"

He purred, butting his head against my chin.

"Do you want a drink?" I asked Juke as I walked into the kitchen.

Juke nodded. "Sure. It's not like anyone cares about drinking on the job anymore. In fact, it's sort of considered self-care at this point."

Putting Mittens on the counter, I opened the fridge and got out some leftover steak from when Bishop had cooked me dinner last night, and two beers. The steak went into the microwave. That's when I realized I had no power.

"Sorry bud. Cold steak it is." I set the dish in front of Mittens.

The cat wrinkled his nose, but began to eat the meat with delicate bites. I popped the cap on the beers and handed one to Juke.

"Your mom's neighborhood was attacked. Your neighborhood was attacked." Juke took a swig of her beer. "It's almost like they're gunning for you, Alvaro."

"I've never met the plague demon," I protested. "I'm pretty sure he's not in league with Desiree, and she's the only one of the three who has a reason to be gunning for me. The attack here? I am worried that one's because of me."

"Don't count out that the plague demon hasn't got his eye on you. That warmonger either. You've got a reputation," Juke said. "That whole thing at the press conference probably brought a lot of attention to you. Then there was what happened at the stadium with everyone watching on the big screens. Desiree could have talked. Those tax demons could have talked. Hell, for all you know, that Low of yours could have talked. I doubt you're anonymous anymore, Alvaro. These demons probably know who you are and see you as a threat to their territories—a minor threat, but still a threat."

Fuck. "So you think the hits on Bea's neighborhood and here aren't coincidental?"

She shrugged. "They could be coincidental, but I'm a cop and I'm suspicious of anything that shows a pattern. Let's chug down these beers and go talk to your neighbors. This isn't exactly my beat, but I should probably go ahead and file a report anyway. Save some other cop the time."

Ugh. I really didn't want to talk to my neighbors. We'd had a love-hate relationship ever since I'd originally tried to claim this house under the squatter's rights laws and failed. I'd needed to fight some dude for the right to live here and had lost, barely getting out of the neighborhood with my life. Then I'd been approached by the "leader," the snow cloud leopard shifter, Kevin, and informed that I had earned the right to live here on the basis of my relationship with Bishop.

I'm a feminist, but I'm also an opportunist, and I hadn't turned down a sweet house just because some guy was trying to suck up to my angel boyfriend, so I'd moved in. They'd watched me like I was a clown-dressing serial killer until Isha had told them I'd freed the captive shifters who'd been forced to fight in the stadium. Suddenly I'd become their Protector in place of Bishop. I'd arrived home every day to find gifts of food, cosmetics, and booze on my porch.

It had been a short-lived celebrity. After the press conference where our governor had been murdered along with Doriel, the Fallen Angel in charge of New Hell, as well as a Morgana, powerful sorcerer, the big cats of my neighborhood had decided that I was a risk they didn't want to take. They'd returned the Protector title to Bishop, and were back to eyeing me with distrust and wary watchfulness.

But Juke was right. Clearly something had happened in my absence, and as a resident here, I needed to ask about it, not hide in my house and pretend we hadn't seen the destruction.

We both finished our beers. I poured a bowl of fresh water for Mittens from a jug in the fridge, then Juke and I went outside.

About twenty shifters were outside, watching us as we approached the house to the left of mine.

"I'm Detective Juke and I wanted to ask what happened here," Juke said to the woman who stood in her driveway.

"Demons attacked us." Her jaw firmed. "They always stayed away before. Two years ago when they first came to LA some tried to rob us, but we fought them off. The Protector made a deal with them, and we haven't had any problems since then. Until now."

"What kind of demons were they?" Juke asked. "How many? Was there anything in particular they wanted?"

"They wanted her." She pointed to me. "There were about ten of them. When they found out you weren't here, they attacked us. I don't know what kind of demons they were but they had fire weapons, lightning, acid, and brutal physical attacks. They were harder to injure than shifters. And they didn't seem at all bothered by what should have been mortal wounds."

"How did you manage to fight them off?" I asked.

She glared at me. "Thankfully Kevin was here. He lead us in as a group and we pushed them out of the neighborhood, focusing on inflicting as many injuries as possible. There were ten of them and forty of us, so we prevailed. But four of us are so injured it will take them weeks to fully heal. We might be able to fend off a second attack, but a third will probably do us in."

I cringed, knowing this was because of me.

"They'll probably keep attacking until I deal with Desiree," I said as Juke and I walked back to the house.

Juke snorted. "These neighbors of yours seem like they can defend themselves. And next time you'll be here to help them fight. That'll go a long way towards regaining their trust."

Her words made me feel better. But how could I be two places at once?

"Do you think…" I eyed the houses and dropped my voice to a whisper. "Do you think they might hand me over to Desiree? She's got to be behind this attack and she made it clear this kind of violence will continue until she gets me. How much longer until the neighbors get fed up and give me up?"

Juke shrugged. "I think that people are at the point where they're pissed off and not about to be pushed around. Demands like that will just make them more determined to fight it out. Everyone remaining in New Hell right now is scrappy and ready to throw down. They wouldn't turn over a neighbor. Not when they need the alliance of their neighbors to stay safe. Plus, if they give you up today, then someone is gonna give them up next time a demon makes demands."

"I used to be their Protector," I mused. "And I think they still turn to Bishop for help. They've got to know Bishop won't be pleased if they give his girlfriend to Desiree."

Juke nodded. "Rule one, don't piss off an angel."

She was right. I thanked Juke again for the ride and watched her leave before heading inside to sit down with another beer.

Plague demon. Warmonger. Desiree. Dragon.

The demons who'd attacked Suerte had wanted to know where "she" was. And the ones who'd attacked here had clearly been looking for me. Was Desiree working with the plague demon? Had the attack on Bea's neighborhood been a coincidence, or were they looking for me as well? The three places I was known to live at or frequent were attacked. Looking at the big picture, lots of other places had been attacked as well. But I still had a bad feeling that Desiree and the plague demon might have some sort of extradition agreement going on when it came to me.

I'd never planned on approaching the plague demon with any sort of partnership deal, and Desiree was low on my list of potential allies as well. The dragon seemed like a terrifying long shot. But the warmonger…

Or someone else. I remembered Juke fighting the demons outside Suerte. I needed allies, but maybe those allies didn't necessarily have to be demons.

I'd been underestimating the humans, even though I'd believed myself to be one up until recently. It was time to stop discounting the people who had the most to lose if New Hell fell into chaos.

Finishing off my beer, I put on jeans and a T-shirt and my leather jacket. Then I got on my bike and headed south.

CHAPTER 17

I knocked on the door of a modest house in Juneau, Alaska, somewhat surprised when the archangel Raphael answered the door. I knew he was there. Raphael didn't throw his power around like some angels did, but there was no mistaking his presence. What surprised me was that he answered the door, and that he was naked aside for neon-pink flannel pajama pants that were covered in images of frolicking otters.

We did the guy stare, assessing each other. He wasn't hostile, just…wary.

"You're Bishop," he said.

I wasn't a question. "Yeah. I'm here to see Ahia."

"I don't recognize you," he went on, ignoring my statement. "What choir are you in? What are you called in Aaru?"

"I don't go by that name anymore, and I'm not affiliated with any choir." I didn't want to antagonize two archangels in one year, but my history was none of his business.

"Bishop!" Ahia elbowed Raphael aside with a glare. "Stop swinging your dick and let him in."

The archangel stepped aside and Ahia dragged me in by

the arm, hauling me along with her to a kitchen with a small table against one wall.

"Sit," she commanded. "We just finished breakfast, but I'll get you a cup of coffee."

Raphael had followed us, but instead of sitting down while Ahia poured coffee into three mugs, he went over to the sink and started to load dishes into the washer. Ahia kissed him and put his cup on the counter, carrying the other two over and sitting across from me.

I took a sip, eyeing Raphael. The archangel was slowly and carefully rinsing off each piece of silverware individually. Obviously he wanted to linger and overhear our conversation. Not that it mattered to me. Of all the archangels, Raphael was probably the least likely to get his shorts in a knot over what I was planning.

"So, what's up?" Ahia said with a warm smile. "Do you need our help in LA after all?"

"I need your help, but not necessarily in LA." I leaned back in my chair, mug warming my hands. "What you said about humans and magic is true. That's their only chance to be able to stand up against the demons. We can't do this alone. There are too many demons, and we just can't fight them all without the humans having the ability to help."

She nodded. "Did you find a sorcerer willing to help? Will your mages band together?"

"A…friend is working on getting the mages to help," I told her, reluctant to let her or Raphael know about Eden's existence. Eden didn't need a hoard of curious angels popping into LA to gawk at her and speculate on her parentage. "What we really need is a large quantity of magical weaponry, anti-magic guns and ammo."

She grimaced. "You *can* buy that stuff, but it's gotten ridiculously expensive, and there's a waiting list. Even if you've got billions lying around, by the time you get the weapons, most of your humans will either have fled or been killed."

"I know. That's why I'm not going to buy it. I'm going to steal it."

Ahia laughed and nearly choked on her coffee. Raphael wasn't even pretending to wash dishes any more. He'd shut the sink off and was openly staring at me, an amused gleam in his eyes.

"The main supplier of magical weaponry is a company owned by the sorcerer Gareth. It's headquartered in Florida, and their company defensive and surveillance systems are magical," Raphael said. "I think it's pretty close to impossible to break in to the facility, let alone try to sneak anything out."

"I'm not stealing from the manufacturer. I'm stealing from their customers," I told him.

"But most police departments only have one, maybe two, anti-magic guns, and few have any of the other stuff," Ahia said. "You'd be hopping around to thousands of locations all over the country, picking up a piece here and another piece there. Within twenty-four hours, they'd have an alert out and every police department in the world will have their magic stuff hidden away behind illusion spells and wards. You'd be lucky if you managed to grab a few dozen before the gig was up."

"I'm not stealing from local police departments, I'm stealing from the U.S. military," I said.

Ahia's eyes widened. Raphael burst out laughing. "You're right. I *do* like this guy."

"Do you know where they store the magic stuff?" Ahia asked. "There are military depots all over the country. You'd need to find out where they keep everything, how it's guarded, and the best way to get it out of there."

"Which is why I need help." I looked from her to Raphael, then back again. "Ideally I'd like to teleport everything out.

Grab and go. But I don't have enough knowledge and don't want to go in blind. I need one or more partners to help me pull this off, and I don't have time to plan a detailed heist."

"This is crazy, you know," Raphael told me. "Which is why you can count me in."

"Me too." Ahia grinned. "Robbing the government sounds way more fun than going to that craft fair by the docks or hiking. The only problem is that I don't know anything about the military, and I doubt my one former-military friend could be convinced to help us with this caper, even if she did know where they'd store magical weaponry."

I'd been hoping Ahia would know someone with all the air force and army bases in Alaska, but it was a big state, and she'd spent most of her life with natives and shifters.

Glancing over at Raphael, I raised my eyebrows. "How about you?"

"I'm not exactly an expert on military logistics, security, or high-stakes burglary," the archangel said. "But I know a guy who's pretty good at theft. And if he's not an expert at the other stuff, I'm willing to bet he's got experts on speed dial."

"How much does this guy cost?" I mentally calculated the sum of my various checking and investment accounts.

"For a gig like this?" Raphael grinned. "At most a few nights of babysitting."

CHAPTER 18

EDEN

*S*outh LA didn't look much better than the rest of the city. I took the scenic route, avoiding the freeway that had been so torn up by the demons that it was down to one lane in sections. Weaving my way west, I rode past the airport and turned south once more, toward where the Disciples had their stronghold.

SoFi stadium looked unoccupied. I went by the old school that the gang had been using for distribution and it looked abandoned as well. Uncertain as to the gang's other haunts, I finally pulled over in the parking lot of an adult bookstore, and called Piers.

"What?"

I smiled at the curt greeting. "Demon problems, Piers?"

"I don't have time for chit-chat, Eden," he snapped. "And I can't help you with any bullshit you've got going on."

"I might be able to help you with *your* problem," I replied.

I counted five seconds of silence before he responded.

"What problem?"

I rolled my eyes. "Warmonger? Rolling into your neighborhoods and fucking shit up? Disrupting your supply and distribution businesses? Clearly picking a fight because they want you to meet them on their version of a battlefield?"

"And how are you supposed to help with that? Another troll? I still haven't washed off the stench from the last one."

"Meet with me and find out." That was greeted with another long silence, so I went on. "I'm looking to do a deal. A supply of anti-magic guns and ammo to help you fight off this asshole and in return, you help me deal with the asshole up in the Valley, and Desiree."

"How many guns? How many bullets?" he demanded.

Shit. I had no idea what quantities Bishop was going to return with and I wanted to hold enough back for the police and others in the Valley. I never thought for a second that the angel would return empty-handed, but a dozen guns would give me a whole lot less to bargain with than a thousand.

"Let's meet so we can talk face-to-face and discuss a deal," I countered, thinking I'd do a better job of selling this in person than over the phone.

"You got a sample on you? So I can see what we're trading for?" Piers asked.

"No. Right now I just want to talk possibilities." I was totally dancing around this.

"Can't do a drug deal without a sample of the goods, and the same goes for guns. I don't got time for possibilities, Eden. We're neck-deep in shit right now," he grumbled.

"Let's talk, and if we work out a handshake deal, I'll help you handle any immediate problem," I offered.

He snorted. "You're one hell of a fighter and you're gutsy, but I can't see how an extra pistol is going to make any difference here. Call me when you've got the guns in hand, and we'll talk. If we're all still alive, that is."

"Wait," I said before he hung up. "I *can* help. I'm not…I'm not human, Piers. And I'm proposing an alliance. My help for yours. I'll outfit your fighters. I'll help, if you help me."

"You a shifter or something?" he asked. "'Cause you'll need to be a Godzilla-shifter to take this guy out."

"I'm a Demon."

That was greeted with silence that oozed disbelief.

"How do you think I took those guys out in the customs warehouse?" I asked. "And escaped Desiree? How do you think I survived fighting in that gladiatorial ring? How do you think I managed to live with a huge tax debt and bounty hunters on my ass? There's only so much luck a gutsy human fighter can have, Piers. I'm a demon."

Piers barked out a laugh. "I knew there was a reason I shouldn't be trusting you. But I'm a desperate guy, and desperate guys do stupid shit. There's a liquor store near the corner of Rosecrans and Inglewood," he told me. "Tell the guy behind the counter that you're looking for a pint of Crown Royal for Emmanuel's wedding. He'll lead you to a back room. Wait there for me."

He disconnected the call. I stared at my phone, hoping that I could deliver what I intended to promise. Then I pulled my bike out of the lot and drove to Rosecrans and Inglewood.

* * *

I CIRCLED the block three times before I spotted the liquor store among the boarded-up shops and burned-out shells of concrete that constituted the other buildings. The liquor store had no signs or the usual alcoholic beverage posters. It was a heavy metal door next to a plywood-covered window. The only indication that this place sold liquor was the name "Boris's Booze written in small, black-Sharpie'd letters under the door handle.

Years ago I would have assumed this was a money laundering front that didn't really give a shit whether they sold any booze or not, but this was a different world we lived in. There was no need to launder money, and anyone who wanted liquor in this neighborhood probably knew where this place was without the need for any signage.

The Disciples pretty much owned the area south of LA, but they still needed stealthy places to meet where they'd be reasonably free from attack. A backroom of a liquor store might be an obvious meeting spot, but if no one could find the damned liquor store, they'd most likely be safe.

I parked my bike and went inside, stumbling my way through the password phrase. The ancient white guy behind the counter sighed and looked at me over his reading glasses.

"You're lucky I got a description, or I would have booted your butt right out that door."

I eyed him, because he looked like he was still undecided whether or not to let me in. Finally he dug a ring of keys out from under the register drawer and motioned for me to follow him. We went back into a storeroom, then into a room with a long folding table that had six wooden chairs on each side. There was one light—a naked bulb dangling from some wires above the table. The walls were a battered, smoke-stained white, and the vinyl flooring was chipped in places, revealing concrete underneath. I walked in, more than a little disturbed when the old guy closed and locked the door behind me.

There were no windows and no other doors, but I couldn't believe that the gang would hold meetings in a place without some sort of escape route, so instead of sitting at the table and playing games on my phone, I took the opportunity to search the room. The walls revealed nothing beyond some graffiti in light pencil and bullet holes in a nice grouping about two feet from the door. The floor, however, was not what it seemed. The filthy, brown filigree patterned vinyl definitely had some actual damage, but one section seemed to be carefully chipped and dinged to look the same age as the rest of the floor. I ran my fingers along the seams, found a raised section, and pressed down.

With a soft "snick" a two foot square section of the floor popped up. Hooking my fingers under the edge, I raised it and saw that the section was hinged underneath and opened up to a dark hole. A rope ladder was affixed to a floor support, leading downward. I pulled my phone out and turned on the flashlight app to shine down the hole. The drop looked to be about twelve feet, and I could see nothing except dirt on the ground below. My flashlight app didn't provide all that much light, but I couldn't see any footsteps or signs that the dirt had been disturbed, but there was a chance it could be packed hard and not the sort of ground that would show activity.

Turning off the app and pocketing my phone, I eased the floor section back in place. It closed with another "snick," looking pretty much the same as the rest of the floor unless someone examined it closely.

The rest of the room revealed one more hideaway in the floor, this one a compartment that held a series of loaded firearms. I checked a pistol, noting that one was in the chamber, ready to go. Clearly the Disciples had all their bases covered in this meeting room.

I popped the bullet out, then replaced everything, closing the compartment.

Finding nothing else, I sat at the table and tapped my foot, waiting. The door opened ten minutes later. I'd tensed at the sound of the handle turning, my hands sparking with electricity just in case this was some sort of setup. When the door opened, it revealed the old white guy. Behind him was Piers with a giant pistol aimed into the room.

"Nice fifty cal," I told him, impressed by the gun.

"Thanks. It was a birthday present from my mother." He

walked into the room and the old dude closed it behind him, locking it again.

I didn't raise an eyebrow, knowing that some people's parents had interesting ideas of appropriate gifts. Not that I'd mind one bit if Bea gave me a pistol for my birthday. Bags had once given me a box of ammo, but that was as close to weaponry-as-a-gift as I'd ever received.

Piers holstered the gun and sat down across from me. I was well aware that the pistol was loaded, ready, and within quick reach, and that Piers didn't really trust me in spite of our past dealings.

Or maybe *because* of our past dealings.

He'd once interviewed me for a job, thinking I was someone else. Piers had hooked me up with Desiree, enabling me to rescue my sister who had been kidnapped and was about to be sold into sexual slavery. He'd also asked me out. All that had ended when he'd connected me to the death and destruction that had happened at the customs warehouse where they'd been holding the trafficked kids.

And when I'd stolen his motorcycle helmet.

We'd come to a reluctant truce after I'd helped him get rid of the gladiatorial games that Desiree had organized at the SoFi stadium in their territory. Of course, that solution had required luring a very smelly troll into the stadium, so I wasn't sure how grateful Piers was.

"You said you were a demon?" Piers grumbled, still eyeing me with distrust. "Prove it."

I lifted a hand and sent a stream of electricity toward the outlet on the wall to my left. It sizzled, blew up in a shower of sparks, and smoked, the plastic melted and singed black.

"Nice parlor trick." Piers folded his arms across his chest and leaned back, looking bored.

Looking around, I spotted a stapler at the end of the table. With a wave of my hand, I sent it flying against the door.

"Come on. Really? Where are your wings? Horns? Forked tail?"

Fuck this shit. I reached down inside myself, searching for any bit of demon energy that I'd managed to retain from this morning's fight. Seizing the tiny scrap, I pushed it into the table. The metal top cracked, and a stem surged upward, branching out into four leaves and a yellow zinnia flower.

Piers blinked. "Okay. That's pretty damned freaky, but I'm not sure exactly how flowers are going to help us defeat a warmonger."

"I do more than create plants from nothing," I snapped, embarrassed at the whole botanical theme I seemed to have going on. "I can fight. You've seen me fight. You've seen the aftermaths of my battles. And not only can I fight, but I'm pretty indestructible when it comes to demon attacks. I absorb their energy and…redirect it." Sometimes killing the demon, sometimes landscaping a beautiful garden.

"So how exactly will this work? You supply us with an unspecified amount of anti-magic weaponry and ammo and we back each other up in fighting these guys?"

I nodded. "I arm you and your gang. You help me defeat the plague demon and his followers that have taken hold of the Valley. Then I'll help you and your gang get rid of the warmonger. Then we all go after Desiree."

Piers raised his eyebrows. "How about you arm us and help us get rid of the warmonger, then we help you with the plague demon. You're on your own with Desiree."

I scowled. "If I'm supplying you with weapons, then you need to be there for the war, not just a couple of battles."

Piers raised his hands. "We don't have any beef with Desiree. After that gladiatorial place shut down, we came to an agreement. The Disciples are not about to break that agreement for some woman who says she might have anti-magic guns and who can pull flowers out of thin air."

He kinda had a point. This would be a lot easier if I had a warehouse full of weapons right now to tempt him with instead of a bunch of promises.

"Let's table the Desiree thing," I said. "But the plague demon has to come first."

Piers stared at me for what felt like an hour. "A hundred anti-magic guns and five thousand bullets."

My palms sweated as I tried to guess what Bishop would be bringing back and what would be left for the police and others.

"Ten guns and a thousand rounds," I countered.

Piers made a "pffft" noise.

"Chicago and New York cops combined don't even have a hundred guns," I said, totally guessing. "Ten guns in the hands of your best shooters can disable dozens of demons while the rest of you kill them."

"But we're not talking dozens of demons," he pointed out. "We're talking thousands. And a fucking warmonger. Fifty guns and five thousand rounds."

"You won't be fighting alone though," I pointed out. "Some of my team will have anti-magic weaponry also. And we've got an angel and magic users. Twenty guns and two thousand rounds."

Piers's phone rang. He glanced down at it, then up at me as he answered. After a few grunts he disconnected the call and put the phone facedown on the table.

"Twenty guns. Two thousand rounds. The Disciples will help with your plague demon and you help with our warmonger. But you come with me right now and show me you're bringing more to the fight than a couple of guns and some cheap magic tricks. We've got a situation. It's the perfect opportunity to prove your value."

I glanced at his phone, feeling uneasy about this whole thing. "What's happened?"

"That asshole grabbed four of our shipments. He says if we want them back, we need to show up and get them." Piers stood. "It's not our first go-round with him. We show up. We fight. And we either retreat because we're getting our asses whooped, or we win and get our shit back. You in?"

I could say "no" and I was sure Piers would still be willing to cut a deal. He wanted the anti-magic weaponry more than my assistance. But this would be the perfect chance to cement our alliance as more than just a guns-for-manpower swap.

Of course, everything would fall apart if I ended up getting killed in this fight. I'd managed to stay alive so far, so I stood and nodded.

"You've got a deal. I'm in."

I followed Piers on my bike, because I had no fucking idea where the Rolling Hills Country Club was. Beyond that, I was a little confused why this was all going down at a country club at all. I'd assumed we would show up at an abandoned warehouse or used car lot, and exchange gunfire. What were we supposed to do at a country club? Discuss the stolen trucks over some martinis and nine holes of golf?

As we pulled up to the entrance, I realized that I knew this particular country club, but certainly not from any personal experience. I didn't golf. I didn't live on the neighboring luxurious estate. But I had watched a lot of movies growing up, and this course was the one used when filming the movie *Caddy Shack*.

Piers parked in the lot in front of a sprawling clubhouse. The lot was more than half full, so I assumed either members were still making their tee times or the Disciples were taking this truck-jacking seriously. I parked my bike in a space behind Piers's truck. He led me up the walkway and into the clubhouse.

"This place looks great," I marveled at the lack of graffiti or damage. "I expect Ted Knight and Rodney Dangerfield to come walking by any moment."

"Lots of rich folks were living in the estates up until last week," Piers said. "The Boss likes golf and was friends with some of the members, so we've always provided protection."

I glanced around. "Is there some kind of parley here in the bar? I'm assuming you're not actually fighting here." I imagined a battle at the ninth hole and almost laughed.

Piers turned down a hallway. "There's more of a shouted exchange than any parley, and I assume it's outside. Calvin said to meet him at the driving range. It's quicker to cut through the clubhouse, and less chance for us to get tagged by a stray bullet."

I frowned, still following Piers. According to Alfie's book, this warmonger was a fan of old-school fighting. If so, then a driving range was probably just as suitable an open space for a fight as a parking lot.

"How do these battles go? You said there's some shouting? Then does everyone start shooting?" I had no idea what to expect here.

He snorted. "Fuck if I know. Last ones we tried to distract them with gunfire while a few of our guys tried to sneak in and grab the trucks. Didn't go so well."

Piers opened a pair of heavy double doors and we walked outside.

Pausing to let my eyes adjust to the bright sunlight, I saw that we were looking out over the driving range. There was a small outdoor bar to our right, and a line of golf carts to my left. In front of me stood a line of natural grass sectioned off by lines of sprayed white chalk. The first five tees were under roof, while the rest were open. I glanced down the expanse of green, wondering who the hell could possibly hit a ball that far. The driving range had to be over four hundred feet long, and at least a hundred feet wide. It was huge.

And at the end of that huge expanse were three tractor-trailers.

"What the fuck?" I muttered. How did the demons get these huge things out in the middle of the grassy expanse? And why?

A bald, white guy covered in tattoos jogged up to Piers and they stepped aside whispering together while I gawked at the whole scene.

The trucks didn't look like they were in bad shape, and the driving range wasn't dug up with muddy tire tracks, so I was guessing either the warmonger or one of his household had teleported them to their current location. Demons milled around near the trucks, all in weird animal mash-up forms. None of those dudes seemed like they were in charge, so I assumed these were the foot soldiers while the higher-level demons held back.

"Does the warmonger show up to these things, or does he just leave it to his household?" I asked, interrupting Piers's conversation.

"He likes to watch," Piers told me. "If one of our fighters doesn't die and we can't get to him in time, he gets taken to the warmonger. We never see those people again."

The guy next to him shuddered. "If we see it happening, we try to shoot and kill our brother. Dying is a better option than whatever they'll get with that asshole."

"I'm guessing you haven't won any of these battles yet?"

Piers shifted his weight and looked at the trucks at the end of the driving range. "No. We've lost two hundred and sixteen men, and haven't yet been able to recover any of the stolen trucks."

"What's in them?" I wondered what could be worth losing that many men. If it had been me, I would have just chalked it all up as an acceptable loss and let the asshole keep his trucks.

"Fruit." Piers frowned as I cut short a laugh. "California supplies the majority of fruit and other produce to the U.S. and we make a huge percentage of our revenue ensuring those shipments get through unmolested. It's not just about the products, it's about our reputation."

Now *that* I understood. A damaged reputation would cost the Disciples both business and members. The most powerful gang in LA was on the edge of obsolescence. No wonder Piers wanted me at this fight. The anti-magic guns were valuable, but winning this fight was more important to their survival.

Piers and the other guy walked out to the sheltered part of the driving range where there were thirty humans, all heavily armed, and all looking across at the demons like this might be their last day among the living. Piers strode forward, down in front of the awnings, but still close enough to duck behind our line.

"Leave, and let us have the trucks you stole, and we will not retaliate," Piers yelled.

The demons laughed and began chanting "come and get it."

"Final chance to take our offer," Piers shouted.

This time the demons didn't reply. Instead they raced toward us across the gentle slopes of the driving range. Piers jumped back, pulling out his pistol. The Disciples opened fire, those with rifles shooting first, then as the demons got closer, those with pistols joined in.

Behind the lines I saw a giant demon on horseback. He was wearing mismatched pieces of armor on a body that looked like it had been dipped in lava and cooled. Red coal eyes glowed from a helm, and fire sparked at the joints of his body. The horse looked more like a skeleton than a living animal. It also had red glowing eyes and orange flames at the joints just like its rider. Lava Boy and Lava Horse moved across the back of the demon line, watching.

I let loose a few rounds, quickly realized that the bullets were doing no damage at all, and holstered my guns. A few bursts of lightning did nothing except scorch some of the grass and give everyone beside me a case of static electricity. The demons were quickly gaining ground, and in spite of my confidence earlier, I had nothing. Nobody was throwing energy attacks for me to absorb and redirect. Bullets and electricity weren't doing shit. All I had left was my fists and my wits.

Piers shouted something I couldn't make out and the gunfire stopped. A dozen men ran between the shooters, tearing across the grass toward the demons. My eyes widened, anticipating a slaughter of epic proportions. As the humans hit the advancing demon line, I winced, briefly shutting my eyes. When I opened them, I was amazed to see the humans holding their own. Yes, the demons were ripping off arms and punching through abdominal walls, but the humans were undeterred. With howls of rage, they continued to fight, biting and stabbing with a severity that surprised me. A few demons broke past the line, and I jumped forward, grabbing a nearby golf club.

My first swing bent the club but hit hard enough to knock the demon onto the ground. I grabbed one of my pistols and shot him in the head, then holstered the gun and proceeded to whale away at his skull with the bent club until it was a smear of red and white on the green grass. Another demon plowed into me, throwing me backward. He was on me before I could get a good swing in, so I abandoned the club and grappled with him, more than a little concerned about how long it would take me to heal from evisceration, or even if I could manage to regrow a torn-off limb. Thankfully the demon didn't cause any more than minimal damage before one of the humans grabbed his head, wrenched it off his neck, and pitched it halfway across the driving range.

That's when I realized there was something not exactly normal about these Disciple hand-to-hand combatants. They were stronger than they should be. They had an insane level of pain resistance and endurance. And their eyes glowed with a psychotic gleam.

Holy fuck. The Disciples had managed to score some of the Aries drug and were fueling their fighters with it. I wasn't particularly upset about the hypocrisy of a group who'd sworn opposition to the drug and were now utilizing it. Desperate times called for desperate measures, and I was sure that these fighters had willingly risked the addiction and maiming for the chance to prove their valor and loyalty.

I scrambled to my feet, continuing to fight with my increasingly bent golf club and pistols. Slowly we were being driven back toward the canopied section of the driving range, the demons proving very hard to kill. Still none of them used any energy attacks that would allow me to seize the advantage, and I began to feel...not exactly useless, but definitely not the asset I'd expected to be in this fight.

Jumping back to the white-lined sections of the range, I ditched my horribly damaged club, grabbed another, and nearly faceplanted tripping on a bucket of golf balls. Pissed off, I whacked one into the range as I regained my balance.

The ball flew with a sonic boom, plowing through two demons and vanishing off the edge of the range. I sucked in a breath, staring for a few seconds as I wondered where the hell this particular skill had come from. Then I started hitting balls.

The Disciples beside me were continuing to shoot with rifles, trying to take out the demon fighters without getting too close to the trucks with their valuable produce. Those with pistols were beginning to back up, taking their time firing as they tried not to hit their Aries-fueled fighters in the fray. I just kept hitting the golf balls. I'd never played this game, and I wasn't particularly known for my aim when it had come to those pickup sports I'd played with the neighborhood kids in the alleyways, so a lot of my balls whistled past demons, probably taking down trees a mile away.

There were a whole lot of balls in this bucket, but with only one out of ten shots hitting, I wasn't exactly winning this battle. I needed to have better aim, and not just launch projectiles all over the country club. Taking a wide stance and wiggling my hips like I'd seen golfers do on TV, I actually aimed this time and took the shot. The ball flew like a bullet, missing my intended target but hitting the demon beside him. The guy's head exploded, and the ball kept going, killing one more demon before losing lethal speed. The third demon didn't die, but the ball distracted him enough for a human to kill him.

"Four," I yelled, although I think I was probably supposed to shout that before I hit the ball. Not that anyone on the driving range could hear me with all the shouting and shooting going on.

I kept swinging with results that varied widely. Sometimes I missed. Sometimes I knocked off arms or legs or blew through torsos. Sometimes I accidently took out a human. Clearly this was a sport that required a lot of practice, but I had a good eye and a bucket of balls. That should be enough to at least make a serious dent in the warmonger's forces.

My shoulders and arms were killing me about fifty shots in. Was there something wrong with my stance? I wished there was a golf pro handy to give me a quick critique, because my somewhat shitty aim was getting worse with every ball I hit.

With a dozen balls left I suddenly saw him. That fucking warmonger on his fucking horse. With a muttered curse, I took aim and hit another ball his way. It screamed through the air missing the warmonger and nailing Lava Horse in the butt instead. The animal screamed and reared, Lava Boy flying of the back and sprawling on the ground. The skeletal horse took off once it had four feet on the ground, vanishing into the recesses of the golf course.

Oh God. I'd hit a horse. I felt horrible, even if the thing had been an undead demon horse. Hopefully its injuries were minor and its infernal master could fix the wound because it would haunt me for the rest of my days if I'd seriously hurt or killed a horse.

A strange thing had happened when the warmonger hit the ground, and in my concern for the horse, I was only just now realizing it. All the demons on the field had paused, turned to look at their master, then shifted their gaze toward me. The Disciples took advantage of their distraction, taking out a few more of the demons. Then as the warmonger got to his feet, staggering a little, his army once more advanced.

This time they shifted their forward progress, heading for me.

I frantically hit a few more golf balls with lousy aim, then realized to win this battle, I'd need to focus less on the lion-chicken-elephant-hawk weirdos heading my way, and on the warmonger himself.

Taking careful aim once more, I fired another ball at Lava Boy. It missed, but knocked the head off a demon beside him. The dead demon fell to the ground, and the warmonger looked straight at me, snarling.

I swung again, and this time I my aim was true. The ball was a streak of light, breaking the sound barrier as it flew toward the warmonger's head. Just before it hit, he lifted his hand and caught the ball.

Thunder rolled through the air and I stared, shocked that the ball hadn't gone through his hand.

Lava Boy's red eyes locked onto me. I froze, wondering if I should run, or duck or hit another ball his way when he opened his mouth and breathed out a wave of fire.

The fire came fast—almost as fast as my golf ball had headed toward him. It tore through his own army, incinerating them and the Aries-fueled humans fighting them. I heard screaming, and vaguely registered that the Disciples beside me were fleeing the area. Rooted to the ground, time slowed as the fire roared my way.

With a last-minute surge of self-preservation, I hit the ground, covering my head with hands, but like the dragon's fire, the warmonger's was volcano-hot. The heat scorched me, stealing my breath. When I felt the temperature lower slightly, I took a tentative inhale and looked up. The grass around me was black and dead. The clubs were melted into blobs of metal and the remaining golf balls were charcoal. The overhang had completely burned off, leaving the skeleton structure of softened metal supports behind. I got to my knees and saw the only green spot was the area I'd shielded with my body.

As I felt my back and rear, fabric fell away in ashes leaving me to touch my bare skin—skin that thankfully was unharmed. Struggling to my feet, I saw the blackened husks of bodies on the field. In the distance there was no warmonger, no horse, no other demons. The tractor trailers still stood at the end of the range, untouched.

I ran my hands over my hair, relieved that it hadn't been burnt off. Naked I could deal with. Bald was not a look I really wanted to be sporting.

There were some noises behind me so I turned, not wanting to be flashing my bare ass, even though I'd just fought demons naked in my neighborhood this morning.

Piers came forward, his dark hair singed, and his eyebrows half missing. The Disciples following him had various stages of burns from blisters to a mild sunburn. I glanced behind myself, just to make sure that no demons were alive and still ready to attack. When I saw nothing but carnage on the driving range, I turned back to face Piers.

"Uh. Thanks. I guess. I'm not sure whether to call this a win or not," he said.

"You got your trucks back, so it's a win," I told him.

"Yeah, but we lost around thirty," the guy beside him spoke up.

Time to push the advantage. I had a deal I needed to close with Piers, and the costs of this battle were something I could worry about later. "True, but you won. This is the first win against this asshole, and you've proved to him, the other Disciples, and your clients, that you're not going to be squashed by some fucking demon."

The atmosphere lightened considerably at that.

"Get your trucks to the border," I told Piers. "Bury and mourn your dead. And know that this guy will think twice before taking your shipments again."

That was total bravado, but a girl had to do what a girl had to do.

"The Disciples appreciate your assistance," Piers said with a hand to his chest. Then he gestured toward the clubhouse. I hesitated a second, then walked on, well aware that my total backside was visible.

No one said a word. Piers and I walked through the hallways, out the front door, and to my bike. I climbed on, the seat feeling weird on my bare ass.

"We have a deal," Piers said. "Twenty anti-magic guns. Two thousand rounds of ammo. The Disciples help you kill the plague demon and his forces in the Valley, and you and your fighters help us get rid of the warmonger. I'm not thrilled with the body count today, but a win is a win and a deal is a deal. You have my word on this."

I started my bike and picked up my helmet. "I'll text you," I told him before I put on the helmet and drove out of the country club parking lot.

And hopefully Bishop would return with enough weapons and bullets to at least cover the deal I'd just made.

CHAPTER 20

EDEN

*I*t was past seven in the evening by the time I roared into my driveway. Shifters have insanely good night vision, so I was sure all my neighbors got a view of my bare back and ass as my burned clothing flapped around the front of my body.

Inside I grabbed a flashlight and took a quick cold shower, dressing in the dark. Then I packed a duffle bag because there was no way I was sleeping here tonight when my family might face another attack by the plague demon. Upstairs I downed a glass of water, then texted Sebastian, an ex-boyfriend who had been a long-time member of the Gray Dogs gang since we were in high school.

Mittens was nowhere to be found, so I put out some luncheon meat, refiled a water bowl, and got back on the road. There was one more stop I wanted to make before I went to Bea's, so I took the 101 and headed to yet another country club.

This meeting should go a lot easier than the one with the Disciples. Sebastian and I had history, and although our relationship hadn't ended amicably, we'd recently put that behind us. Plus he owed me for getting his younger brother out of a fix down in Disciples territory, and I was totally going to leverage that favor.

There was also the fact that he still had a thing for me, and although I had no intention of cheating on Bishop, I wasn't averse to a little flirting if that would help.

Even though it was too late for golf there a dozen vehicles at the country club, and the lights were on in the clubhouse. A big dude I didn't recognize stood at the doorway, a pistol at each hip and a bandolier of knives across his chest. He scowled as I walked up.

"Eden to see Sebastian," I told him. "He's expecting me."

A walkie-talkie miraculously appeared in his hand. He spoke into it and the only words I recognized were "Eden" and "Sebastian."

I waited, forcing myself not to do a stare-down with this guy. The Gray Dogs didn't really like me. They saw me as someone who could take Sebastian, wrap him around my finger, and force my way into an organization whose exclusively male members normally regarded women as an appendage. They respected women at a level that depended on which guy they were dating, but someone like me would be a threat. Sebastian's current girlfriend, while temperamental, understood the game and played it.

I, on the other hand, would not play their game. And they knew it.

The walkie-talkie squawked, and bouncer-guy motioned toward the door. "Go in. Third room on the left."

The clubhouse was silent except for the faint hum of conversation from some distant room. I counted doorways and walked into a small bar. The golden lights were dimmed. The dark wood furniture gleamed. Sebastian sat at the bar, a tumbler of booze in one hand. His black hair shown, the light highlighting his sharp cheekbones and the golden tone of his skin. He sipped his drink, those dark brown eyes fixed on me as I approached.

"Eden." His voice was smooth as velvet. "I was happy to receive your text. What can I do for you?"

Not what you're thinking buddy.

I sat down beside him, my knee brushing his thigh totally by accident. I swear.

"I'd like to discuss business," I told him.

His posture shifted slightly. As much of a horndog as Sebastian was, he was first and foremost a businessman. The Gray Dogs were his life, and while he'd made no secret of wanting me back by his side, he'd always be wedded to his work.

"Drink?" He held up the glass. Knowing him as I did, I was sure it held some expensive whisky.

"I'll have what you're having."

He got up, making sure his leg brushed against mine. Behind the bar, Sebastian poured the amber liquid into a rocks glass, and somehow the whole thing was laced with sexual tension. Instead of sliding the drink over to me, he came back around the bar, sat down and held it out. Yes, our fingers touched as I took the glass from him. Yes there were sparks. But those sparks had more to do with our turbulent history than any current desire on my part.

He watched as I took a sip.

This seductive shit was getting a little old, but I didn't want to slap him down and ruin any chance I had at a collaboration. Not for the first time today, I wished Bishop was back.

"A plague demon with an army of two thousand has decided the Valley is his territory. I intend to kill him." I said, hoping to break the porn-vibe going on here.

It worked.

Sebastian sat up straight. "You're a psychotic badass Eden,

but this isn't a fight you want. Get your family safe and stay away from this guy."

I shrugged. "Too late. Some of his goons attacked our neighborhood early this morning. I took out the plague demon and one other guy. The third took off. So I've got an interest in sending this guy to his eternal resting place."

Sebastian's eyes widened. "You killed a plague demon? How the fuck did you kill a plague demon?"

Too late I remembered that Sebastian thought I was human, even though his younger brother had claimed I was actually a demon. Sebastian had thought his ramblings were the effect of detoxing from Aries, and hadn't taken him seriously. I wasn't sure if I wanted him to know the truth. Sebastian was part of my past, and I hated to ruin those memories with the confession that I wasn't the human he'd believed me to be.

"I used some magic," I lied.

His eyes narrowed. "I don't always know when you're feeding me a line of shit, Eden, but this time I know. Was it that boyfriend of yours?"

If it had been Bishop, all three demons would have been a pile of sand within seconds of attacking us. I hesitated, not sure whether to admit to my abilities, or let Bishop take the credit.

"It doesn't matter," I finally said. "But no one attacks my family. And I'm not going to wait for them to destroy the Valley. I'm bringing this fight to them."

Sebastian blew out a breath and sat back in his chair. "This guy hasn't targeted us, Babe. I'm reluctant to put the Gray Dogs on his radar, even to help you."

"I'm expecting a delivery of anti-magic guns and ammo," I told him. "I'm willing to arm anyone who helps me defeat this plague demon, the warmonger who's taken control of south LA, and Desiree, who is claiming the west of the city as her territory."

"I'm interested in any deal involving the weapons, but I'm not going to commit to what amounts to three wars," Sebastian cautioned. "How many guns and how much ammo are you offering? I'll be fair with you, Eden, but I'm not going to send my brothers to their deaths for a couple of pistols and a handful of bullets."

"I don't know exactly the quantity I'm getting." I was reluctant to commit myself to a certain amount when I'd already promised Piers two hundred weapons and bullets. "Can you let me know what you'd expect? My priority is the plague demon, but once he's gone it will be only a matter of time until one of the other two tries to take the Valley."

Sebastian winced. "Tell you what. Let me know what you've got to offer when the stock comes in, and I'll tell you what I'm willing to commit the Gray Dogs to."

Fair enough. I stood and downed my whiskey. "Thanks, Sebastian. I appreciate it."

I did. I appreciated his honesty and the lack of bullshit in dealing with him. We would never have sex again, but I wanted to count him as one of my friends—a close friend."

"Eden."

I turned to look at him.

"Even if I can't commit the Gray Dogs to a fight, I'll be there for you. You tell me when and where, and I'll be there."

My heart warmed at that. It wasn't just a ploy to get me into bed. He meant it.

"And if you ever need me, Sebastian, I'll be there for you too," I vowed.

He smiled, saluting me with his whisky glass. "You always have, Eden. You always have."

* * *

THE WARDS BIT as my skin as I drove through them, causing me to gasp. I wasn't sure what Genevieve had done to them, but she had clearly leveled up the protections here.

Pulling into the driveway, I parked my bike beside Bea's faded tomato-red car, and unstrapped my duffle bag from the back. The houses on the street were dark aside from a faint flickering glow, letting me know that the electricity was still out. Shouldering my bag, I went to the front door and knocked. The curtain twitched, and I gave the passwords. Seconds later, the door opened and I saw Sadie beaming up at me.

"Peanut." I folded her into a hug, my bag falling off my shoulder and banging against the door jamb.

"Bea is in the backyard. Nevarra is over at Javier's. We finished dinner hours ago, but there are leftovers I can warm up on the cook stove."

I hated for her to go to the trouble. "I'm fine," I said, even though I *was* hungry.

Sadie pulled away from me, her gaze running over my body from head to feet. "At least have some cheese and ham," she said. "I don't think you're always eating right, Eden."

I laughed at how much like Bea the girl sounded. "Fine. Come join me in the kitchen. I've got a present for you."

She squealed and hopped, clapping her hands. I locked the door behind me and followed her into the kitchen, waiting until she'd fixed the plate of cheese and ham chunks before putting the giant book on the table.

"It's about dragons," I told her as I pushed it over. "The only catch is you need to tell me all about it. I don't have time to read a book this size, but I think I should know as much as possible about dragons."

Her eyes gleamed as she snatched the book from me and clasped it to her chest. "Dragons! I love it! Thank you, Eden."

Bea walked in from outside. "A book? That's really sweet of you, Eden. Sadie loves books."

"It's about dragons," the girl announced. "Can I go upstairs and read it? Eden's spending the night. She can stay in my bed if she wants. I'll sleep on the floor."

"The living room couch is fine with me," I told her, giving her a quick kiss on the head as she slid off her chair. "Go read your book. I'll see you in the morning."

Sadie ran off and Bea took her seat. "You do know she'll be up all night with that thing. She's been obsessed with dragons ever since you told her there was one downtown."

"I'll totally cheat off her notes," I told Bea. "The Disciples are on board to help us take down this plague demon, and we'll probably be able to count on the Gray Dogs as well."

Bea scowled. "What did you have to promise to get those two gangs on board?"

"Anti-magic weapons." I ate a piece of cheese. "Bishop is off trying to score a bunch of them. How much help I get will depend on what he brings back."

"Make sure you keep some for the police," Bea said. "I don't trust these gangs to do the right thing once we get the demon situation under control. It won't be fair if you supply them with weaponry, only to have them shake us down for protection later."

"They won't," I growled.

Bea rolled her eyes. "You are twenty-three-year-old woman. Grateful as I am for your assistance, I am not going to have you spend your life hovering over us like a mother hen. I dealt with gangs before you came into my house, and I'm capable of handling them when you're off living your own life, Eden."

"Sorry," I muttered. "But I do want to spend the night tonight, just in case. And tomorrow I'm going to arrange for some help here in the neighborhood."

"I appreciate that." Bea smiled warmly. "And you are always welcome to spend the night. We've got fresh eggs for breakfast, and I traded sewing for avocados and tomatoes."

It sounded wonderful—so much better than spending the night in my house alone. Funny how I savored my independence when I'd first scored the house in Los Feliz, yet now I realized how much I missed having my family around.

I finished my cheese and ham, then shooed Bea away and cleaned up the dishes myself. When Nevarra came home, we went upstairs and bribed Sadie away from the dragon book with the promise of a game. After three rounds of Uno, we turned off the flashlights and settled in to bed.

I curled up on the couch under my favorite afghan and slept better than I had in days.

CHAPTER 21

BISHOP

Raphael, Ahia, and I were standing in front of a fancy marble-and-glass high-rise building. The wind roared down the streets, hurtling trash and lost hats by us. Shoppers bustled along the sidewalks, hunkered down against the wind, clutching their bags and briefcases tightly. They ignored us, even though Ahia was the only one dressed appropriately for the Chicago weather. At least Raphael had changed out of the pajama pants and put on a shirt, otherwise we probably would be attracting a lot of attention.

"We're meeting this guy at his apartment?" I asked. It was after business hours, but I'd assumed he'd have us go to his office, or a trusted restaurant.

"Yeah. It's the nanny's day off, and his wife had plans for the evening. He couldn't get a sitter, so he said to meet him here."

None of that inspired confidence in me about this guy's ability to help us pull off a major robbery. What happened if the dude couldn't get a sitter when this was going down? Would he call it off, or drag his kids along with us?

Raphael's phone buzzed. He looked down at the text, then walked up to the doorman. "Penthouse. He's expecting us."

The man's eyes glowed yellow as he stared at Raphael, then he nodded and opened the door, ushering us in.

Rat shifter. There weren't many of them in LA and few ever came to me for assistance. The ones I'd met over the last ten thousand years had been intelligent with a strong sense of self preservation. They were also ruthless in a fight, although they tended to avoid fighting as much as they could. They were also very social. Where there was one there would be at least ten others nearby. As we rode the elevator, I wondered if this guy of Raphael's was a rat shifter. It made sense.

The elevator stopped, and the doors opened into the penthouse apartment. Whoever this guy was, he or his wife had a good eye for interior design. Vintage Persian rugs covered the floors in red and gold. All of the furniture was inlaid mahogany in light, clean Sheridan-style lines. The couches were in a similar style with high backs and rounded edges. The paintings on the walls were an ode to American Fauvism. Andrew Dasburg. Alma Brockerman Wright. Bob Thompson. It was a little eclectic, but everything complimented the other seamlessly.

A demon walked around the corner of the living room. His human form was of medium height with a slightly heavy build. His black hair was silver at the temples, and his dark eyes were shrewd with a glint of humor. He wore an expensive suit, and strapped across his chest was a baby in a sling carrier—an angel baby.

An Angel of Chaos baby.

"Daddy, Daddy! I want to be at the meeting with you!" A young girl ran up to his side, this one an Angel of Order. While the baby resembled his father in appearance, this child was all golden-brown skin, hair, and eyes.

"This meeting is for grownups, Karrae," the demon told the girl. "Go organize the spice cabinet, or sort the Legos by color and size."

"But Maitor gets to stay." She pouted. "That's not fair. Why does Maitor get to stay?"

"Because Maitor will set the building on fire if he's not supervised." The demon leaned down and kissed the girl on the top of the head. "Go. And I promise later we'll have ice cream."

I wasn't an idiot. Whoever this demon was, he was mated to an angel, and the pair of them had gotten busy creating offspring. And the demon was no slouch. He might come across as the middle-management businessman who also was an indulgent father, but I saw the intelligence in his eyes, and I noticed the intensity of his energy, revealed then quickly hidden. Not conventionally powerful, but the sort of sneaky, steady, strong power that splintered giant oaks and cracked boulders.

The girl danced off, clearly excited at the idea of ice cream and the demon turned to me.

"I'm Dar." He held out his hand.

"Bishop." I reached out to shake his hand, watching him assess me as much as I was him.

"Raphael says you've got a job that might interest me?" His dark eyes gleamed.

"I want to rob the U.S. Military of their magical weaponry and take it to New Hell so I can arm the humans to fight back against the demons." Might as well get right to the point here. Demons weren't known for their loyalty outside of their households, so I wasn't worried that he'd take a moral objection to humans fighting against others of his own kind. But if he wasn't willing to join in, or had reservations about the project, I didn't want to waste any of our time here.

The baby squealed, kicking his legs and raising his arms at my statement.

"That sounds like a fuckload of fun to me," Dar said, clearly agreeing with his son. The demon rubbed his hands together. "As long as I'm in on the action, I'm game. Just don't tell my wife. Or my daughter. Oh, and Raphael and Ahia will owe us ten days of babysitting."

"Two," Raphael countered.

Ahia elbowed him. "Ten days is fine. We're always happy to watch Karrae and Maitor."

Raphael grimaced at that, but didn't argue. "You're welcome to join in, Dar," he said. "But primarily we need intel. Where are the weapons held? What sort of security do they have? When and how should we pull this thing off?"

"*When* needs to be in a week at most," I told the demon. "Ideally this needs to go down in the next few days."

"That can happen," Dar said. "Why don't we plan to do it late tomorrow or the following day. Come over here to the dining room table and we'll plot this thing out."

We all sat down while Dar got us a round of drinks. Once everyone had a bottle of beer, including the baby, he got down to business.

"I've been immersing myself into human politics for the last few years," he said. "Not only am I now the Mayor of Chicago, but I'm on a first name basis with most of the cabinet, and foreign heads of state."

Raphael rolled his eyes. "We don't have time to discuss your resume. Let's get right to the job and skip the bullshit."

Dar glared, then took a swig of his beer. The baby mirrored him, drinking from his own, nipple-topped beer bottle.

"Fine," the demon said. "The military stores their magical weaponry in three locations: Letterkenny Army Depot in Pennsylvania, Hawthorne Army Depot in Nevada, and

McAlester Army Ammunition Plant in Oklahoma. McAlester has mostly anti-magic guns and ammo. Letterkenny has defensive stuff to set up warded perimeters, block teleportation, shield aircraft from magical attacks. Hawthorne has the scary shit that's highly classified."

"Which is?" Ahia asked.

Dar shrugged. "Fuck if I know. None of the people whispering in my ears has that level of clearance, so I'm assuming whatever is there, it's probably the equivalent of a magical nuclear bomb."

"Let's focus on Letterkenny and McAlester then," I said. "I'm not interested in blowing California off the side of the continent, or transforming everyone into zombies."

I was mildly uncomfortable about whatever might be at Hawthorne, but that wasn't my problem to solve. Let the Ruling Council of Angels or the human organizations deal with magical weapons of mass destruction.

"Then let's talk McAlester first," Dar said, pulling a pad of paper over and drawing a crude map. "Their mission used to be basic logistics and distribution for all branches of the military with a huge percentage of civilians working on base. Last year they added a new warehouse as well as some military supply chain and contract personnel with higher clearance levels. This is where the new building is, and judging from the security, I'm guessing that's where the anti-magic guns and ammo are kept."

"Can we teleport in? And more importantly, can we teleport out with the stock?" Raphael asked. "What sort of wards will they have around and in the building?"

"I'll need to double-check with one of my contacts, but last I heard they were more concerned about human theft than anything else. We might be facing only electronic alarm systems and a couple of guards with rifles."

Ahia grinned. "If so, then we can be in and out without anyone knowing."

"I think we need to do a little reconnaissance beforehand," Dar warned. "I've got a presidential pardon in my back pocket, but I don't want to have to use it on something like this."

"How about Letterkenney?" I asked. Anti-magic guns and ammo were the priority, but defensive magic would really be useful. If we could set a large perimeter of powerful wards around a city, then we'd need less manpower to defend our sanctuary areas.

"That one's going to be more of a challenge. It's a huge site specializing in air and missile defense including high-altitude and space weaponry. All the high-tech stuff goes through there, so their security is tight."

"I'm guessing that means wards to keep us from teleporting in," Raphael said.

"I'll make a few calls, but I'm thinking the best way to pull this one off would be to go in as humans with security clearance. Inspectors or auditors or something. Maybe even have a senator show up on the same day for a visit. I'd also want a mage to supply us with some detection amulets to know if there's tracking on any of the crates, or self-detonation, or anything like that."

Ahia winced. "Self-detonation? Maybe we should wait on Letterkenny. Hit McAlester tomorrow, then gather more information, and formulate a solid plan to rob Letterkenny in a few weeks or even a month."

"If we don't do it right after McAlester, our window closes," Dar warned. "Once they realize we've stolen their shit, they'll lock down the other depots so tight a mouse won't be able to get in. If we're going to do Letterkenny, we're better off going in semi-blind than waiting."

"Unless everything explodes while we're teleporting it,"

Raphael said. "Magic doesn't do well when it blows up. If I know it's coming, I might be able to open an interdimensional gate midway through our teleportation and shove it all through, but there's no guarantee I'll get it in and the gate closed before it goes off."

That was impressive. Teleportation took a fraction of a second. For Raphael to even be able to open an interdimensional gate mid-teleport was unbelievable. I glanced over at him and sensed he wasn't lying or exaggerating his abilities. Raphael had always been looked upon as the weakest of the archangels, but clearly the guy had skills beyond those of his siblings.

"Let's focus our attentions on McAlester," I said. "We can plan for Letterkenny, but if we get there and the job holds too much risk, we'll bail."

Dar stood. "Then let's get started. I'll order a food delivery and put on a pot of coffee. We'll work through the night, and pull this all off tomorrow."

The baby strapped to his chest waved his hands, his eyes glowing green. I could swear I heard him say something that sounded a lot like "Fuck yeah."

CHAPTER 22

EDEN

The next morning I woke after a long and restful sleep on Bea's couch. The aroma of coffee wafted in from the kitchen. I heard the murmur of soft voices and realized everyone but me was already up.

"Good thing we didn't get attacked last night. I would have probably slept right through it," I said as I joined them.

"That's good. You needed the rest," Bea said, putting a plate of eggs and sliced tomatoes and avocado at the empty spot on the table. "Water's on, but still no electricity. Sit and eat. Then afterward, you can take a shower if you don't mind cold water."

"We've got another box for Jayla," Nevarra told me. "I don't think it will fit on your bike though. Maybe you can borrow Bea's car to deliver it?"

I shoveled in a bite of eggs and avocado, marveling at how food always tasted better when Bea made it. "I'll be back later this afternoon, so I'll take it then."

"Are you spending the night again?" Sadie asked.

"Probably not tonight." I smiled at her. "I'm hoping to

bring a friend by to help keep everyone in the neighborhood safe. Do you remember Addy?"

I'd never brought her by, but I'd told the girls about the mage. And I'd told Bea about what I'd done. I was still upset about the whole minion thing, but Bea had made me feel better about it all, echoing Bishop that I hadn't intended to do anything other than save the woman's life, and although I regretted the side effects of that action, I shouldn't beat myself up over something that was done and out of my control.

I ate and chatted with Bea and the girls. Nevarra and Sadie warmed up water and washed the dishes, making a second pot of coffee and refilling all of the water jugs in anticipation of another outage.

Then Bea settled in at her pedal-powered sewing machine, Sadie went upstairs to read the dragon book, and Nevarra went out back to take care of the chickens. I took a cold shower, and put on my clothes.

After sending a few texts, I said goodbye to Bea and the girls. Then I hopped on my bike and headed south to Telaney's house in Silver Lake. She'd reluctantly agreed to put Addy up when she'd found the woman trying to sleep under a bridge with nothing but the clothes on her back. I'd felt a responsibility to take care of the mage since I was the reason she'd been kicked out of the only home she'd known since she was twelve, but it was clear that Addy was uncomfortable staying in my home. Neither of us had been happy about the whole minion thing, but I could see where living under my roof might be a constant unwelcome reminder of the situation. Addy and Telaney didn't get along either, but the two of them didn't have the same weird obligation thing as Addy and I, plus as Telaney said, it wasn't like she had a boyfriend or girlfriend where a houseguest would cramp her style.

The two argued. Constantly. And since Addy didn't have a vehicle, Telaney had to drive the mage everywhere. I'd tried to help by supplying Addy with a cell phone, clothing, and necessities all courtesy of my Vulture job. I planned on putting some money in an account with Mathias so she could begin to replace the magical supplies she'd been forced to leave behind, but we didn't really have time for that. I needed Addy to have the tools that allowed her to do her magic. And I was hoping Mathias would extend me the same sort of credit plan that Alfie had been willing to do.

As I drove into Silver Lake, I kept an eye out for signs of any recent attacks. Thankfully, it didn't seem as if the roving bands of demons had made it to this neighborhood yet. This area, just like mine, was now part of that warmonger's territory, so I expected eventually an infernal gang would show up with death and destruction on their agenda, but right now all I saw was the damage that had taken place over the last two years and the steady efforts the new residents had taken to fix up their homes.

I pulled up to the curb in front of Telaney's house, admiring her flower beds and the fresh coat of white paint on the stucco house. Climbing the steps to her porch, I opened the screen door and knocked.

There was the thump of quick footsteps, and the noise of several deadbolts being drawn. Telaney swung open the door, and my eyes widened. My friend was clearly flustered, adjusting a shirt that was on backwards and barely covering the top of her naked thighs.

"Umm..." Had I interrupted something? Should I come back later?

"Who is it?" Addy came around the corner, her hair mussed and a sheet wrapped carelessly around her body. She had the swollen lips, the flushed face, the sparkle in her eyes that could only come from one activity.

She saw me, squeaked and dashed out of view. I heard the bedroom door slam and started to laugh.

"Stop," Telaney hissed, stepping out onto the front porch. "It's not what you think."

"Oh, it's not?" I tried to be serious but ended up snort-laughing. "'Cause it looks like you two have been getting it on. What happened to 'she's a total bitch' and 'I hate her'?"

"She is, and I do." Telaney tugged her shirt lower. "It's… complicated. There's an attraction, and the friction between us kind of sparked a flame."

"Flame? How about bonfire?" I teased. "Is this the first inferno, or have these fires been going on between the two of you for a while?"

Telaney glanced behind her, then back at me, a sheepish grin spreading across her face. "It started the night I brought her home. And then I felt guilty, because it wasn't like she had anywhere else to go besides your place. I was worried that maybe I was taking advantage of the situation. But a few nights later we had an argument, like we seem to do every second of every day, and next thing I knew we were in bed again. We've been screwing like rabbits ever since."

"Excellent." I nodded. Hopefully this would turn into something more, because Telaney deserved to have someone who loved her after all the shit she'd been through. But if not, at least this was a great way to blow off steam and soak up the endorphins.

"So are you here about a job?" Telaney asked. "Or maybe you need me to do a security detail somewhere?"

I suddenly felt bad that I was here for Addy and not her. Telaney was my best friend. She was inner-circle as far as people I trusted. Why was I discounting human skills aside from magic? Why did I place shifters and magic users above regular humans when it came to what we were facing? I'd counted myself as human up until the last few months of my life. I'd seen what humans could do to protect those they loved, and they were far from powerless. I needed to stop coddling them and thinking of them as not up to this task. I needed to start treating humans as the equals I'd always believed them to be.

"Not a Vulture job," I told her, since those had seemed to have dried up in the last few weeks. "This is personal. The demons are attacking my neighborhood in Los Feliz. That plague demon took out a couple of blocks in the Valley and went after my family's street yesterday morning."

Telaney sucked in a breath. "Is everyone okay?"

"Yes. I teleported there while I was sleeping and was luckily there to defend them, but I'm worried. That plague demon can kill humans in minutes and they've no way to fight off his diseases if they get through the wards. So I'm making the Valley my priority."

Telaney's eyebrows rose. "How did you...? Are you psychic? Did you sense your family was in danger and so you teleported there? Is this some new superpower?"

I blew out a breath. "I don't know. I was asleep, and it might have all been a coincidence. Plus I've got no idea how to teleport again. But I do know that this plague demon is the most pressing of our threats."

"What can I do to help?" Telaney asked.

"Help me plan, strategize, and scout. Help me defend the Valley, fight, and kill this guy. But only if you're comfortable with that. This is a plague demon, and I'm not sure how you can protect yourself against that sort of attack. Regular bullets might not work. Bishop is trying to get more anti-magic guns and ammo, but until then, I understand if you'd rather sit this one out."

Telaney bristled, just like I thought she would. "Like hell I'm going to sit this one out. We'll take out this plague demon first, then the other two afterward. So what's your plan?"

And here's where I sucked. Strategy and planning was not my skill.

"Figure out where he is, what his strengths and weaknesses are," I said. "Make a plan to attack and kill him. If Bishop gets here with anti-magic weaponry, I'll have the police, the Disciples, and the Gray Dogs on my side. If he can't deliver, then we're on our own."

Telaney's brows knitted. "This guy's got an army of two thousand. That's a lot of demons to kill if we end up having to do this on our own."

She was right, but I didn't know what else to do.

"But we *do* need to find out more about the head guy—Itinder or whatever his name is. Ideally we won't *have* to fight two thousand demons. Maybe we can figure out a way to sneak by all of them and assassinate Itinder," Telaney suggested. "Nip this thing in the bud. Kill the head plague dude, then his army will fall apart and go back to Hel, right?"

"They might just join up with another demon," I told her. "And I'm not sure we're strong enough to kill the head plague dude. I had a hard time killing one of his lower plague demons yesterday morning. I'm not confident that I could put Itinder down."

"Okay. Maybe if we whittle away at his army, he might decide the losses are too great and the gains too little to stay," Telaney suggested. "He'll pick up his toys and go home because we're not easy pickings."

"That's what I'm hoping," I said, even though I doubted this guy would leave unless we killed at least half, if not more, of his army.

"Let's focus on defending against his attacks, and figuring out what we're up against," Telaney said. "We'll figure out a strategy to kill this guy later, once we know more, and once we know what kind of anti-magic weaponry and other support we'll be able to count on. If we find out where this diseased fucker lives, that'd be a start."

Telaney clearly needed to be in charge of this thing, not me.

"What about the warmonger?" she asked. "At the meeting you were thinking of maybe partnering with him to get rid of the plague demon. Is that still on the table?"

I winced. "Yeah, that's probably not going to happen. I went to talk to the Disciples yesterday about a partnership, and ended up helping them get some of their hijacked trucks back from the warmonger."

Telaney shrugged. "He'll probably not recognize you with all the Disciples fighting him. Unless you started sucking in his energy attacks and launching them back, that is. Even then, that might make him respect you enough to grant you an audience and consider some kind of deal with you."

"Nope. First, I already made a deal with the Disciples, and I don't want to double cross them. Second...I launched a super-sonic golf ball and accidently hit the demon horse the warmonger was riding. It reared and took off, throwing him to the ground. I don't think he'll forgive or forget that sort of humiliation."

Telaney burst out laughing, then slapped a hand over her mouth. "Oh Lord. That's hysterical. Only you, Eden. Only you."

Yeah, only me. Now I probably had a warmonger gunning for me as well as Desiree. Making demon friends everywhere I go. That's me.

"So we forget about the warmonger for now, and focus on the plague demon." Telaney patted me on the shoulder. "What's first on our list?"

"Finding out where Itinder and his army are staying," I told her. "Blister is gathering information for me, but I don't know if she has the contacts to find the details out."

"She's more of a big-picture spy," Telaney agreed.

I nodded. "If you were some bigwig disease demon living in the Valley, where would you call home?"

Telaney snorted. "Me? A secluded bungalow in Altadena or one a few miles from Mt. Baldy. Or beachfront in Santa Monica. No, I'll take the mountains over the beach. Even now there's too many people at the beach."

"Okay, *not* you," I laughed. "Think bigwig plague demon."

"Bigwig? Well, all the Karens flock to Porter Ranch. Gated community. Nice views of the city and the Santa Susana Mountains. Cookie cutter homes all built two inches from each other. Planned within an inch of its life with groomed walking and hiking trails, high-end shopping, pretentious hillside villas, spas and fine dining, all without ever having to leave the safety of those guarded gates."

I nodded. "Studio City has some pretty nice neighborhoods too."

Telaney held up both hands, palms upward. "So you think this plague demon is a trendy millennial with money?" She raised one palm and lowered the other. "Or is he an old school conservative who sticks to expensive cuts of steak and after dinner brandy, and is afraid of the riffraff?"

"You're right. Porter Ranch it is," I eyed her outfit. "Feel like taking a field trip today?"

She glanced behind her at the slightly open door. "I'm pretty sure Addy's managed to get some clothes on by now. Come inside, make us all a pot of coffee, and I'll be ready in ten—twenty if I can actually score a hot shower this morning."

addy and I had a few awkward moments while I made coffee in an actual coffee maker since Telaney's neighborhood seemed to be the only one in LA with power at the moment. We talked about the unseasonably warm fall weather, how the demonic damage of our freeway system was causing just as much gridlock as during a pre-demon rush hour and how over three quarters of the residents had fled to the States. I poured the two of us a mug, leaving Telaney's empty for when she got out of the shower. We both walked over to the sofas, sat with the coffee table between us, and looked everywhere but at each other.

"Um, I had something I wanted to ask you. I mean tell you about. Because I don't want to inadvertently compel you," I started out. "Three demons attacked my family's neighborhood yesterday morning. One was a plague demon. I fought them off, killing two of them, but what really saved the neighborhood was a set of wards that Genevieve Planteaux, one of the neighbors, erected. They held the demons at bay and gave me enough time to get out there and fight. And when I threw one demon into the wards, it killed him."

Addy eyed me with curiosity. "Is she a mage or a witch?"

I blinked. "I don't know. Is there a difference?"

"Witch magic is similar to ours. It comes from the same source, but the methodology is different." Addy took a quick sip of her coffee. "I ask because witches can create some amazingly powerful wards. Their defensive magic abilities are very strong. Mages tend to specialize, but few of us focus on wards and defensive systems."

"Oh." So maybe my great idea wasn't so great after all. "I know you do illusions, but other than that, what magics are you skilled in? What's your specialty?"

"Morgana focused on high level illusions, enchantments, and the creation of pocket dimensions, so that's what I learned. There were some basics in other disciplines we all needed to be proficient in, though."

I caught my breath. High level illusions, I figured, but *pocket dimensions*? Was that what the whole hiker trail thing had been?

Addy smiled as if she read my mind. "The hiker trail was an illusion. If Morgana had sent you to a pocket dimension, you might not have come back. Once you let an illusion spell fall, those caught in it are just in their normal surroundings. Pocket dimensions can be cut off, meaning there's no return, or they can be dismissed entirely, which spits the person out in a random location—which isn't always in this dimension."

"Holy shit," I whispered.

She nodded. "I never got that far. None of us did. I tried, but the best I could do is create a tunnel, a kind of gate between dimensions. They weren't always stable, and I never knew where they ended up, but I'd hoped with practice someday I'd reach Morgana's level of skill."

"So...no wards?" I wondered if unstable interdimensional tunnels could work as a weapon. Open one, shove some demons in, close the door.

"Oh, I can do wards, although probably not as good as your neighbor. I was pretty skilled at setting traps. And don't discount the ability of illusions. They can confuse your opponents, terrify them, lead them to blindly race off a cliff they didn't even realize was there."

Okay, this was sounding better and better.

"I know you've been trying to collect spell materials, and I'd like to help with that if I can." I grimaced as Addy shot me a wary look. "Just informing you that I've got an account at Mathias's Magic Shop and at Artemis Books, and that any of my team who need supplies from either place to help them defend the city are welcome to purchase stuff on my account."

A smile twitched one corner of her lips. "Nicely worded. I'll be happy to take advantage of that. And I'd like to meet your neighbor, Genevieve Planteaux, if you don't mind. I've lost contact with everyone I know. None of my new acquaintances does magic. Even if she is a witch and not a mage, it would be nice to talk to someone and maybe share information and experiences."

"She might be willing to put you up in a guest room, if you're interested."

Addy nodded. "So I can help defend your family's neighborhood, and maybe teach this Genevieve a few new tricks, I'm guessing." She glanced behind her toward the hallway that led to the bedrooms and the bathroom where we could still hear the noise of the shower. "It's probably a good idea. Put some much needed distance between us to think. And, as I said, it will be nice to talk to another magic user."

* * *

I RODE my bike and Telaney and Addy followed in Telaney's car. First we went to Mathias's store, where Addy was definitely a kid in a candy shop. She and Mathias chatted about spells while she gathered up a basket full of stones, herbs, wands, and packets of what looked like dirt. Telaney and I followed Isaac into the back room where he served us tea and chocolate macadamia cookies he'd made just this morning.

"Do you know if Mathias and the other mages in LA have some sort of guild?" I asked Isaac as we sipped our tea.

He nodded. "I wouldn't call it a guild, but he's got about ten other mages on an e-mail chain. They help each other out when someone is short a batch of herbs, or needs hemlock branches for a rush wand order. They talk a lot about what products and supplies are in high demand, and if there are any threats that might affect our businesses."

"Do you think they would be willing to provide products and services either free or at a discount to ensure a peaceful Los Angeles, and New Hell?" I asked.

Isaac wrinkled his nose. "I'm not sure. I know Mathias is fed up with the instability. Demons don't tend to mess with us, and their being a threat definitely means we have a lot of humans lining up to buy our products. From a profit standpoint, peace doesn't lead to profit. But I know it bothers Mathias to see his city torn apart like this. He'd support you, Eden. I don't know if any of the others would."

"Maybe he needs to remind the other mages about all we've lost. The vibrant neighborhoods that are now abandoned rubble. The businesses shuttered. The people who have fled. There're no more weekends at the beach, lazy afternoons wandering through open-air markets. No more football or baseball or even pickup games at the local parks. No more kids laughing and playing in the schoolyards during recess."

Isaac swiped a hand across his eyes. "Yeah. Everyone likes money, but not at the expense of those experiences. I'll get

Mathias to e-mail everyone and let you know what they say. What are you thinking in terms of assistance?"

"If there are any mages who are willing to fight, we'd welcome their help," I told him. "If they're not comfortable with that, then any magical products that would help us defend against demons, specifically plague demons, warmongers, or high-level demons, would help."

"Wands, amulets, and scrolls." Isaac thought for a second. "I've got some herbal combinations I've been working on to negate the effects of certain magic. I'd be happy to provide those if you think they'd help."

Isaac had always denied having magical ability, claiming Mathias was the expert there, but his herbal teas and concoctions had unusual benefits. I wasn't sure if some of that was a collaboration between the two men, or if Isaac had unrealized powers of his own.

"Anything that would guard against plague demon diseases?" Telaney asked.

Isaac grinned, rubbing his hands together. "Garlic. Echinacea. Green tea. Ginger. Ginseng. Sambucus. Honey. Holy Basil. There are so many herbs and spices that boost the immune system."

I thought about Mrs. Vandergriff and her family. "Black veins and red sores. Very quick death."

Isaac thought for a second. "Sounds like something that got into the blood stream and triggered a severe immune response. Maybe an anaphylactic shock or cardiac arrest, although it couldn't have been that sudden if there were sores on their skin. Perhaps a breathing issue resulting in incapacitation, then the disease went through their circulatory system to kill them while they were out."

Telaney shuddered. "Do you have anything that might be an antidote to that?"

"Or better yet, guard against the infection?" I said.

Isaac got up and went into a pantry. A few minutes later he returned with a bag of what looked like lemon candies.

"This is something Mathias and I were working on. I'm not going to promise it will work because we haven't been able to test it out yet, but in theory it should ward off a conventional disease attack, even if it's supercharged or spread by magical or demonic means."

"Then I guess we're your test subjects," Telaney said, taking the bag. "What's the dosing protocol for these things?"

"We concocted them so the protective effects would last eight to twelve hours," Isaac said. "Suck one as if they're cough drops. I used lots of lemon and sugar, but I'm warning you that they still taste bad. For them to have a long-lasting effect, don't chew them up."

I eyed the bag, estimating a hundred in there. It should be enough to split them between my family, Telaney, and Addy.

"How long would it take you to make more of these?" I asked Isaac.

"Once we're confident that the mixture and magic works, I can produce a few hundred a day," he replied.

I quickly calculated the Gray Dogs, the police, the Disciples, and my own team, as well as my family and the neighbors. "Go ahead and get started. I'll pay for any you produce even if you end up needing to tweak the formula. I'd rather have them ready than not."

Isaac smiled. "No charge. LA is my home, and I want my home back. If that means I spend days crafting lozenges, then so be it. Anything to help, Eden."

We finished our tea and cookies then went back into the shop. Addy had an enormous supply of herbs, stones, spices, and wands on the counter. I winced, hoping that I had enough money to pay for this and that Mathias would be willing to allow me to run a tab since I'd told Addy I already had one in place.

The bill was far less than I'd expected, and Mathias told me to settle up with him later before I'd even broached the topic. As we left, Addy admitted that she'd bargained with Mathias for supplies in exchange for her work enchanting several of his objects with illusion spells. It seems the mage was very impressed with her abilities, and had suggested an ongoing partnership where Addy could make money on commission for jobs she was better skilled to handle than he was. It was absolutely a win-win agreement.

As I followed Telaney's car, I hoped Addy could work the same kind of bargain with Alfie, because those books of his were expensive and I was pretty sure I was nearing the end of my credit limit with him.

CHAPTER 24

We pulled into the parking lot for Artemis Books. Telaney and Addy gawked as they got out of the car. Every other building in the strip mall was currently a blasted shell with splintered plywood over the windows and doors. Graffiti had been spray painted across everything. But Artemis Books stood untouched, pristine in its concrete and glass glory.

"How did…how did his shop escape whatever the hell happened to the other stores?" Telaney asked.

Addy shrugged. "Either he has some powerful magic, or he's got friends in high places."

I held up my hands. "I've got no idea. I don't ask, and Alfie has never offered an explanation."

The bell chimed as we walked in. I winced passing through whatever magic Alfie was using to protect his entrance. Telaney seemed unaffected by the spell, but Addy's grin widened. Alfie looked up from behind the counter and gave me a nod before returning to his computer.

There were three other customers in the store that I could see, two women looking through the history section and one man sitting at a table, paging through a book. The lights were a soft golden glow, and the store was cozy and warm despite the power outage that had seemed to affect most of the LA area.

Addy took off into the racks of books. Telaney rolled her eyes and went over to look through the bargain section. I headed for the counter, lurking close but not close enough to annoy Alfie, who was clearly busy with administrative stuff.

"Looking for something specific, Eden?" Alfie asked, not looking up from the computer screen.

"I brought in my friend. The one I told you about, who is a mage specialized in illusions—"

"I noticed that this mage is tied to you. You've marked her with an excessively large ownership claim."

I felt my face heat up.

"I'll admit, I'm impressed that you scored someone so capable," he continued, "but I really had thought this sort of thing would be beneath you, Eden."

"I didn't mean to do it." My voice was a whole lot more defensive than I'd wanted it to be, but Alfie's gentle criticism stung. "I was trying to save her life and I didn't realize that was the price."

Alfie looked up from the laptop and scowled. "Everything has a cost. Everything. Especially resurrection."

As if I didn't feel bad enough. "I, uh, I did it again, but this time the guy wasn't actually dead. He was just dying. He begged me. I told him what had happened before, and he said he didn't have any problem with that."

"Is it truly consent when someone is facing their own demise?" Alfie asked. "What's next? Owning souls and torturing them for all of eternity?"

"No!" I glared at him. "Look, I'm kind of dealing with stuff as I go here. It's not like my asshole parents gave me an owner's manual of what to expect. I've been raised by humans, and for most of my life I wasn't able to do more than electrical attacks, some minor telekinesis, and a resistance to illness. Cut me some slack, Alfie."

"Never," he said with a teasing smile on his thin face.

"That's fair. It's not like I need any additional accountability partners, though. My foster mother, my sisters, and my friends seem to be doing a good job of keeping my amoral tendencies in line."

"I hope so." He flipped the long mane of hair from one side of his head to the other, revealing the shaved undercut. "So tell me more about your illusionist friend."

"She's…lost all of her spell books and supplies, and I'd like to help her rebuild her library. Is there anything behind the counter that she might be interested in?" Not that I could afford anything behind the counter, but hopefully Addy could work out some sort of trade deal like she'd done with Mathias.

"Who did she study under?" Alfie asked as he pulled a notebook off a shelf.

I glanced at the rows of bookshelves, not sure if I was supposed to be telling anyone this or not. "Morgana Silver-Moon."

His eyebrows rose. "Morgana Silver-Moon? Morgana was elven-taught as a changeling. Not quite sorcerer level, but very high in her training before she escaped to the human world as a teenager. She had a price on her head from her owner."

I felt a bit sick over that. Not that any of her past excused what Morgana had done, but nobody should have to go through that as a child, or even as an adult.

"I've got three books in the back that your friend might be interested in, but they're expensive."

Alfie quoted a price that made my eyes water. Should I ask him to bring them out, let Addy look at them, and hope she could cut a deal? I'd hate for her to get excited about one of those spell books only to have me tell her that there was no way I could afford the price, but maybe there was a work-around. Alfie had often sold me stuff on payment plans, and had even helped me in return for a favor. I hated to not explore all of our options.

"Let's see what she finds on the shelves," I told him. "But I do think she might like to take a look at those three books before she makes a decision."

Alfie came out from behind the counter. "I'll go give her some assistance. You stay here, and make sure you look at the new selection of postcards I've got on the spinning rack over there."

I walked over to the postcard rack, not because I had anyone to send postcards to, but because I'd learned to take Alfie's suggestions seriously. He was like a creature in a video game that suddenly appeared with a weird side-quest, or gift that ended up being critical to achieving the next level.

As far as I could tell the postcards were just postcards. There was the typical shit—the Hollywood Sign, the Griffith Observatory, Venice Beach, the Chinese Theater with the sidewalk stars, Santa Monica Pier, La Brea Tar Pits, The Getty, and pics of Sunset Strip.

I grabbed five, trusting my intuition since I saw most of these sights every day and none of them were particularly appealing in terms of a visual keepsake. Addy appeared from one of the rows of bookshelves, her arms full of books. Alfie followed behind her, as she chatted about dark moon energy and planetary alignment. The mage set the books on the counter and I caught my breath, wondering if I'd need to sell my soul for these.

I owed her. I owed her big. Yes, I'd resurrected her when that demon had killed her, but she hadn't asked for it, and she absolutely hadn't asked to serve me for the rest of her natural life—which could be an elongated, unnatural life for all either of us knew.

"Let me show you the really amazing spell books I've got behind lock and key," Alfie said. "I think these will really benefit you, especially with your level of skill and expertise."

Addy's eyes sparkled with excitement, her cheeks growing pink with the praise. I'd never seen her so animated. It made me determined to get her whatever she needed, no matter the cost.

Alfie brought out the three spell books. They were leather bound, the bindings worn and softened with age. The pages were vellum with spidery writing in black ink. Illustrations filled the margins, and there were notations in several different hands from the original author in between the lines of text.

I couldn't understand any of it, but clearly Addy could. She oo'd and ah'd over the pages, carefully flipping through them with cotton gloves on her hands. After twenty minutes of enraptured examination, she pointed to one of the books.

"I'll take this one and these three from the bookshelves."

I clamped my teeth together, waiting for Alfie's quote and hating that I'd need to say no to probably all but the cheapest of these purchases.

Instead, Alfie rang the sale up on his cash register, closed the drawer, and put the three bookshelf books in a bag, carefully wrapping the expensive one in a cotton sheet, then in a linen bag.

"Here you go, Sweetie. Come back soon, you hear?"

Addy did a little hop-dance, taking the bags like she was a Bel Air socialite shopping on Rodeo Drive. "Thank you. I appreciate all of your help."

She strutted over to where Telaney was still looking through the bargain bin, while I remained behind, stunned and more than a little apprehensive.

"What…who… Who's paying for that?" I asked.

"You are." Alfie shot me a smug look. "Eventually."

"I didn't realize my credit was that good."

He shrugged. "There are debts you skip and debts you pay. I'm gambling that this is a debt you pay."

Alfie knew far more about me than I'd ever expected. "I will pay you back, although it might take more than your lifetime."

He chuckled. "Dear girl, you have no idea how long my lifespan is. I trust that I will eventually receive full payment for the debt."

Did mages live longer than most humans? Or was Alfie not a mage? I shrugged away the questions as "none of my business" and decided I wasn't going to be looking any gift horses in the mouth.

"I'm trying to gather forces, arm them and go after those three demons I told you about," I said, figuring that if Alfie was a mage, I might as well ask for his assistance too. "I'm also asking the mages in the city if they'll support us either with magical items or fighting beside us. I don't know your talents outside of the bookstore, but I'm hoping you can help?"

"I won't get involved, and you shouldn't either." Alfie gave a one shoulder shrug. "The pendulum of Chaos and Order swings one way and then the other, but in the end it all balances. Ride out the storm, and the tide will turn."

Remembering how his store stood untouched in a strip mall of rubble, I wondered if Alfie had the same sort of deal with the demons that Bishop had once had. If so I didn't blame him for sitting this whole thing out. He didn't look physically strong, and I could be wrong about him having magical abilities. For all I knew he was an occult-book loving human, who'd somehow paid the demons to leave him alone.

"No problem. I get why you might not want to get

involved, but I have to do this. I can't wait for the pendulum to swing." Especially when that pendulum didn't seem to be on a human-life time clock, and my family and friends were at risk.

"This is a small matter that has no importance on a universal scale," Alfie pointed out.

"Maybe, but it has great importance to the humans and shifters that call this place their home," I shot back. "I've got a responsibility to them, especially those in LA."

His gaze narrowed. "Exactly what sort of responsibility?"

Ugh. I so didn't want to get into the details of this shit.

"I claimed the city," I told him. "It's mine, and I have to do something to bring peace to the area."

Alfie leaned his elbows on the counter. "Peace is a fleeting concept. And sometimes peace comes at a great price. Dictators provide peace."

"I don't want to be a dictator." As if I could. I couldn't even manage to keep one small neighborhood safe. I wasn't a leader. I'd tried to be a Protector, a lone-warrior type, but in spite of all those Hollywood action movies, there really wasn't much a lone-warrior could do against tens of thousands of demons overrunning a sprawling city.

"As for the claiming thing..." Alfie pursed his lips. "Did anyone hear you? You claiming the city, that is?"

I blinked. "Um, maybe Bishop?"

Alfie snorted. "He doesn't count. You're screwing him. He won't hold you to any hastily made vow. If Bishop is the only one who heard you claim the city, you're good. There's no loss of face. Just pretend it never happened and go about your business. Take a Vulture job. Play with the tiger cubs in your neighborhood. Teach your minions something."

"*I* know I claimed it," I countered. "And even if I didn't, people are dying. Humans are fleeing, abandoning everything they own. They're piled up at the borders, frantically trying to get out of New Hell. And the ones remaining here are being slaughtered or enslaved."

"Don't claim what you can't defend." Alfie shrugged. "You can't defend New Hell. Even Doriel couldn't control it all. I'm not even sure the Iblis could."

I knew he was right, but I couldn't help it. I had to do *something*.

Don't claim what you can't defend. Too late. Even though Bishop might forgive me if I went back on that vow, I'd never be able to forgive myself.

Telaney came up to the counter. She put an armful of books down, and I eyed them as Alfie rang the purchases up. Romances. Sapphic romances.

You go, girl.

She paid for her books. Alfie bagged them up, then the three of us walked out of the store.

It wasn't until I was getting on my bike that I realized I'd forgotten to pay for my postcards. Oh well. I owed Alfie so much at this point that I doubted ten bucks worth of tourist crap was going to be a deal breaker. When I came in a few weeks from now to make a payment, I'd tell him to add the price to my bill.

Unless he'd already done so. Alfie had some skills, and I wasn't sure that they were mage skills, but I had a feeling that he'd already added the cost of those postcards to my bill, and that I'd be paying for far more than the cost of goods sold sometime in the future.

CHAPTER 25

I pulled into the driveway at Bea's house; Telaney parked at the curb. Waving for them to follow me, I led the pair up to the door, and knocked, shouting out the passwords I'd made up for Nevarra and Sadie.

I heard a giggle, then Sadie unlocked the door, ushering us in. I made the introductions and she led us into the kitchen where Bea was still sewing and Nevarra was taking care of baby chickens in a box under a battery powered light.

"Hey girls," I said. "And hi, Bea."

I introduced Addy and Telaney. Waving for them to sit at the table, I went over and fired up the camp stove to make us all coffee. I could tell that Addy felt awkward, but Bea and the girls quickly made her relax. By the time I passed out mugs of coffee, Addy and Telaney were both cuddling downy chicks on their laps and chatting with Bea about gardening.

"What did Jayla like best about the care package we sent?" Sadie asked me. "Did she give you any ideas of what she might need or what?"

"She loved everything," I lied. In reality I had no clue what she'd thought since she hadn't answered the door when I'd delivered it. "She didn't specify needing anything in particular, but I know she was happy with what you both sent."

"The next box is ready to go," she told me. "There's a rug, and it's too big to carry on your bike, so you might need to borrow Bea's car."

Telaney eyed me. "Jayla?"

"A homeless teen I pulled out of downtown earlier this week," I told her. "She's staying at Suerte, living in the shed behind the bar. The girls have been getting care packages together for her since she doesn't have much in the way of personal possessions."

"That's sweet." Addy smiled at Sadie and Nevarra.

"We know what it's like to do without," Nevarra told her. "And what it's like to have no one to help you. Family is everything. And when you find that family, then you truly feel at home."

That was so very true.

"Did you talk with Genevieve Planteaux about Addy?" I asked Bea.

She nodded. "Genevieve is excited at the idea of talking craft with another magic user. And she has her spare room all ready."

Addy glanced briefly at Telaney before turning to me. "I'd like to go ahead and meet her, if that's okay. I've got my ingredients to sort through and my new spell books to read as well. It's probably a good idea for me to start right away."

"Nevarra can walk you over and introduce you," Bea said to Addy. "When you're settled in, stop by and one of us will take you around to meet the neighbors and get an idea of where everyone lives. I'm sure Genevieve will want to show you where she's placed her wards as well."

Nevarra stood. After another quick glance at Telaney, Addy stood as well.

"I'll help carry your stuff," Telaney finally said. "You and

Nevarra go on to the house. I'll grab your bags out of the car and meet you there."

Sadie went with them as well, leaving me and Bea in the kitchen.

"I get the feeling there's some romance going on between those two, and neither one of them knows where they stand with the other." Bea nodded toward the front door.

I followed her gaze. Maybe this separation *would* be good for them. Give them time to think, and time to trust.

* * *

SADIE WAS RIGHT. The carpet would never have fit on my bike. Instead Telaney and I stuffed it in the trunk of her car along with the box, and we left my bike behind to pick up later.

"I'm sorry to be yanking Addy away like this when you both seem to be..." I wasn't sure how to label whatever Telaney and Addy had. Was it just releasing tension and relieving stress through sex? Was it more than sex?

"Like I said, I think it's probably good for us to have some time and space." Telaney sighed. "Though I *could* use some bestie advice right now."

"I'm here for you," I said. "But fair warning, I don't exactly have a great track record in healthy relationships. This thing with Bishop is the first time a boyfriend and I haven't been trying to kill each other on the regular."

"That's still an improvement on my background," she countered.

Telaney had been sex trafficked as a young teen, and she'd confided in me that the experience had made it hard for her to trust and be emotionally vulnerable to her partners. I could see where that would make any relationship difficult.

"I don't trust her. I'm not even sure I like her," Telaney

admitted. "But all the arguing and digs at each other kinda does it for me. How sick is that?"

"Not sick at all," I assured her. "Tell me what you *do* like about her."

"She's brilliant," Telaney said without the slightest hesitation. "I don't know much about magic, but I can tell she's very gifted and a hell of a good fighter. I don't want to be on the opposite side of her in a battle. The woman can be totally ruthless, and I admire that."

"Mmmm." I waited for Telaney to continue, because I knew my friend, and I knew there was more.

"She's very loyal, which is why this thing with Morgana bothers her so much. I think she's hurt and confused, and not sure who is worthy of her loyalty right now. In spite of being tossed into this weird obligation with you, she's quickly processing it all and dealing with it. And I believe down deep, she really wants to do what's right for the city and the humans here."

"Those are good traits," I pointed out.

"Yeah. Except I think she's not sure *we're* what's right for the city and the humans. I mean, I get it. This stuff will take time after a life of brainwashing. I don't know if she'll ever really be on our side or anyone's side. And I don't know if I'm just serving as some sort of balm for getting thrown out of her mage group and getting rejected by her boyfriend."

I nodded. "You worry she's just proving to herself that she's attractive to others, that she can form, at a minimum, a sexual relationship with someone outside of her former mage family."

"That, plus I need to decide what I really want from her, and if that's something she can even give me. Is she the sort of person I need in my life? And she probably needs to think about that too. We can't do that thinking when we're boinking all over the place. Sex releases endorphins and I can't tell you the number of times those fucking endorphins have convinced me I'm in love with some unsuitable asshole."

We pulled into the parking lot of Suerte and Telaney maneuvered her car into a spot near the door.

"I'll go inside and have a beer," she told me. "Come in when you're done with the gift-giving."

I struggled to get the box and carpet out of the trunk and all of it in my arms. Staggering a little, I managed to carry it all around the bar and to the shed without dropping anything.

With my hands full, I kicked at the door. "Jayla! It's me, Eden. I've got more gifts for you from my sisters."

This time the door opened. Jayla squealed, clapping her hands together.

"Can you get the carpet?" I asked. "I don't think I can get it through your door while I'm carrying this box."

She grabbed the carpet and went back inside. Since she'd left the door open, I took that as an invitation and walked in after her, carefully setting the box on the floor. Jayla had unfolded the carpet and was exclaiming over it while pivoting around, clearly deciding where she should put it in the small twelve-by-twelve shed. I'd only gotten a quick glimpse through the crack of a door before, so I took this opportunity to really look around. The place was cluttered, but no more clutter than other teenagers' rooms. She'd hung several posters on the walls, and had set up a stack of apple crates to serve as shelves. They were crammed full of books, Pokémon figures, bobble heads, and stuffed animals. Her bed had several colorful throw pillows and a pastel blanket that I recognized from home. Scattered across the end of the mattress were coloring books with crayons, board games, and a pile of inexpensive necklaces and bracelets.

Unrolling the rug, Jayla grabbed the box from the floor, ripping the cardboard top open. She vibrated with excitement as she went through the assorted items, carefully placing each on her bed as she debated where she was going to display each one. At the bottom of the box was a card. Opening it, Jayla's eyes widened.

"I've been invited to visit your sisters. And have lunch."

I'd warned them that Jayla didn't seem to bathe regularly and that the odor inside the enclosed space of the house might be eye-watering. Both girls had assured me that they wouldn't insult their guest, and that any odor could be aired out after the visit was over. Sadie even commented that if the weather was nice, they could have their lunch outside, in the tiny backyard.

"I want to go but..." Jayla looked around the shed with clear anxiety.

I understood her reluctance. The unhoused were always having their stuff stolen. It would be very difficult for Jayla to leave all these treasures behind for a day without constant worry that they might not be here when she got back.

"HB will ensure the safety of your home and belongings," I told her. "No one understands territory like a shifter. They're crazy possessive about their homes and their stuff."

She glanced around once more, then nodded. "Your sisters said tomorrow?"

I'd been planning on having Bea come pick the girl up, but I worried she might not want to get in a car with someone she didn't know. That left the transportation up to me. Hopefully girl wouldn't mind riding on the back of my bike.

I confirmed when I'd pick Jayla up, then went into Suerte through the kitchen door.

The bar was surprisingly busy. The tables were filled. Everyone had at least a drink in front of them if not a plate of food. As I looked around I noticed duffle bags and luggage stacked against the back wall. Telaney was at the bar chatting with a woman wearing a baseball hat while HB set an iced tea in front of them.

"What's up with the luggage?" I asked HB as I slid onto a bar stool next to Telaney.

"Their pack's territory was attacked and destroyed," HB told me. "They lost all of their houses, and their food stores."

"The children and elderly hid in an old bomb shelter in the woods," the woman with the baseball hat said. "When it was clear we were losing the fight, we retreated and scattered. We tended to our wounded and checked on the young and the elders while a few of us went back to see if the attackers had left. When we were sure they were gone, we gathered up anything that remained of our possessions and fled here, to the safety of our Protector."

I flinched, remembering that most of the shifters no longer considered me to be their Protector.

"Where was your pack's territory?" I asked the woman.

"Yorba Linda." She shrugged. "We will rebuild again. This is not the first time in our history that we have needed to flee our homes. God provides."

I respected her faith, and hoped that someday soon, these shifters could once more reclaim their territory and rebuild.

"You ready?" Telaney asked, downing the rest of her tea.

"Yeah." I turned to HB. "I'm taking Jayla over to visit with my sisters tomorrow afternoon. I told her that you would ensure her stuff remained untouched."

HB nodded. "Of course. I'm glad she's getting out and maybe making some friends. She won't come in the bar, even when I'm the only one here. She's so isolated out there. It worries me."

It worried me too, but I understood how hard it could be to trust strangers. The fact that Jayla had agreed to meet my sisters was a huge step.

CHAPTER 26

elaney and I headed west on the 118. Traffic had picked up, and I'd noticed that quite a few of the cars going east were loaded down with people and boxes. Stuffed trunks were bungie-corded closed. Luggage was tied to the roofs. Just past the 405, everyone came to an abrupt stop. We followed the vehicles ahead of us merging into the far left lane and slowly edging ahead. Half an hour later, we were all detoured into the east-bound lane through an open section in the concrete barrier to get around four tractor-trailers piled up across the freeway. I smelled gasoline through the closed window and sadly noted the bruised and battered vegetables and fruit scattered across the pavement. We were forced to get off the freeway at Havenhurst Avenue, and detour a bit south due to road closures and debris.

The neighborhoods we drove through were deathly silent. Vultures circled overhead, and perched on lawns. This time the smell coming through the car windows wasn't gasoline, but decay.

"Circle around," I told Telaney. "I want to see if all the

neighborhoods surrounding Porter Ranch are like this, and how far out the vacant areas extend."

She made a left, then glanced over at me. "Lots of people are leaving New Hell. These aren't poor neighborhoods. I'm sure they were packed and out of here hours after the Governor was killed."

"Everyone?" There were cars in most of the driveways, but no sign that these homes were currently occupied. And places this luxurious should have been snapped up as squatter's-rights homes. "And what about that?" I pointed to a group of vultures and a coyote trotting down the sidewalk with what looked like an arm in its mouth.

"Raiding the garbage that probably hasn't been picked up in a week." Telaney winced at the coyote. "Or maybe not."

"Pull over," I said. "Let's check."

"Are you kidding?" Telaney pulled over, then dug a bag of what looked like lemon candies out of her center console and popped one in her mouth. "If a plague demon killed all these people, then there might be some horrible disease microbes out there, just waiting for a new host. I don't want that new host to be me. Or you."

"Good idea." These were the disease-protection candies that Mathias and Isaac had made. Telaney offered me one and I took it, not sure if I'd be immune to demonic plagues or not. I'd neutralized what the demon outside of Bea's neighborhood had been trying to spread, but that didn't mean I'd be unaffected by another strain, or by disease launched by a more powerful demon.

"Hope these things work." Telaney screwed up her face. "Ugh. They taste like nail polish remover and tar flavored with sugar and lemon."

She wasn't wrong. I tried to keep from gagging and got out of the car. Telaney slid out of the driver's side, pulling a shotgun and a nylon bag from the back seat. "Kinda wish I had a hazmat suit and a flame thrower. Or at least a jug of bleach and some Lysol spray."

As we made our way through the streets, the same desolate scene greeted us. Two blocks down, we saw several bodies lying in yards, a few more sprawled across the sidewalk, and one poor dude who was actually in the middle of the road. They were covered with red blistering sores, black necrotic flesh, and yellow-tinged fluid.

"I wonder if anyone made it out alive," Telaney whispered.

I hoped so. Somehow I doubted it. This plague demon seemed to hit hard and fast, with people dropping dead before they had a chance to defend themselves. The only way someone would have survived this was if they'd left before it happened.

After walking for almost an hour, we discovered that a four-block circle around the gated community had the same apocalyptic appearance. The "dead zone" encircled Porter Ranch. Houses west of the dead zone were clearly abandoned, no doubt by residents who didn't want to wait around for disease to reach them. There were no cars in those driveways, and the homes showed clear signs of a rapid evacuation. Doors stood open. Abandoned belongings littered lawns—probably items that wouldn't fit in the vehicles that were left behind in favor of more important or valuable possessions.

South of the dead zone was a different story.

Here the houses were destroyed, blasted chunks of stucco and concrete littering formerly manicured lawns. Vehicles were blackened, on their sides, a few of them precariously balanced on tree tops. The timber frames that once lay under the concrete and tile roofs smoldered, looking like blackened fingers splayed from a scorched foundation.

And these bodies… They were gutted, burned, or twisted.

Sometimes all three. A dozen were displayed in some sort of sick tableau. I might be a demon, but I never understood the fascination for this sort of violence, this careless disregard for life.

These humans had gone down fighting something physical instead of a plague.

"Why aren't they dead of disease?" Telaney wondered as we walked through the rubble.

I shrugged. "A different band of Itinder's army? One without a plague demon? Blister did say that some of his army were warmongers. This sort of killing and damage seems more like it would be their thing."

"Maybe Itinder took care of the few blocks closest to his hideout. A protective ring to warn anyone what might happen if they come too close," Telaney said with a shiver.

Walking over to a pile of bodies, I nudged a few over, surprised to see that some of the corpses were demons. And it wasn't just conventional firearms that had taken these demons out. Some had torn limbs, twisted bodies, and a few seemed to have had their heads ripped from their bodies. I'd seen these kinds of injuries before—in the makeshift gladiatorial ring at SoFi stadium.

"Aries," I said to Telaney. "The Disciples have even given in and started giving it to members of the gang. I'm guessing some of the residents up here had a supply of the drug as well."

"Fat lot of good it did them," she grumbled.

True, but better to take out a handful of demons first if you're going to die anyway.

There was a faint scuffle, like a foot slipping on gravel. Telaney ducked behind an upside-down Prius and pulled out her pistol. I froze, listening, but heard nothing else.

"Get down," Telaney hissed, waving me over.

"Probably just a vulture," I whispered.

Just in case, I pulled my gun from the shoulder holster, and crept forward. It could be a vulture with a small "v," a Vulture with a large "V," a demon, or an injured human needing help.

Or a human who didn't need help.

Licensed Vultures weren't the only looters. The past few months of chaos and lawlessness in New Hell had brought out the worst in people. It was everyone for themselves, and no one hesitated to shoot another person over a case of ramen noodles or a six-pack of Diet Coke. What should have brought humans together, only served to completely rend the fabric of society.

Another scuffle, clear behind a blackened Nissan up on its side. Before I could take more than another step, a figure darted out from behind the vehicle, shooting as she ran. I hit the ground, but not before one of the bullets grazed my arm, tearing through the leather of my jacket and leaving a slash of red in its wake.

Telaney opened fire from behind the Prius while I tried to take cover. The bullet wound felt like someone had slapped me with a hot knife. I grimaced at the pain, rolling behind a broken piece of statuary for cover. I was face-to-face with a white concrete Venus. She was close enough that I could have kissed her white lips. Her face was pitted and in a weird train of thought that I attributed to pain, I thought the marks looked like acne scars. We were in LA. Even in a city run by demons, this girl should have been able to find a decent dermabrasion or laser skin resurfacing.

Venus's ear flew off in a spray of white concrete, bringing me back to the dangerous reality of our situation. Scrambling into a crouch, I tried to determine exactly where my assailant was now. In the seconds I'd spent contemplating a statue's dermatological problems, she'd could be anywhere.

Silence stretched on for what felt like forever. I couldn't

see Telaney, but she probably had a better idea of where this woman was than me. The fact that she was holding fire meant neither of us would have a clear shot.

I heard another scuffle of feet on gravel. Telaney shot, so I popped up over Venus and did a quick sweep, spraying bullets from the Glock. On instinct, I'd aimed in the woman's general direction with my first shot, but she whirled behind a concrete fence, ducking down for cover.

I kept low, my gun resting on Venus's shoulder as I stared at the fence. My arm was on fire, and using both hands to hold the gun wasn't helping. I doubted firing one-handed and letting my injured arm dangle by my side would be any better for the injury and it sure as hell wouldn't improve my aim, so I sucked it up and bore through the pain.

"We're not here to hurt you," I shouted, as some sort of Hail Mary to the situation. "We're just scoping out the area for injured and survivors."

"We're the good guys here," Telaney added.

The "Good guys"? I glanced back at Telaney and saw her shrug.

If I thought any of that would convince the woman to come walking out from behind the barrier, gun lowered, I was wrong.

"You're a demon, you fucking piece of shit," the woman shouted back. "And anyone with you is just as bad. I'm not letting you kill me, or enslave me, or steal my soul."

I frowned, recognizing the voice. Telaney must have as well, because I heard her shout "Poodle?"

Poodle was another Vulture who I'd occasionally seen at jobs in the Valley. We'd always respected each other, given the other polite space when salvaging the same job. She'd never shot at me before, and I wasn't sure what had changed that she was now eager to blow my head off.

I knew what had changed.

"I'm not what you think. I'm still Eden—the same Eden you've always known," I told her.

"She's okay, Poodle. And so am I," Telaney added. "We're not here to compete with you for any salvage. We're just checking for survivors. Stop shooting and we'll talk."

Poodle didn't come out, but she didn't continue shooting at me.

"I saw what you did during that press conference. It was on live TV. You're not human," Poodle said. "I always thought there was something weird about you, and no wonder. You're a demon."

"She was raised here among humans as a human, you idiot," Telaney snapped. "She's on our side, and you should know that if you watched that press conference. We're out here gathering information because we're going to take this fucking plague demon down and save the Valley. So either stop shooting and get out of here, come out and help us, or die. Your choice, Poodle."

Whoa. Telaney was completely out of fucks.

The silence stretched on again, then I tensed as I heard the shuffle of feet on gravel once more.

Poodle came out, pistol raised. With fingers spread and clearly not on the trigger, she lowered the gun and holstered it. Telaney and I did the same, coming out of our hiding places. Poodle glanced at my shoulder where her bullet had hit.

"Sorry," she muttered. "Guessing you can fix that, though?"

"Eventually," I told her, hoping my healing abilities hurried up because this gunshot wound hurt like a mofo.

"This was my neighborhood." Poodle did a slow three-sixty. "I grew up here. And now everyone's dead or gone. That pile of concrete there? That was my house. And next door was where Naomi Delson lived."

I stood silent, feeling awkward with these obviously painful memories of Poodle's.

"Fucking demons." Poodle glanced at me. "No offense."

"None taken." I looked over at the wreckage she'd said had been her home. "You here for work, or trying to find keepsakes from your childhood?"

"Just came to take a sad, sad walk down memory lane." A muscle in her jaw twitched. "You two planning to kill these fuckers?"

"As soon as possible," Telaney told her. "Right now we're just scouting the area and gathering info. You know anything about Porter Ranch?"

Poodle shrugged. "What's there to know? Nice homes. Pretty much every one of them has a pool. The residents managed to stay clear of the demons for two years, paying them off and hiring private protection. This guy shows up right after that press conference when the governor was killed, and takes the entire place. I'm guessing anyone inside the gates is either dead or enslaved. Immediately after, that plague demon sends his goons out to clear the perimeter."

"To send a warning and a message," Telaney said, echoing what we'd discussed earlier. "I wonder what it's like inside the gates?"

"Let's go see," I told her.

We weren't insane enough to walk right up to the wrought iron gates with the tiny guard shack, just in case Itinder had a demon there on duty. Instead we headed west and circled around the community. The iron fences were only seven feet tall, but there was thick, spikey foliage on the inside of them, blocking our view.

Poodle jumped up on a burned-out car, climbing up to stand on the hood. She took off her backpack, pulled a pair of binoculars out, and looked through them.

"Got some demons walking around the streets closest to

the fence. They look bored. Dude at the guardhouse is focused on a magazine. The houses look occupied, but if the guy's got two thousand demons he needs to put up, then that makes sense."

"Where do you think Itinder would be staying?" I asked her.

She hopped off the car. "Not sure. I've never been inside, but I heard the houses on the east side of the community are pretty swag. The clubhouse is big, but I don't know if anyone would actually want to live there."

It was good info, but if I was going to lead an army of my own to attack these guys, I needed to know more.

"I'm going in." I took a step toward the fence, only to have Telaney grab my arm.

"Remember what I said about a hazmat suit and bleach? I wasn't kidding."

"I'm not planning to fight anyone," I told her. "I'm just going to sneak around and get a better sense of the layout, the demons he's got here, and where he might be staying."

With an army of two thousand, how many were at Porter Ranch, and how many were spreading their ick around the Valley? Had he deployed some of his household to scout out the other territories and see if there were opportunities to expand? Or were all two thousand right there inside?

"What if you get caught?" Telaney asked.

"I'll be fine," I told her. "Text me if anything comes up where you and Poodle need to get out of here. Otherwise, I'll be back in less than an hour."

"I'm not letting you go in there alone," Telaney snapped.

Poodle's eyebrows rose. "Well I'm not staying out here all by myself. If you two are going in, then I am as well."

Telaney opened up her bag and took out the candies, offering one to Poodle. "Here. Don't chew them and don't spit it out even though it tastes like crap. It's supposed to help you fight off disease."

Poodle popped one in her mouth and made a face.

Telaney reached into her bag and waved a blue spray bottle of Febreze at me. "It's not Lysol, but it'll have to do. Any demon tries to infect me, he's getting this in the face."

"I've got some Chlorox wipes in my bag," Poodle said. "Think that'll help? Maybe I can just throw them at the plague demons?"

Jesus.

"I really think you two should stay here," I told them. "That way if I get in trouble, you can call for backup."

Telaney rolled her eyes. "So we wait here for hours, then call HB and Addy? And then I'll need to explain to Bishop that you died by demon small pox and that we should gather your friends and family for a memorial service? Eden, this is stupid. I'm not letting you go in there alone."

"Fine." I walked up and climbed the fence, vaulting over the top into a very thorny bush. Telaney followed, with Poodle bringing up the rear as I watched for guards, or any demons who might be looking out the windows of the houses across the street. Broad daylight normally wouldn't have been the best time to sneak around a demon encampment, but given that most demons could see in the dark as well as the day, it probably didn't matter much.

There was a six-foot strip of well-manicured green grass between the thorny green bushes we were hiding in and the road. On the other side of the road were a line of houses placed closer together than I'd expected for such a swanky neighborhood. The lawns were a lush green with artistically arranged plants mulched in cocoa husks and stone. The houses were variations on a pueblo theme with bricked driveways, spacious garages, and huge tinted windows. They were pretty, but the whole thing felt sanitized—which made it a weird choice of neighborhood for a plague demon.

There was no movement visible from the houses, and no hint of the walking guard-demons from either side of the street. I gestured over to one of the houses with a huge row of shrubs near the garage.

"Go," I whispered.

The three of us ran, then crowded behind the bush.

"We need to split up," Telaney said in a hushed voice. "We'll get out of here quicker and attract less attention if we go it alone."

"I'll go south," Poodle said. "Telaney, you go north. Eden, you cut across the back of these lawns and head to the east. We'll all meet back here in thirty."

I hesitated, not really wanting them to risk getting caught without me nearby to provide some nonhuman backup. But I needed to trust that humans could hold their own in a fight, otherwise this was going to be a very short war with a very bad ending.

"Okay. If the crap hits the fan, then get the hell out of here," I told them. "Don't wait for the rest of us, just go."

"Got it."

The expression on Telaney's face let me know that she was absolutely not on board with that plan. But there was nothing I could do about that. We checked for any demon patrols, then took off, each of us on our separate routes.

I ran between two houses, hopping over a fence and crouching low. There was a large kidney-shaped pool in the backyard with a circular spa tub attached. The bricked patio had a comfy seating arrangement of three outdoor sofas and two chairs around a rectangular fire pit. A screen-enclosed area had a table, chairs, and a wrought-iron shelf. It was beautiful aside from all the blood.

The brick patio was blotched with thickened red. A long

streak led to the pool where a bloated body floated face-down. A man had been impaled on a lamp post in the center of the yard, and a head with long blonde hair covering its face was over by the sofa.

I darted across the lawn, but dove down behind the sofa when I heard a voice talking in an unfamiliar language.

The patio door slid open and two demons walked out, one a seven-foot-tall zombie-looking guy, and the other a goat-cobra-lion mix. GCL was the one talking, waving his hands as he spoke.

That bitch who took out Rouex is gonna pay. I don't know whose household she's with, but this is our territory and she's poaching.

I sucked in a breath, not knowing how I was understanding their weird language.

Did you hear what she did? the zombie guy asked. *He pushed out enough disease to kill half the city, and she sucked it all in. She turned it and Rouex into some damned flowers. I'm not fucking with that, I don't care what Itinder says.*

Crap. That was me. Rouex must have been the plague demon.

You gonna leave and join up with Desiree? GCL asked. *She's put the word out that she's looking to expand her household.*

Better her than end up dead in a patch of daisies or some shit. Zombie guy breathed out a rattle sound. *Something smells...off.*

Damn it. I flatted myself against the brick pavers, peeking around the side of the sofa. Were these guys like shifters? Could they scent me out like Bob, the were-dog, could?

GCL inhaled. *Smells like demon, like one of the Fallen, but not as much brimstone. Kind of like an angel, but not.*

Zombie-demon made a raspy sound that was probably meant to be a laugh. *Why would an angel ever come here? Maybe Itinder has a guest? He would love to join up with a Fallen. Butt kisser.*

If he's making alliances with a Fallen, then we should stay, GCL said.

Tomorrow night's the big night. We need to decide now if we want to get out before it all goes down.

Fuck it. Let's stay. I heard the swish of the sliding door, then a scream. *Dinner's ready. Let's get inside before he's dead.*

CHAPTER 27

I should have left. Whoever was in there was probably not in any condition to survive even if I managed to save them, and this whole thing was supposed to be an intel-gathering reconnaissance mission. If I went in there, I'd end up battling three or more demons, attracting the attention of any other demons in the community, and I'd be endangering not only myself, but Telaney and Poodle as well. I should have left, gone over the backyard fence, and kept heading east on my mission to find out where Itinder was holed up and how he'd structured his defenses.

Spoiler alert. I didn't leave.

Whoever was in there might have been one of my sisters, Bea, Bags, or another of my friends. He was someone's son, someone's husband, brother, friend. He didn't deserve to die this way.

No one deserved to die this way.

Creeping around the sofa, I ran for the patio door and slid it open. Another scream sounded from a nearby room, so I ran in that direction, bursting into the kitchen just as a demon was bending over a man duct-taped to the counter.

"Hey," I shouted.

All three demons turned toward me.

"Get the fuck out. This is our dinner," Zombie-demon said.

"Who the fuck are you?" GCL said.

"Eden Alvaro." I pulled out my pistol and shot the third demon in the head.

He rocked backward, smashing against the cabinets, but not dying. The other two demons jumped on me, one punching me in the stomach and the other blasting me with demon energy. I grabbed it and sent it back into the demon. It wasn't enough to kill him, but it did knock him back and singe his fur.

Putting three bullets into Zombie-demon, I turned and shot the other two. It didn't kill them, but it bought me enough time to dash forward, grab a knife from the knife block, and cut the guy loose from the counter.

He wasn't in the best of shape with bruises, cuts, and small burns all over his skin. One eye was swollen shut in a colorful mess of bruises, and his head was bleeding, but he still managed to roll off the counter and stagger upright.

"Run," I told him as I shot the demons once more.

He took off, and I kept shooting until the pistol clicked empty. There was another magazine in my pocket, but the three demons were on me before I could exchange it for the empty one.

"That was our dinner," I heard one roar as they all pummeled me. I hit them with my pistol, kicked, bit, and pulled fur, zapping all three with electricity—anything to keep their attention on me and away from the injured human who probably hadn't even made it to the fence yet. I hoped that our fight hadn't drawn any of the neighboring demons, or that poor human would quickly be right back where I found him.

I held my own and after five or so minutes, we were all slowing down. Ten minutes later, the four of us were bloodied, battered, and bruised, sprawled across the kitchen floor.

"Damn, you're a good brawler," Zombie-demon said to me. "I haven't had this much fun in a decade. It was worth losing our dinner."

"Agreed," wheezed Third-guy. "What was your name again? Garden of Eden, or something?"

"She said it was Eden Alcatraz." GCL snapped a broken leg back into place before turning to me. "You must be new in the household. Next time we'll share dinner with you."

"Thanks," I staggered to my feet, wiping my bloody nose on my sleeve. "Since dinner got away, I guess I better get going and warm up some ramen noodles."

Zombie-guy stood. "There's some of that in these cabinets. It any good?"

"Yeah," I told him. "Throw some extra stuff from the fridge in there and add hot sauce, and it's a decent meal."

They were all raiding the fridge and arguing over what to put in their ramen as I left by the patio door. Instead of vaulting the back fence, I used the gate and walked between two houses whose backyards adjoined the one I'd just left.

Heading east, I stuck to cutting through yards, trying to save time since the roads seemed to wind all over the place. It would be easy to get lost in this place with row after row of similar houses, everyone with a kidney-shaped pool in the backyard. The beatdown I'd taken made it difficult for me to walk, so there was no running or stealthy darting between shrubberies. At this point I didn't give a fuck if anyone saw me. I hurt. I was grumpy. And any demon who tried to mess with me would feel the wrath of my temper. A few demons were out and about, but no one even gave me a second glance. I'd even stumbled past the patrol, so focused on keeping one foot in front of the other that I hadn't seen them until too late.

They waved. They kept on going.

I kept cutting through backyards. At one point I tripped over a lawn sprinkler, setting the system off. By the time I made it out of the yard I was drenched in addition to bruised and bloody. The next yard I fell over a kid's toy and landed in the largest pile of dog shit I'd ever seen.

I was about to give up when I saw a gelatinous blob of a demon oozing down the sidewalk. At this point I was feeling like I really had nothing to lose, so I went up to him.

"How do I get to Itinder's place?" I asked. "These fucking houses all look the same."

The blob nodded, blinking a dozen eyes at once. *I hate this place,* his voice said inside my head. *Can't wait to go back to Hel. Go two blocks straight, then turn left and go another block, then right and five blocks. Can't miss it with all the bodies on the lawn.*

I wasn't sure what the correct protocol was for thanking demons, so I just grunted at him, then followed his directions. No one accosted me, and Blob was right, I did recognize Itinder's house as soon as I saw it. Evenly arranged dead bodies flanked the walkway to the porch. The railings and porch columns were garlanded with entrails. Heads swung in a line from the edge of the roof like they were Christmas lights. I was starting to feel a little better, so I opted not to risk suicide by demon, and avoided the front door, going around the side yard between Itinder's and the neighbor's house instead.

The guy had clearly never heard of privacy shades. Every window was a clear view into the house. It was absolutely not my style. White walls, white marble floors, white furniture. The wrought iron staircase leading to the upper floor was black, but everything else in the damned place was white —and splattered with bloodstains.

I wasn't sure what it said about me that I thought the bloodstains were an improvement.

Making a note of the house number and street name, I went a few blocks north, then tried to retrace my path. There hadn't been any guards around Itinder's house, and I hadn't noticed any demon presence there, so I assumed the guy and his first-string of demons were out.

This whole thing would make an attack much easier. The plague demon clearly thought the decimation of the surrounding neighborhoods and the minimal patrol inside the perimeter along with the guard at the gate would be enough to keep any attackers at bay. He'd probably figured his biggest threat would come from one of the other two demons who were busy consolidating their own holdings right now. I doubt he ever considered that humans might attack him here in his enclave.

And that's where we were about to prove him wrong.

It took me forever to get back to the fence and find the spot where we'd come in. Not that I expected Telaney and Poodle to be waiting for me at this point. There was no sign of them at the fence, although the crushed state of the bushes gave me hope that they'd safely returned and been able to scale the fence to the other side.

It took me a few tries to get over the fence. The thorny limbs scratched my face and snagged my clothes, and my body was not happy with the additional exertion. Swinging my legs over the top, I went to drop down, only to find I'd hooked my jeans on the top of the iron fence. I swung there for a few seconds, scrambling to get enough of a hold on the fence to pull myself up. Before I could manage that, my pants ripped and I fell, landing hard on the ground.

Telaney and Poodle were nowhere to be seen, so I pulled my phone out, hoping to call someone for a lift.

It was dead. Which was just the icing on the cake for what was gearing up to be the shittiest day ever.

I walked south through the dead zone, then through the bombed-out neighborhood. Once I was a few blocks past the wreckage, I turned east, hoping I could find a non-destroyed car to steal, or someone I could hitch a ride from.

I hurt. I was wet. I stank. My pants were ripped in an unfortunate location. Thankfully there was no one around to see the right butt cheek I was flashing. Ten blocks later I still hadn't found a working vehicle or seen another living being. I was about to break into one of the houses and sleep until I was healed, maybe finding clothing my size that had been left behind, when I heard the sound of a car coming my way.

Jumping into the street, I waved. Not that I expected anyone would want to give me a ride looking like I did right now, but a girl could dream.

Telaney's car turned down the block heading my way. I nearly wept with joy.

"Need a ride?" She asked as she pulled even with me.

"Fuck yes, I do."

I climbed in. Her eyes widened as she saw me, then her nose wrinkled.

"Jesus, Eden. What the hell happened to you."

I gave her the short version of the story, reclining the seat and leaning my head back.

"What about you and Poodle? Did she make it out okay?" I asked as Telaney drove.

"Yeah. When we were due to meet, we found some naked guy trying to climb the fence. Looked like he'd been beaten up pretty bad. We helped him out and to Poodle's car. She offered to give him a lift and put him up at her place until he found his people." Telaney glanced over at me. "And now I know why there was a naked guy running around a demon compound in hysterics."

"Glad he got out before someone else caught him," I said. "Did you two manage to find anything out while you were there?"

"They were all talking in some weird language, but I did find out that security is minimal. The patrols are bored to death and doing a half-hearted job. The dude at the guard shack is equally bored and unmotivated. Everyone seems confident that no one would mess with them, especially at their home base. Poodle said they all seemed to be spread out in different houses, and from what she could see, they were having a hard time telling one place from another. She saw a big fight between two demons because one evidently walked into the wrong house."

That was actually kind of funny.

"I heard one of them said there was something big going down tomorrow night," I told her. "We can't move on them until Bishop gets back with some weaponry and we can organize our forces, but I'm going to ask Blister to see if she can find out what they might be planning."

Telaney shot me a surprised look. "They were speaking English? Or Spanish?"

I felt my face heat up. "No. Sometimes I can understand them when they're talking demon, or whatever language it is. Most of the time it just sounds like gibberish but sometimes it all falls into place and I understand them."

"We should definitely try to figure out what's going down tomorrow night," Telaney agreed. "If we can get Juke and some others on board, we might be able to fight them off and defend whoever they're expecting to attack."

That was the plan.

CHAPTER 28

BISHOP

I pushed the cap down over my hair, eyeing my fatigues with the name "Henderson" emblazoned across the upper left side of the shirt. Raphael was "Smith" and Ahia was "Becker." Originally Ahia had been "Boobs," but she'd pitched a fit so Dar had changed it. I was pretty sure the demon would have changed it even if Ahia hadn't protested, since the idea was for us to be unremarkable and unnoticed.

"You trust this Dar?" I asked for what was probably the fifth time.

Ahia snorted. "No."

"I trust him to do anything for a babysitter," Raphael said. "And I trust him to act in his own self-interest."

It wasn't exactly reassuring, but I didn't have any other option. We needed these weapons and there was no way I was going back to LA empty-handed.

"Are we ready?" Ahia asked.

Raphael and I nodded. I patted my pocket where I'd stored the fake ID Dar had provided us with. This was a surprisingly human heist aside from some difficult angelic actions on my part. If it went off well, we were set to enact a near identical plan at Letterkenny this afternoon. With any luck, we'd be in and out and long gone before any of the theft had been noticed. I had more faith in that happening here, at McAlester, then at Letterkenney where there was a better than good chance we'd get snagged by some sort of magical alarm system.

Ahia got in the driver's seat of the Jeep. Raphael sat next to her and I hopped into the back. As she pulled up to the gate of the base, she stopped, smiling over at the MP.

He smiled back, then asked for our ID. I dug the plastic card out of my pocket, handing it over. So much for step one. We'd hoped he would wave us on as we were dressed like soldiers and driving a base Jeep that Dar had managed to swipe for us.

The MP glanced at our ID and handed it back. "Who are you all here to see?"

Crap. Ahia went to give the name of Dar's contact. It was our plan-B, and we hadn't wanted to involve him, but there seemed to be no other way to get on base.

"Incoming," the MP's partner announced nodding behind us.

I turned around to see a line of black, tinted-window automobiles approaching with a pair of police on motorcycles leading and following.

"Damn." The MP frowned, a muscle in his jaw clenching. "Were we expecting a VIP visit?"

His buddy snorted. "Wouldn't be the first time some general forgot to let the Commander know. I'll get on the phone. You stall them."

The MP waved us on. "Y'all go on through. Can't have the big wigs waiting in line at the gate."

Plan A was back on track. We drove past the gate, circling around to the motor pool, and parking the Jeep. We got out, separated, then waited until Ahia came out of the motor pool building. When no one was nearby to see us, she and I jumped into a box truck. Ahia inserted the keys she'd lifted, then started it up.

"Got the paperwork?" She asked Raphael, who was to remain behind as backup in case everything went sideways.

Raphael slid a folder out from under his shirt and handed it to her. Ahia put the truck in gear and we drove through the base, down roads we'd memorized from Dar's map to the warehouse. Two guards stood outside, rifles in hand.

Ahia hopped down, trotting up to them with the folder. "Contracts sent us down here. Expedited shipment to the western border."

One guard slung his rifle over his shoulder, taking the folder. "Fucking demons. We've never had this many people asking for asylum before. It's insane."

"They used to be citizens," the other guard said. "I hate that we're treating them like illegals. On day they're part of the US, the next they're huddled in some building waiting for an immigration hearing just to leave the coast."

The first guard shrugged. "I don't make the rules. I just do what I'm told." He finished reading the contents of the folder and handed it back to Ahia. "Only one of you can go in the building, and they gotta be escorted."

Ahia rolled her eyes. "I know. I know. Not my first rodeo with this stuff." She turned to the truck. "Henderson. You go in and get the boxes."

I hopped out of the truck. The second guard unlocked and opened the door to the warehouse, ushering me in.

"A46592H are down here on the left," he told me, waiting for the door to close and the lock to engage before falling in beside me.

We walked in silence for a few seconds.

"She native?" the guy asked, nodding toward the entrance. "Or Asian?"

I grunted. "Hell if I know."

"Becker doesn't sound Asian," he continued. "Maybe her mom's Chinese and her dad's Mexican. She's got kind of a Latina look about her.

"I think she's got a boyfriend," I cautioned him. Raphael would probably put the guy ten feet under if he tried anything with Ahia.

"Boyfriend an officer?" the guy asked, eyeing the door again.

"No idea. She's expecting a ring for Christmas, so you might be out of luck."

He shrugged. "It's not too late until they walk down the aisle. Sometimes there's a chance even after that. She's cute. I like the curvy ones."

I grunted, hoping that he took the hint and just shut the hell up.

"Really nice tits. I'll bet that black hair of hers goes down to her fine ass as well.."

This guy would be dead and the mission blown if Raphael had been the one in the warehouse instead of me. Although the archangel didn't strike me as the insanely jealous type, this guy was being a dick.

It was hard to love an Angel of Chaos if you were at all possessive. I'd learned long ago to trust, and to be flexible about what my idea of faithful was when it came to relationships.

"Here are the crates," the guy said, pointing to a stack of boxes on a pallet with a bright blue A46592H stamped on the side.

I grabbed two boxes, putting one under each arm. The guard looked over toward the door, confident that I couldn't manage to smuggle more boxes out under my shirt. That's when I did what no one in Aaru had ever known I could do. I separated myself into two aspects. One of me hid behind the crates, while the other adjusted the boxes and headed toward the door.

I'd concealed a lot of my abilities when I was in Aaru, oddly reluctant to let anyone know the unusual powers a supposed middle-level angel had. I liked being invisible. I liked being free to do my own thing without attracting undue attention. But all the rules were being broken since I'd met Eden. For the first time in my life, I truly loved. And I'd do anything, even reveal my abilities to two angels and a demon I didn't know, to help her.

With the boxes loaded in the truck, Ahia left. We were to pick up Raphael, leave through the gate with the fake IDs and the fake contract for the weapons. Then once Ahia had driven a few hours, Raphael would transport them and the boxes to a warehouse in LA while my one aspect waited here.

I remained behind the crates, hearing the locks slide free on the door once more. Voices filled the warehouse—commanding, ego-filled voices, and obsequious, fawning voices.

"McAlester supplies magical weaponry and ammunition to our joint military forces all over the world," a voice boomed. "This facility is constantly guarded, and any fulfillment is carefully monitored."

"Very impressive, Senator," Dar replied. "My, what a lot of weaponry and ammo! I doubt we'd need such a military response in Chicago, but it's reassuring to know if we're ever under attack, that such munitions would be readily available."

They walked around. I ducked between two crates, but Dar skillfully led the Senator and their security away from where I was hidden, wanting to see some boxes in another aisle. I had to give the demon credit. He was oily and the perfect politician.

And the perfect thief.

After a ridiculous amount of time with interminable, flattering small talk, they finally left, the lock snicking closed behind the last security guy.

There. The guards had seen us leave with only two boxes. They'd been back in here after and seen a warehouse still full of stock during a VIP tour. I waited for another hour, until the shift change when a guard from each shift did another inspection of the warehouse. Then when the door closed, I transported the whole lot, teleporting it to the warehouse in LA where I met Ahia and Raphael.

Stepping outside the warehouse, I waved Bob over. "You all got this?"

He scowled. "I find things. I don't guard things."

"I know," I told him. "But if you like calling LA your home, you and your friends will make sure this place is locked down tight and secure."

He nodded. "Fine. But only for you, boss."

I smiled. "Thanks, Bob."

I turned and headed back inside. There weren't many I trusted, but Bob was a member of that tight circle. We'd been together for even longer than HB and I. Thousands of years, and three continents.

"Ready for round two?" Raphael asked?

I nodded. And we teleported to Pennsylvania, to meet up with Dar and do this all over again at Letterkenny.

'd charged my phone in Telaney's car, showered and changed clothes back at Bea's, then spent the rest of the evening texting. Turns out that Blister wasn't the only one gathering intel. Juke let it slip that they had a whole roster of confidential informants now telling them what the various demon groups had planned. By the next morning, both of my sources had agreed that the word on the street was a huge attack was planned on Reseda.

I spent the whole morning coordinating a defense. Juke and the police were working to evacuate the city while I tried to gather as many people as possible to fight these guys off. Piers immediately asked me if I had the anti-magic guns yet. When I said no he hung up on me. Sebastian was sympathetic, but didn't want to risk his guys trying to hold an evacuated town with no weaponry that would give them at least a level playing field. In the end, it was just my team and the police. My team minus Addy, that is. I wanted her to stay put and continue to work with Genevieve.

Bea offered me her car, so I took that to Suerte to pick up Jayla, thinking that would be a more enjoyable ride than on the back of my bike. She still reeked of garbage, but her braids were neat and her face, hands, and clothing clean. She chatted excitedly during our drive, then fell silent as we turned off the freeway. Her hands were a white-knuckled knot on her lap, and she bit her lip. When we turned down the road and went through the wards, she yelped.

Was she sensitive to magic? Could she have some demon in her ancestry? None of the humans who lived here had ever expressed discomfort when passing through the wards.

"You felt that?" I asked her. "I've gotten used to it, but it hurts me too."

She shrugged, not replying. As we pulled into Bea's driveway, her anxiety was palpable. Then the front door flew open and Nevarra and Sadie raced for the car. As Jayla got out, they greeted her enthusiastically, peppering her with questions about the ride here, as well as which of the gifts she'd liked best.

"The carpet was great," she said, "and I really liked the posters."

"That was my idea." Nevarra grinned.

"I brought the Pokémon cards with me," Jayla said, digging into her pocket. "I used to play on the app before my phone got stolen, but I really want to learn to play the card version."

Sadie bounced. "Totally! I love Pokémon. I'll loan Nevarra some of my card decks so she can play with us too."

"That sucks about your phone being stolen," Nevarra told her. "Maybe Eden can find one for you. She's a Vulture, you know. If there's a fight and people die, she's licensed to take their stuff. That's how Sadie and I got our phones."

It had cost me money to have someone wipe them and move the numbers to a pay-as-you-go plan once the dead-guy's contract had expired, but I hadn't told them, or Bea, that.

Jayla followed the girls inside, far more relaxed than she'd been when we arrived. I went over to Genevieve's house to see her and Addy, figuring I'd give the girls some time alone. When I came back, they were upstairs playing Pokémon and munching through a bowl of Doritos—a rare treat that Bea had managed to find at one of the few remaining convenience stores.

I helped get lunch together, then made myself scarce while they all ate, grabbing an egg salad sandwich and heading across the street to the transfer station that was now serving as the town's dump. As I walked past piles of garbage and demolition debris, I heard a tiny "meow." A grey kitten with neon-green eyes crawled out from under a box, shaking his fur and running toward me.

"Mittens!"

I hadn't been home in days, and was worried that the cat had thought I'd abandoned him. Scooping the furry guy up in my arms, I cuddled him as he purred.

"Are you keeping our house safe?" I asked.

The kitten hissed, extending claws three times as long as his tiny paws.

"Of course you are, you scary, lethal, gorgeous boy, you," I praised him. "I'm sorry I haven't been home. While you're defending our house, I've needed to stay here, to protect my family."

He let out a plaintive yowl at the last word. I rubbed my face on the top of his head, wondering if Mittens had family. Were there other hellkitties in Hel? Littermates he missed? Feline friends? I suddenly felt sad for the kitten, all alone in this world.

"I'll be your family," I told him. "Bea and the girls? They're human, and they're not biologically related to me, but sometimes family are the ones you choose. I've got a big family I chose, and you're a part of it. I hope you consider me part of your family as well."

He purred, butting his head up against my cheek, and licking my hand with his sand-papery tongue. Then suddenly he was gone. Vanished. With no warning whatsoever.

Cats. There was really no understanding them sometimes.

I wandered around the rest of the afternoon, helping neighbors with repairs and their gardens. At four o'clock, I headed back to Bea's to return a very reluctant Jayla to Suerte. The three girls hugged, Nevarra and Sadie promising to have Jayla over again soon. In a surprising move, Jayla returned the gesture, telling the girls she would like them to come to Suerte and see her little home as well.

It was a touching display of trust from a girl who probably hadn't had reason to trust anyone in a long, long time. I'd make sure future visits happened on both sides, and I was sure HB would be happy to provide lunch for the girls when Jayla was playing host.

Jayla smiled the entire ride back to Suerte, a jewelry box on her lap. Every now and then she'd peek inside the box, running her fingers through buttons, hair-ties, necklaces, and keychains.

While she skipped around the side of the building to her shed, I popped inside, weaving through the crowd of shifters toward the bar. There were cots and sleeping bags along the walls. Children sat at tables, playing board games and doing puzzles. Adults were in small groups, whispering in hushed tones.

HB slid an iced tea over to me when I sat on a barstool. "Got some folks who want to help out tonight." She nodded toward one of the groups of shifters. "They want action. We might not be fighting to get their territory back, but I told them once we take care of this plague demon, the warmonger is next on our list."

"I appreciate it." I glanced at the children. "Bishop isn't back yet. This might be a really rough battle. I'd hate for any of these kids to end up orphans."

"There are things worth dying for," HB informed me. "Every one of these shifters knows that if they go down in battle, we will take care of their children. And when we get their territory back, their children will be the ones to carry on their traditions, to cherish their memories. Life is short. Make it count."

Her words hit home. I'd been trying to make my life count. I'd been risking my life to make a better world for others. I'd somehow forgotten that the humans and shifters here in New Hell were willing to do the same.

* * *

MY GROUP and several of the police team leads in addition to Juke met at three in the afternoon in Reseda. HB and Isha had managed to round up thirty shifters who'd volunteered to fight. Mathias and Isaac were here with three other mages. Telaney and Poodle had brought two fellow Vultures with them. Juke had fifty officers, and Blister had completely surprised me by arriving with four other Low demons.

Isaac handed out bags of his lemon candies for the fighters, saying that he and Mathias had been up all night tweaking the formula. I hoped they were effective, because they tasted even worse than the previous version. I noticed that Isaac had leather bands around each wrist that were covered in silver runes, and an amulet around his neck. He might be fighting with conventional human weapons, but Mathias had made sure he was going into this battle with magical protections.

"We've done all we can to evacuate the neighborhood," Juke told us. "According to our less-than-perfect estimation, about eight thousand people still live here. They're fairly spread out, and we didn't have a lot of time, but we're hoping only a few hundred have chosen to remain."

"From what we've heard they're planning on coming down Reseda Boulevard," Blister said. "It's a little over six miles, and the demons who can't teleport were bitching about walking that far, so they got a bus."

I stared at her. "A bus? Seriously? Itinder's army is going to show up in a *bus*?"

"Are all two thousand of them in the bus?" Telaney asked. "Because that's totally going on TikTok. I might die tonight, but that's gonna be a viral video."

Blister scowled at her. "No, they're not trying to cram two thousand demons in a bus. The ones who can teleport are bringing the others. It's just the Lows they're making take the bus."

More proof that it sucked to be a Low demon.

"I wonder how many of Itinder's army might be ready to bail on him?" I asked. "I'm thinking we should let any obvious deserters go."

Telaney nodded. "No sense in wasting bullets on them."

"I've got informants who are going to text me when they're approaching and give me an update if they've changed their plans in any way. We're going for the element of surprise here, so take cover anywhere you can. They'll expect humans to be here, but hopefully they won't expect us to be prepared and ready to fight back." Juke's phone beeped and she glanced down at it. "Five minutes out. Let's get everyone in place."

We ran for our groups, hiding behind houses, bushes, and cars. The few police with anti-magic guns were up front, partnered with two other shooters. My team was behind them, prepared to take out anyone who broke through the line. The mages were at the rear, with a SWAT team of ten to assist them.

Five minutes felt like forever. Finally I saw the demons, a giant mob of monsters swarming down the street. Those at the edges darted around parked vehicles, some of them running into houses, then out again as they found them empty. I worried that the miles of vacant houses might tip them off, but so many people had fled the area that it probably wasn't all that suspicious.

The police waited until the demons were practically on top of them before dashing into the open and firing. With amazing accuracy, they splatted thirty demons, their partners killing them before the mob realized what was happening.

The demons reacted quickly, grabbing the dead and using them as shields against the anti-magic bullets. Another of Juke's colleagues jumped into action. These cops were outfitted in tactical gear with huge riot shields. Each followed by an anti-magic and two other shooters, they slammed into the line, knocking the dead demon shields aside so the anti-magic guns could reach their target. Once more, the shooters did their job, killing every blue-splatted demon.

Our success was short-lived. The demons began hitting the police with bolts of energy. Others surged over their fallen and mowed down the cops before they could get out of the way, stomping on them and ripping them with sharp claws. I ran forward, redirecting as much energy into me as I could. The demons kept coming, and I feared for the police they'd just plowed over.

HB, Telaney, Blister, and Isha ran to meet the advancing demons with me. A second line of cops stepped out behind us, shooting any demon they could with anti-magic weaponry. My team took out the disabled demons, while I continued to absorb any energy attacks, redirecting the some into other demons. The streets were littered with bodies, the dead demons outnumbering the deceased humans three to one. But there were too many of them, and as well-armed as Juke's forces were, they had a limited supply of anti-magic guns. Slowly the demons began to push us back down the street. Then I heard a shout that meant the police were out of anti-magic ammo. They fell back, and the mages stepped up.

I waved for my team to stand by, but they ignored me, continuing to fight demons that hadn't been disabled. Trying to make my way closer to them, I was knocked aside by a lizard-lion, and found myself scrambling to get up as demons ripped through my clothes and pummeled me with their energy attacks. I started blasting them back with what I'd stored inside me, giving me enough space to get upright.

HB, Isha, and Telaney were nowhere to be seen. Blister was back with the mages who were waving wands and reading from scrolls. Bursts of light went off like mini bombs in the middle of the demon army. The mob began to thin out as demons vaporized, but others quickly took their place.

There were too many. This was a losing battle, but I hoped we'd make enough of an impact to cause significant desertion and make Itinder think twice about this war.

Plowing into the mass of demons, I absorbed, redirected, and shot, turning as many demons as I could into sand. The whole time, I kept my eyes open for Isha, Telaney, and HB, worried sick that they might be mortally injured, or even dead. Fear for them made me angry, and I recklessly blasted demons left and right, screaming and cursing like a berserker.

"Garden of Eden!" The zombie-demon from Porter Ranch shrieked "I pledge to your household. I swear to serve you and yours as long as you spare my life."

The only reason I spared his life was because he'd dropped to his knees in front of me, and my energy blast went over his head, taking out the two demons behind him.

"Accepted," I shouted. "Now get up and help me."

The zombie-demon didn't hesitate. Jumping to his gray, emaciated feet, he stood at my back, blasting down his former colleagues. Demons poured around us, and suddenly there were no more bursts of light. The mages were tapped out.

I hoped they and the remaining police had managed to retreat to safety. I hoped my team was alive and safe as well. I kept fighting, mainly because there was no clear way to retreat out of this swarm of demons. It was tiring, and the demons were realizing that I was using their own energy attacks against them. They began to switch to a physical assault. Between zombie-demon and myself, we managed to keep killing any that came near, but I knew it was only a matter of time until I ran out of energy reserves. And as scrappy as I was in a physical fight, I was no match for the superior strength, sharp teeth and claws of these opponents.

I sent a blast at a demon who was running toward me. It sputtered, knocking him down but not killing him. I braced myself, ready to go down fighting, when an explosion happened thirty feet away, throwing demons through the air like confetti.

There was a second blast. And a third. That's when I realized that whoever it was launching grenades, they were clearing an exit path for me.

"Go," I shouted at zombie-demon.

He tilted his head. "Run? Isn't that cowardly?"

"Surviving is never cowardly. Now, go," I told him.

We headed down the path, shooting, blasting, and punching any demons in our way. Grenades continued to go off, not always leading us in a straight line. I trusted whoever it was, because I really had no other option at this point. Zombie-demon and I weaved down streets, encountering fewer and fewer demons. Finally we were in the clear. I slapped zombie-demon on the shoulder, and pointed down a side street I recognized. We ran, me leading us to my bike.

And there, standing next to my motorcycle with three other Lows, was Blister. She still had two grenades strapped to a bandolier, cluing me in that she and her pals had been the ones who'd helped us get to safety.

I nearly hugged her. The only thing that held me back was the knowledge that Blister really hated any sign of affection, and would probably doubly hate it in front of her friends.

"Have you seen Telaney? HB? Isha?" I asked her.

She grinned. "Yep. We managed to get them out as well. The shifters looked pretty battered, but nothing they can't heal. Telaney's limping and covered with blood, but she said she'll be okay once she gets a bath and a beer."

I slumped with relief. "Did you see Juke?"

She shook her head, her face grim. "The mages got out okay, but the police took heavy losses. We saw some of them retreating, but none of us noticed Juke among them."

Feeling sick I pulled out my phone and texted Juke first, sending the others e-mails afterward. When I was done, I remembered the zombie-demon standing by my side.

"What's your name?" I asked him.

He bowed. "Reginald."

Reginald? I'd expected something tough like Smasher or Shredder, not Reginald.

"Blister, can you take Reginald with you, and give him the 101 orientation? He's a new member of our household," I told the Low.

"She's a *Low*," Reginald squeaked.

I frowned at him. "Blister is a valuable member of my

household. You should treat her with the same respect you would me."

I didn't think that meant much, but Blister's eyes widened.

"Yes, Mistress," Reginald replied, his head bowed.

I winced. "Call me Eden."

"Yes, Garden of Eden." He bowed again and followed Blister and her friends as they walked down the street toward her car. It would be a tough fit in the tiny vehicle, but being smashed in with a bunch of Lows would give Reginald a good idea of what being in my household would entail.

My phone beeped, everyone checking in except Juke.

I got on my bike and headed back to Bea's, hoping that she was alive and safe, and that she'd reply soon.

CHAPTER 30

I turned the corner to Bea's street and panicked. Blackened buildings and burned foliage greeted me. As I passed through the area where the wards had been, I noticed they were down. Passing by the burned buildings, I saw the charred husks of bodies littering the streets and the lawns. I speeded up, then slid sideways into a stop as I saw Kellen sitting a few houses down from Bea's

In my rush to get things organized for the attack on Reseda, I'd completely forgotten about Kellen. In my defense, I'd just met the guy this week, and hadn't spoken to him since I'd dropped him off from Suerte. Still, I felt bad that I'd left him out of the plan. We could have used him.

But…why was he here?

Kellen stood, walking up to me.

"What happened here?" I asked him as I scanned the other houses. Outside of the ones at the edge of the neighborhood, the others seemed to be undamaged. But that didn't mean the people inside were still alive. Thinking of the plague demon, I pushed down another wave of panic.

"I was at home when I had this weird, urgent feeling. It

was like something psychic. I got Mosi and Lucas into the car and we rushed here. I've never even been here before. I had no idea what was going on, but when we arrived, we saw a couple dozen demons trying to batter their way through some magical wards. Mosi and Lucus went through the wards to assist the humans on the other side, but it hurt when I tried to get through, so I stayed outside and fought the demons. I must have died three or four times, but I kept healing and fighting. It was crazy."

Demons had attacked my neighborhood and I hadn't even known. Where had that sixth sense gone that had let me teleport here in the middle of the night?

"Is everyone okay?" I asked Kellen.

He shook his head. "A lot of people died. I fought off as many demons as I could, but the last time I died, I was out for a while. When I came back to life, the demons were gone, the wards were down, and those houses were burned. Mosi and Lucas are okay. They're going house-to-house to help the injured people."

My family. Kellen had never met them, so he wouldn't know if they were hurt or even alive.

I left my bike and ran to Bea's house, pausing when I saw Addy sitting on the front step. She had a velvet bag clutched in one hand, and was rubbing her forehead with another. Bloodstains led from her nose down to her chin, and she had bruises under each eye.

"Are Bea and the girls okay?" I blurted out, feeling a little guilty that I hadn't led with "are *you* okay?"

She nodded, her eyes welling with tears. "Genevieve is dead. We fought them as long as we could. Her wards were amazing. The woman was so talented. But at the end they didn't hold, and she'd given too much of herself trying to save us. The wards fell, and she dropped. I couldn't revive her. She's gone. The only mage friend I have, and she's gone."

I dropped down and held Addy as she cried, feeling her grief as if it were my own. The woman was so alone in this world, and there was nothing I could do to help her. We couldn't truly be friends, not with our strange bond. She and Telaney had a love-hate thing going on. Hopefully she'd be able to make mage-friends through Mathias and find her place, because Addy really needed to belong somewhere.

Finally she lifted her head and wiped her eyes, pulling away from me. "How did everything go with you all?"

"We killed a lot of demons but had to eventually bail. There were just too many of them," I told her. "Telaney, HB, and Isha are injured but they'll be okay. I haven't heard from Juke yet."

"I'm so sorry, Eden." Addy gave me a watery smile. "I know she's a good friend of yours. You must be really worried."

I was worried. But Juke was tough, and I still had hope that she would text me soon saying she was okay.

"When the wards fell, that werewolf family came out to assist, along with the humans who live here," Addy said. "We all fought, but it was a losing battle. When it became clear that we weren't going to make it, one of the neighbors ran to get the children together and to safety. We were all going to hold the demons for as long as we could so they could get away. Ten humans died. Two of the werewolves died."

Her voice hitched and I rubbed her shoulder. "I can't thank you enough for what you've done here. Fighting to protect people you don't even know? My family? I'm really in your debt, Addy."

She cleared her throat, then took a deep breath. "We were all going to die. I knew we were all going to die. I just wanted to make sure the children made it first. So I fought, figuring I'd end up burning through my magical energy and my life force just like Genevieve. I was ready to die fighting, and then the dragon appeared."

"What? *What?*" I stared at her, open-mouthed.

"I know." Addy laughed. "I couldn't believe it either. I didn't even see the thing coming. Out of nowhere there's some giant lizard with wings, kicking ass and taking names."

"A dragon," I repeated, still not understanding why the hell the dragon had shown up here, in my neighborhood.

Addy nodded. "It burned up all the demons. *All* of them. Fried them to a crispy. Dead, dead, dead. Unfortunately it torched a few of the houses as well, but I'm thinking that's an acceptable price to pay. Oh, and it somehow incinerated the disease one of the plague demons had launched. Burned it all up, then flew off."

I was absolutely shocked. "Did it eat anyone?"

"Nope. Didn't kill any of the humans either even though everyone was running and screaming."

What the fuck?

I might be able to believe that the dragon downtown had somehow gotten my scent and traced me to my neighborhood, even though I hadn't stolen anything of his and had left right after I'd seen him in that mall. But he'd shown up and defended my little neighborhood in the Valley against some attacking demons. And left. Without eating anyone, even the charred demons.

I'd seen that dragon for all of three seconds, but he hadn't struck me as the altruistic type. I'd thought dragons viewed humans as well as demons as enemies or a convenient snack. None of this made any sense at all.

Addy laughed again. "I don't get it either. But I'm happy the thing showed up. If not, we would have all died. Maybe even the kids. That dragon saved us all."

"You, Genevieve, and the others saved the neighborhood

as well," I reminded her. "Did you get a chance to meet Kellen? The werewolf sitting down the street there?"

"The guy with the white eyes and scarred ears?" Addy smiled sadly. "I felt him the moment he arrived. He's one of us, isn't he? A minion?"

I winced. "Yes. He was dying and begged me. He willingly signed up for this. Otherwise I never would have done it again."

She shrugged "It's okay. The guy is one hell of a fighter. And those friends he brought really helped as well. The one guy, Lucas, knows some first aid, so he and the bear shifter are taking care of the injured."

"I'm glad they were able to help," I told her.

"Go in and see your family" Addy tilted her head toward the front door. "I'll stay out here with Kellen in case there are any more attacks."

I thanked her, climbed the steps, and went inside. Hearing Bea and the girls talking, I went into the kitchen. Bea and Nevarra seemed unhurt. Sadie was washing off what looked like road rash on her palms and knees.

"Everyone okay?" I asked, thinking that Sadie might have fallen when everyone was trying to get the kids out. She still limped a bit from when she'd been shot, and sometimes took a bad step.

"We're all fine," Bea said. "Sadie just got a little scraped up."

"I almost died," the girl announced with far more excitement than I thought suitable.

"It was a close call," Nevarra added. "The wards fell, and everyone was panicked. Bea and Mr. Lee were trying to get all the kids to his SUV to get out when a really fast demon tried to grab Sadie."

Sadie dabbed at her skinned knees. "I spun around, so he

didn't grab me, but he got in front of me and tried to grab me again. That's when the dragon came and saved me."

"I about wet my pants when that thing landed in the street," Bea said. "I had visions of it gobbling up Sadie and flying off, but instead it pushed her aside with one of its wings and burned up the demon that was trying to get her."

"Then the dragon burned all the demons," Nevarra said. "They were running and screaming and trying to get away, but it got them all."

"When the dragon pushed me aside, I fell and scraped myself up," Sadie said. "Then I just laid there 'cause I was surprised and excited."

Of course she was excited.

"I thought dragons ate humans." And ate demons. And didn't swoop in to save the day.

"They do," Sadie said. "Humans. Demons. Cows. Pretty much anything. They're omnivores, but they prefer a meat-heavy diet. And they eat a lot because they're so big."

Maybe he was on his way back from dining on a whole herd of cows and wasn't hungry, but couldn't resist stopping in to incinerate some demons? They were supposed to be highly intelligent, so maybe he had a grudge against this particular group of Itinder's and decided to indulge in a little post dinner revenge.

"I'm not sure if I should go downtown and thank that dragon or not," I said. "He did save you all, but that might not have been his intention."

"Oh, it was definitely her intention," Sadie told me. "And this wasn't the downtown dragon. You said that one was orange. This one was blue. A really pretty, shiny blue."

A second dragon in LA? This one blue? Great. As if demons weren't enough of a problem.

"Glad as I am that we're okay, not everyone in the neighborhood fared as well," Bea said sadly.

"Addy said ten people died, but we don't know who yet," Nevarra added. "Javier lost one of his older brothers and an aunt, and his father was pretty badly hurt. I was getting ready to go over and see if I can help.

Bea got up. "And I should go check on the neighbors. I'm sure there are plenty of people who are injured, or have lost family."

They left while I got a glass of water for Sadie and me, sitting at the table opposite her. I was glad the attack had occupied everyone's mind and they hadn't asked how my evening had gone. I didn't really want to talk about it and relive the fear I'd felt when I'd lost sight of my friends, the realization that I might not make it out alive, and the horror of seeing so many of Juke's colleagues die.

And Juke… Was she okay? Was she lying dead on that street in Reseda with the other police? Was she lying injured under a car?

Once Bea and Nevarra were back I should go back to see if I could find her…or her body.

"Eden?" Sadie asked.

I smiled at her. "Yes, Peanut?"

She bit her lip. "I know a secret. And I'm not supposed to tell anyone, but I think I should tell you."

"I can't promise to keep it to myself if I think someone might be in danger," I warned her.

"It's about Jayla," she said. "She's scared, and she told me a secret, and I promised not to tell anyone. But after tonight…I think I should let you know what she said."

"What is it?" I asked, worried that Jayla was in some sort of trouble. If there was an abusive family member after her, then I could think of no safer place for the girl to be than at Suerte. HB had a soft spot for kids. She and the other shifters there would make short work of anyone who showed up trying to hurt Jayla.

"She and I were in my room going through my Pokémon cards, and she saw the dragon book you gave me. She asked me about it, and I told her about the one you'd seen downtown, and how I was trying to learn everything I could about them. She said she had a secret, and that the dragon downtown would kill her if he knew, so I couldn't tell anyone."

I leaned forward, my arms on the table as I waited for Sadie to continue.

She took a deep breath and slowly let it out. "Jayla said she is a Sarkan. They're a type of dragon that evolved differently. They were hunted by the other dragons, so they fled eons ago through interdimensional portals. Some came here and Jayla is one of their descendants. But now other dragons are here too, and they'll kill her if they find her."

This all seemed so unbelievable, but then again, two years ago I'd thought angels and demons were the stuff of legends.

"Where is her family?" I asked Sadie. "Do they live in communities or individually? Does she have parents somewhere looking for her?"

Sadie lifted one shoulder. "I don't know. She didn't tell me about any family. I feel kinda bad because I didn't believe her at first. I was nice, and pretended to believe her, but I really didn't. Sometimes kids lie when they feel bad about themselves, and I didn't want to lose Jayla as a friend. I like her."

"What made you decide to believe her?" I asked.

"When the dragon came and saved us, I thought maybe it was Jayla," Sadie said. "I'm still not sure I believe her, but it was weird that dragon showing up right when we were all about to get killed and burning up all the demons. Plus, how would she know about Sarkan? I'd never heard of them before I started reading that book. I don't think that's the sort of thing a teenager would just randomly know."

It might be a coincidence. Jayla could have lied, an insecure girl who wanted to make herself seem special to new friends. Maybe she'd heard about the term in a book, or was really interested in dragons the way some kids loved dinosaurs. She might just be a normal human girl who'd runaway from a bad situation and found herself on the streets.

But just in case, I should probably pay a visit to Jayla and see if what she'd claimed could possibly be true.

CHAPTER 31

I ended up walking up and down the street all night since I couldn't sleep. Kellen and his friends stayed to keep watch, drinking coffee that neighbors brought out to them. Addy came out several times to examine the perimeter where the wards had once been, carrying Genevieve's spell books and referring to them often.

As the sky lightened with the pending sunrise, I left a note for Bea and the girls, then walked my bike down a few blocks before starting it up so I wouldn't wake any neighbors who managed to actually get some sleep.

The sun was just cresting the horizon when I pulled into Reseda. The place was eerily silent. The street where we'd fought was littered with bodies, ash, and sand. I parked and walked through the battlefield.

It was horrifying. Most of the human dead had been wearing police uniforms. They were blackened, disemboweled, beheaded. Quite a few were covered with blisters and black-veined flesh from a plague demon's disease. I'd been searching for Juke, but so many of the bodies were unrecognizable that I left still not sure if she was among the living, or one of these blackened corpses.

Heading back to my bike, I texted her again, kicking myself for not having gotten an alternate contact. Did she have family? A close friend on the force that would know if she was okay? And what did it say about me as a friend that I didn't even know these things? It was true that Juke and I had always had a more business relationship, but I should at least know if she had living parents, siblings, or a significant other.

Leaving Reseda behind, I drove to Suerte, parked, and walked around the building to Jayla's shed. A muffled noise that sounded like crying came from the building, abruptly stopping as I knocked on the plywood door.

When that door opened I saw that Jayla had not only been crying, she'd been packing.

"You're leaving? What happened? Are you okay?" This was not what I'd expected at all. Gone was that excited chatty teen who'd I'd driven yesterday.

"I have to go." She sniffed, wiping her nose on her sleeve. "It's not safe here. I…did something, and it's not safe."

I was silent a few seconds, trying to figure out what to say that wouldn't let her know Sadie had betrayed her confidence.

"Where will you go? Do you have a place to stay?"

She shrugged then shook her head. "North maybe? I'll have to travel far to make sure I'm safe."

I walked by her, sat on the end of her inflated mattress and patted for Jayla to sit beside me. "Who's after you? Is there anything I can do to keep you safe?"

She dropped to the mattress and put her head in her hands. "It's a bad…man. He killed my family. He thinks I'm dead, but I did something and now he might know I'm alive.

I'm not sure if he followed me to LA, or if his being here in a fluke, but I can't risk staying."

Oh, God. I resisted the urge to hug the girl, not sure if she'd welcome that or not. Instead I patted her shoulder, leaving my hand there in a hopefully comforting gesture.

"You know I'll protect you. HB will protect you. There's a bar full of shifters right now who'll protect you. Sometimes you need to stop running, accept help from friends who care about you, and make a stand."

Her laugh was a watery sound. "He'll kill you all. Leaving won't just protect me, it will protect you all too. I don't want Nevarra and Sadie to get hurt. Or your mom. She reminds me of my mom, and I'd feel bad if he killed you all just to get to me."

"Why does he want to kill you so badly?" I rubbed her shoulder.

She sighed, dropping her hands and looking up at me. "Because I'm Sarkan. Because of who my parents were. He sees our very existence as a threat, and his people feel we've betrayed our heritage and our ancestors."

I narrowed my eyes. "Won't be the first time I've beat the shit out of some racist dick. I'm not sure what country Sarkans come from, but you're just as much a citizen of LA as I am. This is your home, and no homicidal Nazi dude is gonna force you to flee your home."

Her shoulders straitened a little at that. "He'll kill you."

"He can try. I'm proving to be rather difficult to kill." I stood and held my hand out to her. "I'm a demon—maybe an angel. I have human friends, shifter friends, demon friends, mage friends, and an angel boyfriend. We're tougher than you think. Especially Nevarra. Did she tell you she was kidnapped? That she fucking killed the bastard who hurt her? Whoever this guy is, he does *not* want to cross Nevarra." She let me pull her up. "I think it's time we talk to HB. And it's time you let us know everything about the Sarkan and this guy who's after you. We'll protect you, but we can't do that unless we know exactly what we're up against."

For a second she pulled against my hand, glancing over at her half-packed bags as if she was deciding whether to leave, or trust a bunch of people she'd just met and stay. For a few seconds I didn't know what she'd do, then she smiled up at me, let go of my hand and walked toward the door of the shed.

"Okay. But I'll need to talk to her out in the parking lot, because there's too many people in the bar right now, and I might not fit."

I texted HB, telling her to meet us outside in the lot and followed Jayla, half afraid the girl would vanish if I lost sight of her. We waited by my bike until the cougar shifter came out the front door, wiping her hands on a bar towel. She was limping, with colorful bruises all over her face. It was a relief, because even though she'd texted me that she was fine after last night's battle, I hadn't been sure if she'd been lying or not.

"What's up." She smiled at Jayla. "We're doing steak and eggs for breakfast if you want to join us. If not, I'll bring a plate out to you."

"I need to tell you something," Jayla blurted.

When she was done with her story about the man who'd killed her family and that she was Sarkan, HB let out a low growl. "We'll protect you. I don't care how many guns the guy has, he's not getting past us. You're safe here."

"He killed my parents," Jayla insisted. "They were totally badass and he killed them. Demons and shifters are no threat to him. I don't want you all to die defending me."

"Then tell us what we're up against," I said.

"You're up against this." She stepped back, and suddenly the teenage girl was gone. A twelve-foot dragon with glossy bright blue scales stood in her place. *He's like this. Only he's bigger and is an experienced fighter. He'll come for me once he knows where I've been hiding, and he'll kill everyone in his path.*

In a blink the dragon was gone and the girl had returned. "It's better for me to leave. Dragons struggle to track Sarkan when they're not in a dragon form, but I shifted last night. If he didn't know I was here before, he does now."

HB didn't seem in the least bit shocked. "If he comes for you, then we'll kill him. But he'll need to get in line, because there's a certain plague demon that needs to go down first. And the warmonger probably second. Maybe we can squeeze this dragon asshole in before we kill Desiree."

"He'll eat you," the girl protested.

"Not if I eat him first." HB grinned. "You have no idea the shit I've killed in my lifetime. And if I can't manage to get the job done, Eden will."

I wasn't certain of that, but I was willing to go down trying.

Jayla's eyes glistened with tears, as she looked back and forth between HB and me. "Okay. I'll stay."

"Good," I said. "And now that I've seen you transform into a blue dragon, I need to thank you for protecting my family and neighborhood last night. If it hadn't been for you, a whole lot more people would have died."

"I bonded with your sisters." Jayla looked down at the ground then gave me an embarrassed smile. "We can't help it. Dragons's hoards are always objects and land, but a Sarkan's precious belongings often include their friends, their mates, and their family. Your sisters were so kind to me, so generous and welcoming. They will always be among my beloveds."

"They're my beloveds as well," I said.

"Come inside," HB said as she put an arm around Jayla's shoulders. "Eat breakfast with us and let me introduce you to some people. And for God's sake, take a damned shower. Rolling in garbage isn't covering up your lizard smell, so you might as well be clean."

Jayla pulled away, staring at HB. "You *knew*?"

"Honestly? I thought you were a crocodile shifter," HB admitted. "They're really rare and secretive, so I didn't blame you for being wary of us. But there's only so much bad hygiene I can handle."

Jayla laughed. "Okay. I'll take a shower and meet the others, and I'll eat breakfast with you all. But I'm still living in that shed."

HB rolled her eyes. "Whatever floats your boat, hon. Now come on and get inside before we all starve to death in this parking lot."

CHAPTER 32

I texted Isha and Telaney to check on them, then placed a quick call to Bishop. It went straight to voicemail. I was going to assume that meant he was in the middle of something, and forcing myself to not worry, I got on my bike and headed south. Isha had been staying in my Los Feliz neighborhood with a friend, and I was confident that any injury she'd sustained could be eventually healed since she was still able to text me. Telaney...I had more worries about her. It wasn't just that she was human and less sturdy than the shifter. My bestie had a bad habit of minimizing any truly horrific injury. I couldn't exactly blame her, since I was kinda the same. Still, I wanted to see her "minor" injuries for myself, so I rode to Silver Lake, parked on the curb in front of her adorable house, and knocked on the door.

I gasped at the sight that greeted me when she answered.

"I know, I know. Not my best look," she said as she ushered me inside. "Thankfully I wasn't exactly pretty before, so this won't destroy my soul."

Telaney had a series of butterfly bandages holding

together a wound that started just under her left breast, vanished under her loose-fit boxer shorts, and reappeared across her right thigh. Her hair was matted with blood, and she had a wad of gauze held in place with a bright pink bandana. There was a blistering red burn on her right cheek, and her left eye was swollen shut.

"You look horrible," I blurted out, realizing too late that was a totally unhelpful thing to say.

"No shit, Sherlock. Come in. And make a pot of coffee for us both while I lay on the couch and moan. Put a shot of brandy in mine. And whipped cream. I deserve whipped cream."

"You deserve a fucking morphine drip," I said as I headed to her kitchen. "Why didn't you tell me you were this bad? I would have come earlier."

"Because Addy texted me what happened in your neighborhood and you needed to be there for your family," she said as she gently eased herself down onto the sofa. "I doctored myself up, and took a pain killer and some antibiotics. I'll be fine."

Telaney's electricity was out, so I fired up her camp stove, put a pot of water on to boil and poured instant coffee into two mugs, adding brandy to hers and getting a can of whipped cream out of her fridge.

"Have you heard from Juke?" I asked as I poured the hot water into the mugs, topped them both with whipped cream, then brought them in. "She hasn't returned any of my texts. I'm really worried."

"No. I lost sight of her early on in the fight." Telaney took the mug I held out. "A lot of cops died last night. I'm worried we don't have the manpower for this war, Eden. We couldn't even manage to hold those demons back from Reseda. How are we going to drive them out, let alone the warmonger,

Desiree, and whoever else jumps in to take their place if we manage to kill them?"

I sat opposite her and drank my coffee, not knowing what to say. We needed the anti-magic weaponry and ammo not just for the police and our team, but to get the Disciples and Gray Dogs on board. It would take an army to oust these demons—a well-armed army. And after last night's losses, I wasn't sure we'd be able to count on the police anymore, especially if Juke had been killed.

"Do you think we should leave? Encourage everyone else to leave as well?" I finally asked Telaney.

"Fuck no." She winced as she sat upright. "Anyone who's left here at this point isn't going anywhere unless it's in a casket. I'm just pointing out that this might not have the ending you're hoping for. Doesn't mean we still shouldn't try."

"I wanted to do a surprise attack on Porter Ranch," I told her. "One of Itinder's demons defected to my household. With his help, I hoped we might have a chance of taking them out. But now I'm worried it would end up being a suicide mission."

"We killed hundreds of demons last night. That has to make an impact," Telaney told me. "I'm sure this Itinder is used to his army going in, slaughtering humans, and waltzing out without a scratch. Last night he lost at least ten percent of his army, and ended up with an almost empty town. We attack him at Porter Ranch, keep picking away at his army every time we can, and he'll eventually decide this isn't fun anymore."

Picking away at his army. I blinked at Telaney. "You're a fucking genius."

She smirked. "I know."

"I'm serious. Both Itinder and the warmonger fight like this is the thirteenth century. Last night their army marched down the damned street in one huge group. We didn't have much choice but to fight them head-on, but it doesn't have to be that way. We need to start picking them off. Chipping away at them when they least expect it."

"Guerilla warfare." She saluted me with her coffee cup. "I approve. We don't need to have the numbers, but we'd still need the right weaponry."

And hopefully Bishop would come through with that.

Telaney picked up a brown bag from the coffee table and waved it at me. "I'm supposed to rub this nasty smelling cream on my cuts, chew on this braided grass shit, then go to sleep with a beaded bracelet on. According to Mathias, it'll all make me heal faster. If it doesn't work, I'm going back to the narcotics."

I stood up. "Text me when you wake up and let me know how you're feeling and if you need anything."

"Will do. Go home. Get some sleep. You look worse than I do," she said.

Making sure she was stocked up with water, snacks, and blankets, I went out to my bike. Telaney was right. I was exhausted from not sleeping last night and my energy was starting to fade fast. The house in Los Feliz was closer than Bea's. It wouldn't hurt for me to swing by and grab a few hours nap. It might help clear my mind.

My phone beeped with a text as I was putting on my helmet. I grabbed it out of my pocket, hoping it was Juke. Instead it was a text from Bishop with an address in Burbank and a message to meet him there.

My heart soared. He was back. Even if he hadn't been able to get any weaponry for us, he was back. And that was all that matter. I'd missed him terribly. I missed talking to him. I missed having him fight beside me, knowing he always had my back. I missed sleeping curled up in his arms.

It took me a while to find the address, but finally I pulled in to an old grocery store that had closed long ago. Any remaining groceries were long gone, leaving a giant empty building. With flashbacks of Morgana, I hesitated, my bike still running as I sat in the parking lot and stared at the abandoned store. Pulling my phone out, I looked at the text, wondering if it was really from Bishop, or if someone had spoofed his number and was luring me here to kill me.

I doubted the plague demon or the warmonger had anyone with that level of tech savvy, but Desiree definitely did.

What's Sadie's safe-phrase? I texted him.

My favorite color is bacon, he immediately texted back.

I doubted anyone but my family and Bishop would know that, but just in case, I sent another question.

What's the first thing I stole from your house?

My heart. And one of my shirts out of the laundry.

I smiled

Now get your fine ass in here, Trouble. I've got something to show you.

Convinced, I drove my bike to the front of the store, got off, and walked through the entrance. Someone had swept the broken glass of the doors aside. Inside the toppled shelves created a bit of a maze. A pair of rats eyed me from the shelter of a wooden box, their whiskers twitching.

Walking through the maze I saw about six more rats. I couldn't imagine there was anything left here for them to eat, but perhaps they'd decided this old store would make an ideal spot to nest. I ignored them as they watched me walk by.

On the other side of the maze I saw a huge quantity of boxes stacked up in rows. Thousands of boxes. And from between the rows, Bishop stepped out.

I ran and jumped into his arms. The feel of him against me, the citrus-spice smell of his soap combined with a tantalizing salty sun-and-surf aroma that was all Bishop, and the murmur of his voice as he buried his face in my hair brought tears to my eyes. I tightened my arms around him, never wanting to let him go.

"I missed you," he said. "You would have had so much fun with me the last three days. I hated that you missed it, that you were here fighting alone."

"Fun?" I wasn't angry, but it did suck that he'd been doing something enjoyable when my friends and family had been fighting what truly had been a losing battle.

"I robbed several military arsenals." He pulled back to look at me, running his hands through my hair. "Me, two angels, and a demon. The demon is a genius when it comes to this stuff. We really owe all this to him."

I looked around at all the boxes. "So this is…?"

"I'm guessing it's about four thousand anti-magic pistols and rifles, and two million rounds of ammo. There's also fifty boxes of anti-magic grenades, and four big-ass machine guns with two hundred boxes of ammo."

I gasped, my eyes tearing up, my mouth trembling.

"Then we knocked off Letterkenny," Bishop continued. "Which wasn't quite the walk in the park that McAlester was. Had a few close calls where I was pretty sure we were going to end up in a federal prison. But we pulled it off. I'm not sure what I teleported out of that warehouse, but the demon said it was defensive magic."

I burst into tears, flinging myself once more into Bishop's arms. He laughed, holding and rocking me as I cried. When I'd finally managed to control my emotions, I pulled away, wiped my eyes, and sniffed.

Then I told him about last night. I'd gone over what had happened with Bea, but with Bishop I felt free to pour forth all my fears and anxieties. I told him about when I'd lost sight of my friends, when I'd thought I was going to die. I'd told him about arriving home to discover how close my family had come to death themselves.

I told him about Juke, and my eyes teared up once more. I hadn't cried this much in my entire life—not even when Sadie had been shot and Nevarra kidnapped. But then I'd been filled with purpose and urgency, pushing all my terror away so I could do what I needed to do. But now? Now I had someone I could open up to, someone I could truly share the helplessness, the terror I'd felt last night.

"I'm so sorry I wasn't here to help you, Trouble," he said as he reached out to stroke my hair.

"I'm not. What you were doing was more important." I gestured at the boxes. "This is our key to winning this war. This will help us take back LA and New Hell. Without these weapons, we were standing against a storm that would eventually drown us. Now we have the tools to truly fight back."

He leaned down to kiss me. "We're going to win this. Now, let's get these weapons into the hands of the people who need them.

I had the guns and ammo I'd promised The Disciples. I had enough to supply the Gray Dogs, and the LA police department. I had enough to provide anti-magic weaponry to neighborhood watches all over the city. These demons were about to find that humans were not the easy marks they'd thought.

My phone buzzed. I yanked it from my pocket and for the second time today, my heart leapt.

"Juke?" I was full of hope as I answered the call.

"Who else would have my damned phone?" she snapped, her voice rough and gritty. "I need you to come pick me up at Pacifica Hospital. I'm discharging myself and need a ride. Get this IV out of me. I've got shit to do, and I can't do it with a tube stuck in my arm."

I laughed, both with relief and with amusement that Juke had meant the last bit for some doctor or nurse.

"I'm not riding on your bike," she warned. "And I don't want anyone driving my car. Borrow or hotwire something, and don't tell anyone I said that."

"How do you feel about teleportation? Because Bishop is back." I couldn't stop smiling. Juke was okay. Well, she probably wasn't *okay* since she'd been in the hospital and clearly in no condition to return any of the texts I'd sent her, but her injuries couldn't be too bad if she was yelling at the hospital staff to take out her IV.

"Bishop is back?" She sounded excited, and I knew it wasn't about the teleportation.

"Yep, and he brought gifts."

"Hot damn," Juke shouted. "Come get me out of here and show me what he's got. Christmas came early this year."

It had. "We'll be there in the blink of an eye," I told her before ending the call.

"Juke needs a lift," I said to Bishop. "And I know she wants to pick out what police units are getting what."

He smiled. "Then let's go. I'd appreciate her input on all this defensive stuff."

"Are we okay to leave all this stuff here unguarded?" I asked.

"Did you notice all the rats?" He gestured toward the door. "They're our security guards."

"Rats?" I looked around, noticing again all the rodents milling near the entrance and darting down the aisles of boxes.

"Dar, the demon we worked with, has some affinity with both rodents and rodent shifters. Guess he's sort of the Rat King." Bishop shrugged. "Either way, he offered a discrete security force and I accepted. That said, once we move some of this to the police and the gangs, I'm going to suggest relocating the remaining stock."

It was a good idea. I didn't trust Sebastian or Piers to not decide to raid our warehouse and scoop up additional weaponry. There was a definite risk that individual police, citizens would decide to help themselves, or that the demons would discover this location and try to destroy our stash.

Everything was finally coming together. Juke was alive. Bishop was back. And we now had what we needed to wrestle LA away from the demons.

$\mathcal{B}$ishop teleported us to just outside the hospital entrance, not wanting to cause any additional panic. We walked inside, asked for Detective Sarah Juke, and were directed to the third floor.

Juke was still in bed, with the IV tube still in her arm as she argued with three white-coated medical professionals.

"There." She pointed at us. "That's my ride. And he's an angel. He'll heal anything wrong with me."

"I'm not skilled at healing," Bishop warned her.

"And trust me, you don't want me to heal you," I told her.

Juke glared at us, and I realized too late that we were supposed to just go along with her claims.

The detective didn't look as though she should be walking out of the hospital right now. Her skin was covered with blistery bumps, and a chunk of her bright-red, tightly curled hair had been shaved and was covered with bandages and tape.

"She had a serious concussion and the most severe, rapid-onset case of measles we've ever seen," one of the doctors said. "Plus a case of Norovirus. She should be dead. And the fact that she's not isn't a reason for her to go strolling out of here less than twenty-four hours after we admitted her."

I caught my breath. "What happened?" I asked Juke.

She sighed. "I went in with my team and was up to my elbows in demons when I found myself face-to-face with that plague motherfucker. He sprayed me with this oily ooze, and I felt like I'd gotten an instant case of the flu, but I stayed on my feet and nailed him with my whip. Took one of his arms off, but then the other demons pushed me back. I kept fighting until another demon clocked me in the head and I went down."

"One of her squad pulled her out and got her to the hospital," another doctor said. "We've got a four to six hour wait, but with her having a contagious disease and being concussed, we started to work on her right away. She didn't regain consciousness until an hour ago, and here she is demanding to be discharged."

Clearly Juke should stay right here, at least for another few days. "Do you want to be a minion?" I asked with every bit of stern, Bea-like attitude I could summon. "Because if we take you out of here, and you get worse, that's what's gonna happen. Minion, Juke. Minion."

The detective glared at me. "No way, Alvaro. If I'm dying, you better just let me die. And if you don't get me out of here, I'll start calling everyone on the force until one of them comes and gets me."

Bishop shrugged. "I don't think you can force her to stay if she wants to leave. I can teleport, so if she starts to feel worse we can have her back here in less than a second."

The first doctor grumbled under his breath. "Fine." He reached forward and removed the IV. "Your clothes are in the closet. Your guns are locked away, but I'll clear their release. Someone will be here shortly with the weapons and any valuables you had when you were admitted."

With that, all three doctors stormed out.

Juke jumped out of bed, not at all bothered that she was flashing us her bare ass in the open-backed hospital gown. Flinging open the closet doors, she pulled out her leather attire, her boots, and her unexpectedly lacy underwear and bra.

And her whip. Putting the whip on the bed, she began to lift the gown over her head.

"Um, should we leave?" I asked, not really wanting to see Juke naked.

The gown was off before I finished my question. "I almost died last night, so I really don't give a shit who sees me naked," Juke snapped. "It's a body. Everyone's got one."

True. But Juke's body was especially impressive. Aside from the blistery bumps, the woman was ripped. Someone clearly didn't miss leg day at the gym. Or arm day. Or ab day. Or rest-of-her day.

Completely unselfconscious, Juke pulled on the lacy underclothes, then shimmied into her leathers. She sat on the edge of the bed to slide her boots on, then coiled her whip and attached it to her belt. Walking over to the mirror, she gently patted the bandage on her head and winced.

"Takes my hair forever to grow. If I'd been conscious I never would have let them shave it. Now I'm gonna have to cut it all short or I'll look like a total freak with this chunk missing."

"I think you'd look great with it shaved," Bishop told her. "Number two guard and that bright red? Killer."

She grunted. "Maybe. I wish I'd been clocked lower down and I could just do an edgy undercut. But no, I have to get hit smack on the top of my head."

An armed hospital employee came into the room then, sparing me from any further hair fashion discussion. She sat a case on the bed, typed a code into the keypad, and opened it to reveal three pistols, six knives, and two pair of handcuffs. Putting another case on the bed, she went through the same routine and revealed an anti-magic pistol and a rifle.

"Damn, Juke," I said as she stuffed the weapons into their holsters and strapped them on. "How much does all that shit weigh? You're packing more guns than me."

Which was saying a lot.

"A girls gotta be prepared," she replied. "Okay let's go."

Bishop gathered me close and put a hand on Juke's shoulder. We'd been in the hospital, then a split second later were in the old grocery store. I'd gotten used to Bishop's form of instant transportation, but this was Juke's first time. She staggered back a few steps, steadied by Bishop's hand. Then she bent over and puked on the floor.

"Ugh." She spit a few times. "Guess I shouldn't have had that hospital oatmeal before we left."

"It gets easier," I told her, handing her a napkin from my backpack to wipe her mouth.

Bishop wrinkled his nose, then waved a hand. Instantly the splatter of vomit vanished, leaving only a patch of glossy floor behind. "I should have warned you about that particular effect," he said.

"No problem." Juke stuffed the napkin into a pocket then looked around. "This the stuff?"

"I figure we can distribute a thousand anti-magic guns and a hundred thousand rounds of ammo to start with," I told her. "Once I get the gangs what I've promised them, then the police, I'll know what we've got in reserves for the neighborhood watches."

"That's amazing," she marveled. "If we'd had all this last night, then there might have been a very different result."

I nodded. "And some of the anti-magic weaponry are things like grenades and distance rifles. I'm thinking we might need to do more of an ambush-guerilla warfare approach."

"Makes sense," she replied.

"There is a whole bunch of defensive magic we lifted from…somewhere," Bishop said with an enigmatic smile. "I'd like you to take a look at it and let us know where you think it would be best utilized."

Juke and I followed him down an aisle. Bishop pulled a few boxes off the stacks and ripped them open.

"Holy shit!" Juke pulled a bundle of sticks and a folded instruction manual from one box. "This is a perimeter shield. Super high-tech stuff. Military stuff, and I'm talking militaries with huge budgets. There are countries that would sell their souls for this."

"What does it do?" I asked.

"You know the wards your neighbor put in place?" Juke asked. "Think bigger. Think stronger. This shit would keep an archangel out. And it will protect a large geographic area —like a city large. No magic gets through without being zapped. Humans can enter. Shifters can be keyed to enter. Demons and angels have to be individually cleared, or they can't get in. This will be a game changer. We'll be able to set up sanctuary areas where people will be safe."

"You need to let me know where you want these areas," I told her. "We'll get them in place all over the city. A few in the Valley, a few to the south…just let me know where."

"And this!" Juke squealed, running to the next box. "This allows us to open a secured tunnel from one sanctuary area to the other, in case there's a siege. And these are teleportation amulets similar to what the demons have called elf buttons. They allow someone to instantly retreat to a sanctuary area if they're in danger."

I smiled, putting my arm around Bishop. "Thank you," I whispered to him.

"Thank me later," he growled.

I shivered in anticipation. Oh, I would definitely thank him later.

"What do you think about an attack on Porter Ranch?" I asked Juke. "I know a lot of your squad died last night, and I appreciate that you might not want to risk any more of your colleagues, but I think it's best to attack now, when we have the advantage."

"We're in," Juke said. "I mourn every officer that went down last night, but we can't let that stop us from taking back the city. And with these weapons, we finally have a chance."

I agreed. "So, tomorrow? The next day? The shifters on my team probably need a day or two to recuperate, and Telaney at least needs that much time. Plus I'd like to coordinate with the mages again as well as the gangs who've pledged to help us."

Juke thought for a second. "Let's work on distributing this stuff and strategizing for next three days, then we'll decide when to attack. And in the meantime, we'll think about which areas of the county should get these shields, and I'll figure out on which police stations get what guns and ammo. Text me a list of what you've allocated to me and I'll work with the commissioner to sort it all out."

I felt a surge of excitement. We had a plan. And we finally had the resources to make it all happen.

"Oh, and Eden?" Juke asked. "Get us more of that shitty-tasting lemon candy from your mage friends. Because I'm pretty sure that's the only reason I'm alive here today."

* * *

MY EARLIER EXHAUSTION faded away as I contacted Piers and Sebastian and made arrangements to transfer their weapons.

Bishop helped speed the process along by teleporting me and the boxes of guns and ammo to agreed upon locations. I secured the promises of both men to have armed forces for our attack on Porter Ranch.

By the time I'd finished with that, I was starting to feel fatigued again. Still, I visited Bea's house with Bishop, checking on the girls and on both Addy and Kellen. Then Bishop transported me down to see Telaney again, then back to my house in Los Feliz to see Isha and ensure my house and the neighborhood remained safe.

Bishop convinced me that Addy and Kellen were able to protect my family, and that I should stay in the Los Feliz house that night. I was anxious to protect my family, but exhaustion won out.

It felt good to be home again. Mittens greeted me at the door, wrapping himself around my legs and purring. I fed him while Bishop made a quick omelet, adding whatever was still fresh in the fridge. We curled up on the couch with beers, Mittens a warm ball of fur on my lap. I stared out the windows at the lights of the city, hoping for peace.

"I almost forgot," I said as sleep pushed my eyelids to half-mast. "Jayla is a dragon. Or a dragon shifter. Or something. Sarkan, she called it. Sadie said they were a kind of dragon that was hunted and fled their homeland. Jayla's worried that the dragon downtown who killed her parents is coming after her."

"Does HB know?" Bishop asked, nuzzling the side of my head. "If so, the girl has nothing to worry about."

"She knows. The shifters at Suerte know. But Jayla saved my family. She exposed herself, shifting into her dragon form to protect them when the demons were about to kill everyone. So I owe her. She risked herself to save them, and I owe her."

He kissed my neck. "Which means I owe her as well. She's family now. She'll always have a home with us."

I smiled, loving that Bishop knew me so well and was always willing to protect those I cared about.

"Love you so much," I murmured as I snuggled against him.

"I love you too," he said.

Then everything faded to a warm darkness and I slept, safe and with the knowledge that everything was going to be okay. Sometime that night, Bishop carried me downstairs into the bed. I didn't remember it. I didn't remember anything. But I woke up at sunrise, Bishop warm and snoring by my side. And for the first time in days, I felt hope.

CHAPTER 34

I'd assumed we would distribute weaponry, storm Porter Ranch, and clean house. Thankfully Juke better understood the enormity of what we wanted to accomplish, and that what we wanted to accomplish would require a lot of planning and coordination.

Piers and Sebastian, put their new weapons to immediate use. I'd bargained some extra cases of ammo so Piers could help defend more than just their shipments and gang businesses.

We were ready to roll until news of the "donations" went up Juke's chain of command. The next thing we knew the Commissioner was trying to muscle in on the deal. When I'd informed him I would only work with Juke, he blustered about how he was going to seize the whole lot under some stupid pre-demon law. Then Bishop had a private word with the man, and he left, cheerfully informing everyone that Juke was in charge of the entire project.

The detective had brought in a team to go through the defensive stuff, figuring out what the hell everything was, and deciding what we were going to use where. The goal was to select not only areas where a lot of humans now lived, but also places where shifters and others who preferred a more rural area. Areas that had suffered huge damage were ruled out.

Blister's huge transit map went up on the wall of the grocery store, with a whole lot of additional highlighter. She'd managed to grab another map that only covered The Valley, and highlighted the crap out of that one as well. By the time we were done, we knew where the demon activity hot-spots were, where people were living, and where businesses still functioned.

Finally, we were ready to attack.

"My people will set up here, here, and here, going in from the west and the north," Juke told us, pointing to the map on the wall. "And the mages will be working to back up my groups."

"I've got the Disciples in the south, ready to storm the gate. Other teams of Disciples will remain outside of Porter Ranch in case the demons try to scatter and flee," I said. " The Gray Dogs are going to be at the west and south, and my team is going in at the east where we can target Itinder's and the neighboring homes."

"My group will on the north side," HB said, "fighting alongside the police."

Addy was staying back to help defend Bea's neighborhood in case of an attack. Telaney, Blister, Isha, and Kellen would be with me as well as Bishop. Kellen had asked Mosi and Lucas to stay behind. I was sure that had been a difficult discussion, but Kellen had convinced them that he was pretty close to indestructible thanks to his minion status, and that they were needed to guard Suerte with the refugees.

Reginald was here, still looking like a seven-foot-tall zombie. Telaney had voiced concerns, saying she didn't trust him, but he was our ace in the hole—the only one of us who had inside knowledge about Itinder and his army.

Surprisingly, Poodle had volunteered to fight with us. I'd given her one of the anti-magic guns and a box of ammo, and she'd be working with my team.

"Any demon that surrenders should be disabled and taken prisoner," I reminded Juke.

She grimaced. "I've instructed my guys, but I'm telling you that they're not on board. After what the demons have done here, and how they've treated human non-combatants, no one wants to show them mercy."

"I know. But we're going to be living with demons. They're here to stay. And the best way for us to move forward is to show demons that compliance won't still mean a death sentence."

Juke glanced at Reginald. "I get it. But we'll be slowed down by having to secure demon prisoners. And there's a real fear that they might shrug off the anti-magic effects quickly and decide to attack again. Just know that any demon prisoners might be more than a little injured."

If prisoners were still alive, I'd count it as a win. The demons would heal once the anti-magic finally wore off, and it might do them good to experience the pain that their human victims did.

Juke looked around the room. "Any questions?" Everyone shook their heads. "Good. Be in position by three o'clock."

* * *

I REACHED out to take Bishop's hand as we waited outside the fence. Telaney, Kellen in his half-form, and Blister were to our right, Poodle, Isha in her wolf form, and Reginald to our left. At three o'clock, the first bomb went off.

Smoke curled into the air from the direction of the gatehouse. The rapid fire of automatic weapons filled the brief silence after the bomb explosion. We waited, because bomb this was meant to get the demons out of their houses, running toward the attack. They'd be furious and confident that they could easily defeat whatever humans had dared attack them.

Then the real fight would begin.

I glanced at my watch, my grip on Bishop's hand tightening. This sort of military strategy was foreign to me, but I was quickly learning.

Hearing shouts in that demon language in between the bursts of weapon fire, I counted silently. Five. Four. Three. Two.

More explosions, this time the smoke rising into the air had a blue tint.

"Go," I shouted, letting go of Bishop's hand.

We were over the fence when the automatic weapon fire resumed, this time the noise accompanied by the sound of screams.

A group of three demons blasted us as we hit the ground. I pulled the energy into me. Telaney and Poodle shot two with their anti-magic pistols. Bishop took care of the third as the werewolves tore the other two demons apart. I waved for Telaney's group to head right, down the street and they took off, Bishop going with them. I accompanied the others, a chill shivering through me as we ran in the opposite direction. Bishop had argued against us being separated, but it didn't make sense to have the both of us together when I'd carefully split my team to ensure an equal distribution of skills and abilities.

By the time we'd turned down the street to Itinder's house, explosions were sounding from all over the compound. We'd encountered three more teams of demons and quickly taken them down. Poodle was incredibly accurate with the anti-magic pistol, and had taken to using her other hand to shoot her Beretta M9, finishing the job once she'd disabled a demon. Reginald didn't hesitate to take out any demon that hadn't been disabled, and Isha had quickly become our forward scout, alerting us to any demons and keeping them occupied until we got there to assist.

By the time we reached Itinder's house, Porter Ranch was in chaos. The explosions and weapon fire were louder as each squad worked their way toward the center of the compound. Once they joined up, they'd all make their way east, sweeping through the community. Then when the battle was won, Juke's team would clear each house individually, ensuring no demons remained.

But for any of that to happen, Itinder would need to go down first.

We raced up the steps to the house, Poodle gagging at the display of human dead on the demon's lawn. Reginald blasted in the door as we stood to the side. Going in first, he waved for us to follow and we made our way from room to room in search of the plague demon.

It quickly became evident that the house was empty. We cleared the building, then left out the front entrance.

"Now what?" Poodle asked.

I'd expected to find Itinder here, or to have encountered him on our way. It was critical that we take the plague demon down, but how the heck were we going to find him? I didn't want to accidentally put us in the way of the advancing humans and have my team shot with friendly fire, but I didn't want to hold back either.

And then I felt it—that same thick, oozing, smothering, dread-inducing sensation I'd had when a plague demon had come to Bea's neighborhood, only a thousand times more nauseating.

I took off at a run, motioning for my team to stay behind

me. Even with Isaac's lemon candy, Juke had nearly died from her encounter with Itinder. At the very best, our entire force of humans would be stricken and unable to fight. At worst, they'd all be dead.

I couldn't let the plague demon take out a huge portion of our police force, the Gray Dogs, and half of the Disciples. If he managed to infect them, we'd lose this battle. We'd lose the war.

Putting on a burst of speed, I left Reginald, Isha, and Poodle behind, heading as fast as I could to where I'd sensed the plague demon. Buildings were a blur as I flew by. I rounded a corner, and slammed on the brakes before I plowed into a giant group of demons.

Hundreds of them surrounded a gaunt, jaundiced man with ram's horns curling from a skull's forehead and leathery wings extending from his back. Sick oozed from him in mustard yellow waves.

In the seconds it took for the demon mob to notice my presence, I realized Itinder had held back, surrounding himself by his household so he wouldn't be shot by any of the anti-magic guns. It meant I had a slim margin of time before any diseases reached the humans.

So I pulled, yanking the yellow toward me. It hit, just as the demons saw me and attacked.

Several of their energy blasts managed to nail me before I got enough control of the demon-fueled disease to begin absorbing their attacks. I redirected some of the shots and used the stored energy to blast others, all while continuing to catch incoming energy and keep a tight hold on the disease. It tethered me to Itinder, and he yanked, trying to pull his best weapon free from my reach. I staggered, but kept my grip, juggling defense and offence while trying to ignore the sharp burning pain at the edge of my spirit-being.

This wouldn't work. I couldn't take on hundreds of

demons and Itinder. Something was going to give, and I had a bad feeling it would be me.

The sound of snarls and weapon fire behind me let me know that Poodle, Isha, and Reginald had caught up, but it wasn't enough. I dropped to my knees, a few more energy blasts burned through me as I struggled to hold the disease in check.

The noise of the battle began to blur and I swayed, fighting to stay alert. A roar broke through the buzz, clearing my head and jerking me back to attention. Looking up, I saw a wave of energy hit the demons. It was orange and gold, blue and green-gray, like sunset over the ocean. And it turned every one of the demons it hit into a pile of sand.

Bishop.

Bishop was here to rescue me once more.

CHAPTER 35

I held on to the disease with all my focus, confident that Bishop would make sure no other demon attacked me. With renewed strength, I tugged on Itinder's magic, yanking it toward me. He fought me for a few seconds, then suddenly cut it all free. I fell back onto my ass, spooling the yellow sickness into me and converting it into energy. When I scrambled to my feet I saw Bishop mowing down demons with a holy fury. I saw the humans in their SWAT gear shooting.

And I saw Itinder making his way to the rear of his demon army.

No way was I going to let that fucker escape. I ran to the north, skirting around the piles of sand and dodging fleeing demons. A block away I caught up with him. He saw me, and I slammed into him just as he teleported.

We materialized in the living room of his home. Before I could attack, Itinder grabbed me and threw me across the room. I hit the wall and bounced off it, rolling away just in time to evade a blast that blew a ten foot hole through the floor. Another blast exploded the sofa into bits of wood, fabric, and foam. I returned fire, but Itinder teleported away before the blast hit him, appearing beside me.

I fired again, this time hitting him, and sending him flying backward. He teleported again, vanishing and seizing me around my neck from behind. I grabbed his hands and kicked out as he lifted me up, trying to not end up strangled to death.

Brownish yellow oozed from him, coating my skin. It burrowed into my nose, mouth, eyes and ears, spreading through every cell of my body.

I should have died, but instead I felt something click open inside of me. A fire sparked, burning deep within my spirit being. It expanded, and as it grew, it scorched the disease.

The yellow sickness lit up red, then faded, drifting away. The fire spread, and I felt the thick yellow coating my skin crack, then melt, sizzling as the droplets hit the floor.

Itinder didn't give up. He kept pushing disease into me, and I kept burning it away. He switched to a black sickness, then a green one, and each time that fire inside me used it as fuel.

Then the fire was no longer inside me, it *was* me. My skin heated, becoming blue flame. Itinder screamed, dropping me as his hands turned to ash.

I looked at him, feeling no emotion at all. He was no longer an enemy. He was no longer a plague demon. He was just something to transform, something else to change.

He recoiled as I reached for him. He tried to teleport, but there was no escaping me. I drew him toward me, pulling him back mid-teleport. I felt his terror, but it didn't matter. Fear had no place here where the only law was eternal transformation.

Eden, the me I'd always known vanished, and I had no

idea what happened. All I knew was when that fire died down, locked once more deep inside, I found myself staring at a wall of ivy and clematis. Thick grass had replaced the carpet, and a giant pine tree stood in the center of the room, punching through two stories and the roof.

I knew Itinder was dead, I just wasn't sure exactly how I'd managed to do it. And I really didn't want to know. Whoever I'd been, it wasn't someone I ever wanted to see again.

The sound of gunfire shook me from my reverie. I left the house, and ran through the streets, knowing that even though the plague demon was dead, the fight was far from over. Plenty of demons remained to fight, and even after the battle, we'd still need to go house-to-house to clear the area.

I slowed, seeing Poodle running toward me, a weapon in each hand.

"Reginald's down," she shouted as she slowed to meet me.

"Where's Isha?" I asked her, concerned for my team.

"Fighting with the other shifters," she glanced behind her, as if she was worried that demons might be in pursuit.

Then she turned around and shot me. Twice.

The first shot spread a bloom of blue paint across my chest. The second punched through my abdomen.

I clutched my stomach as blood poured from the wound, gasping with pain. I'd been shot before, but not like this.

Another blast and I fell backwards onto the pavement, blood bubbling up with each exhale.

"Kill every demon." Poodle said as she took aim at my head. "Which includes that freak Reginald and you as well. We'll never be safe unless all the demons are dead. Telaney might think you're okay, but I know better. Demons can never be okay."

She'd killed Reginald. Had she done the same to Isha?

I coughed, choking on the blood filling my lungs. A

shadow moved behind Poodle, and I wasn't sure if it was my imagination, or real.

"I've got a group raiding that warehouse while you're occupied here," she continued. "We'll take all those weapons and put them to good use. Soon humans will be in control once more. So thanks for that."

Her finger tightened on the trigger just as two gray, zombie-like hands grabbed her arm. The shot went wide, splintering the pavement beside me rather than going through my head. Poodle spun around, shooting once more just as Reginald sent a surge of energy through her.

She fell to the ground, a blackened husk, and Reginald fell on top of her, his back splatted with blue paint and the exit wound of a bullet out the rear of his skull.

Then everything went black, and this time there was no inner fire to save me.

* * *

Swirls of light and energy. Vast swaths of deepest darkness. A pulse of conversion, of destruction leading to creation. Nothing was sacred beyond the transition of something into something else. Occasionally I would pause to admire a form, a structure, or even the beauty of the nothingness. Then I reached out and reshaped. Even my creations were in a constant state of change. Atoms splitting and forming anew, excess energy swirling out to fuel another formation.

"Eden. Eden, some back to me."

Everything compressed, compacted into something small. Suddenly, I felt. I felt pain. Fear. Anger.

Love.

I opened my eyes, and there was Bishop. He was dirty and smeared with blood and gore, his wings extended out with a riot of sunset colors.

I'd never seen anything more beautiful in my life.

"I found you dead," he said, his voice husky.

Frowning, I remembered. I should be dead. But the pain was gone and I was breathing like normal. Reaching for my stomach, I felt my torn clothes, realizing that the flesh beneath them was smooth and uninjured.

"What happened?" I asked him.

"We won. All the demons are either dead, or in the handcuffs we took from Letterkenny. I found a tree in the middle of Itinder's house, so I'm assuming that was your doing."

There was a note of humor in his words, but I didn't feel like smiling. "I killed him, but I'm not sure how. I'm not sure I even want to know how."

"Telaney, HB, and Blister are fine," he continued. "And Juke. Her cops suffered very few losses. Same with the two gangs. Everyone is jubilant."

"Isha? Reginald?" I asked.

He shook his head. "Reginald didn't make it. Poodle either. Isha is seriously injured and hasn't regained consciousness."

"It was Poodle," I told him. "I think she probably caused Isha's injuries. She'd shot Reginald and was going to kill me. If Reginald hadn't taken her out, I'm not sure I'd be alive right now."

"You weren't alive right now," Bishop said, his expression grim. "Until right before you opened your eyes, you were dead and cold. I couldn't feel you. I couldn't sense you at all."

I saw his grief and reached out a hand to touch his cheek. "I don't know what's going on. Is this an angel thing?"

He shook his head. "No. But you're alive and nothing else matters."

I had a feeling it all mattered a whole lot, but right now I was too tired to argue.

"Can we go home?" I asked, desperately needing to sleep.

"Let Juke, Telaney, and Bea, and the others know I'm okay and I'll talk to them in the morning. I just need to rest."

Rest in Bishop's arms, so he could keep the nightmares of cold, endless, unfeeling transformation away.

"Absolutely." He bent his head and kissed me. Then he teleported us home.

I slept for four days, Bishop, Bea, and Mittens keeping watch over me. And when I woke, I felt completely renewed.

While I'd been reenacting Sleeping Beauty, Juke's teams with help from the Gray Dogs had swept Porter Ranch, clearing out any remaining demons. They'd begun to set up the first of the magical perimeters around Burbank, planning to expand a little each day. The Disciples had returned to their territories. Several of the shifter groups had teamed up with them to fight back against the warmonger.

Isha was alive and slowly healing at Suerte.

Demons who'd surrendered were in a special wing of the human prison with the anti-magic handcuffs from Letterkenney on twenty-four seven. They were to remain there for transport to the gate in Seattle, where they'd be returned to Hel. Juke had found some nifty devices among the stash from Letterkenney that would tag the demons being sent back to Hel. They were warned that if they came back before fifty years were up, they'd show up on a tracker, be hunted down and killed. I wasn't sure how that would all play out in fifty years, but the demons who were being exiled seem pretty cowed by the threat.

Poodle's attempt to take the warehouse of weapons had failed miserably. The rats had done their job, and so had Bob, who Bishop had left to help protect the facility.

The weirdest bit of news was about what had happened to Kellen and Addy. Evidently both of them had collapsed at the time I'd officially died, them dying as well. When I'd come back in Bishop's arms, the pair of them had also returned, resurrected for a second time.

I didn't want to think too hard about all that. Honestly I didn't have time to think about all that, because we had a warmonger to kill and Desiree to deal with.

And the devil waits for no one.

ACKNOWLEDGMENTS

Thank you to my friends and family who were my sounding boards and helped me connect with resources as I did my research.

I really appreciate the help of Adam Richardson from the Writer's Detective Bureau who gave me a cop's view on how the police might work in a dystopian LA.

Also, big thanks to my copyeditor Kimberly Cannon, whose eagle eyes catch the typos and keep my comma problem in line, and to Damonza for once again providing me with an amazing cover design.

ABOUT THE AUTHOR

Debra lives in a little house in the woods of Maryland with her sons and two slobbery bloodhounds. On a good day, she jogs and horseback rides, hopefully managing to keep the horse between herself and the ground. Her only known super power is 'Identify Roadkill'.

For more information:
www.debradunbar.com

IMP WORLD NOVELS

The Imp Series

A Demon Bound

Satan's Sword

Elven Blood

Devil's Paw

Imp Forsaken

Angel of Chaos

Kingdom of Lies

Exodus

Queen of the Damned

The Morning Star

With This Ring

* * *

California Demon Series

California Demon

Sinners on Sunset

Ventura Hellway

The Devil Went Down to Glendale

Route 666

* * *

Half-breed Series

Demons of Desire

Sins of the Flesh

Cornucopia

Unholy Pleasures

City of Lust

* * *

<u>Imp World Novels</u>

No Man's Land

Stolen Souls

Three Wishes

Northern Lights

Far From Center

Penance

* * *

<u>Northern Wolves</u>

Juneau to Kenai

Rogue

Winter Fae

Bad Seed

* * *

<u>The Templar Series</u>

Dead Rising

Last Breath

Bare Bones

Famine's Feast

Royal Blood

Dark Crossroads

Accidental Witches Series

Brimstone and Broomsticks

Warmongers and Wands

Death and Divination

Hell and Hexes

Minions and Magic

Fiends and Familiars

Devils and the Dead

The Bremen Shifter Band (short story)

* * *

White Lightning Series

Wooden Nickels

Bum's Rush

Clip Joint

Jake Walk

Trouble Boys

Packing Heat (TBD)